Falling in Louvre

By
Fiona Leitch

Copyright © 2021 Fiona Leitch
The right of Fiona Leitch to be identified as the Author of the Work has been asserted by her in accordance with the Copyright, Designs and Patents Act 1998.
Published in 2021 by Fiona Leitch
Apart from any use permitted under copyright law, this publication may only be reproduced, stored, or transmitted, in any form or by any means, with prior permission in writing of the publisher or, in the case of reprographic production, in accordance with the terms of licences issued by the Copyright Licensing Agency.
All characters in this publication are fictitious and any resemblance to real persons, living or dead, is purely coincidental.

Fluctuat nec mergitur

'She is tossed by the waves but does not sink'

\- the motto of Paris

Foreword:

In May/June 2016, Paris was bracing itself for a flood of soccer fans from all across the continent, as they prepared to host the European Football Championships. But they were unexpectedly hit by a flood of a very different kind.

Weeks of heavy rain caused the Seine to burst its banks. The floodwaters found their way into the underground city beneath Paris; a network of sewers, Metro tunnels, catacombs and the basements of some very famous buildings... The lake underneath the Palais Garnier (the opera house) is well known, being the inspiration for the Phantom of the Opera, but it's not so well known that the Louvre, home to some of the most important artworks in the world, has a basement storage facility. On the 2nd of June 2016 this storage facility flooded, forcing the museum to close for several days and move everything out of the basement and onto higher floors. The waters eventually receded, just in time for the opening night of Euro 2016.

This is the story of what *might* have happened during those floods...

PROLOGUE

Paris, January 2016

Bertrand was King of the Pigeons. Unofficially.

He did have the best perch in the city. Oh, his peers might extol the virtues of certain other landmarks, but not for Bertrand the windswept and oft freezing *tour Eiffel*; his seat – the head of a particularly grotesque gargoyle atop Notre Dame – was conveniently close to the Louvre, with the rich pickings of many an abandoned packed lunch in the courtyard, and in the summer *les jardins de Tuileries* could be relied upon for the odd dropped ice cream. Plus you got a better class of tourist among the cathedral's many visitors, visitors who loved all of God's creatures equally, even an old and tattered pigeon whose feathers could only be described as 'manky'.

Bertrand gazed up at the sky. The clouds were thinning. The steady drizzle which had slowly but surely soaked the city over the last few days had finally stopped, and the low winter sun had popped out for one final late afternoon hurrah before clocking off. It shone down on the rain-lashed streets, bathing buildings in a glorious warm glow and making the puddles sparkle.

It shone on the rather nice apartment block in the 6th arrondisement where Sylvie, tense as a bird in a gilded cage, prepared her husband's dinner in a Prozac daydream. It shone on unlucky-in-love Philippe, hopeless romantic and night-time security guard, coasting his bike down the rue de Rochechouart. And it shone on Bertrand himself, who shook his ragged feathers and roused himself from thoughts of subjugating his ungrateful pigeon subjects (or at the very least that fat *cochon* Gerard, who strutted around the Pompidou Centre like Bonaparte himself). One last chance for a scavenge before the sun disappeared and it was time to get his head down.

Bertrand took off. There was magic in the air tonight; he could feel it in the tips of his wings. He soared over Paris, pooped on Philippe's head, then flew into the approaching night and out of the story.

CHAPTER 1

Sylvie Cloutier née Boudain was feeling less than herself. Truth be told, she'd been feeling that way for so long that she wasn't sure that the Sylvie she remembered even existed any more, or indeed that she ever had done.

But she had.

Sylvie Boudain had had an impish grin and eyes that sparkled with mischief. When she laughed she showed all her teeth, and her face lit up so gloriously that nobody even noticed that her two front ones were a little crooked. She was bright and intelligent, but kind; the sort of person who claimed not to suffer fools gladly but who nevertheless bit their tongue and smiled sympathetically when they were invariably confronted with one. She had always attempted to see the good in people, and this attitude had served her well in earlier, happier days. She enjoyed art and music and culture, but having been brought up by her father on his own and having spent school holidays with him in salerooms and auction houses across France, she had also cultivated a love of the kind of fruity language men of business tended to use amongst themselves when their womenfolk were absent. More than one crusty old dealer of *objet d'art* had choked on his Gitanes in surprise at the spectacle of this petite, delicate young flower of femininity unleashing a stream of obscenities when outbid in the saleroom. She'd even been banned from one auction house in Courbevoie after telling the particularly smug auctioneer in no uncertain terms that his mother was known to, ahem, 'entertain sailors' (her father had laughed uproariously at that, knowing that the man's mother did indeed have what could only be described as a colourful past). When it came to business she was hard-headed but not unsentimental; she had been known to pay a little too much for a painting or a statue because it reminded her of her mother, happy to have it hanging around the family antiques shop for a while so she could enjoy owning it. But her father had never reproached her for this, because he was guilty of doing the same thing himself.

In matters of the heart she had known her worth; her father had made sure of that. She'd long been able to twist him around her little finger, but she never felt guilty about this because he was quite clearly a willing victim. Further victims had followed, but none had really captured her heart because they had a lot to live up to; she was too much of a Daddy's girl to accept a man who was any less devoted to her than he was.

She allowed herself a wry smile at that thought. She was beginning to think that a little less devotion might be a good thing.

Sylvie turned on the tap and began to wash lettuce. She watched as a weak but welcome ray of sunlight through the kitchen window made the green and white crinkles of the leaf sparkle like the ripple of waves on the sea. She turned the leaf this way and that, watching the droplets of water dance in the sun, and was suddenly, achingly reminded of a poem she'd studied at school:

Under the Mirabeau Bridge
There flows the Seine,
And our loves recall how then
After each sorrow joy came back again…[1]

She'd learnt it as part of a school recital and had never forgotten it. She remembered her father's look of pride as she stood and spoke the lines, how he'd wiped away a tear as she reached the end and smiled at him. She'd enjoyed school, despite not being overly fond

---

[1] Le Pont Mirabeau by Guillaume Apollinaire translated by Richard Wilbur

of being told what to do; she'd rebelled in her own quiet way, disagreeing (politely and with well-reasoned arguments) with the teachers and doing the absolute bare minimum in Physical Education (she'd much rather have been reading a book than throwing a ball around or – shudder – attempting cartwheels around the gym). She'd enjoyed Music, despite having very little musical talent, and had gone through the obligatory Edith Piaf phase that was mandatory for a certain type of French teenager. She'd excelled in Literature and Art but failed miserably at Mathematics, and the mere thought of algebra was still enough to make her break into a cold sweat. She'd never worked out why *x* equalled *y* or if, indeed, it did.

All love goes by as water to the sea
All love goes by…

'Sylvie!' Henri's voice was loud, harsh. Not the smooth, persuasive timbre he'd used when they first met. 'Day dreaming again, Little Bird? Wake up, I want my dinner.'

She shook, first her head to clear it, then the lettuce to dry it. 'Yes, Henri.'

Henri was the phrase 'Napoleonic complex' made stocky flesh. He was a short but heavy-set man in his 50s, older than her, stronger than her, cleverer than her. More powerful than her. Henri was the Emperor of his home. What he said, went.

Sylvie watched anxiously as he ate his dinner, pushing her own food around the plate and taking an occasional nervous nibble. *Algebra.* That's what being married to Henri reminded her of. She constantly felt like she was about to be handed an algebra test that no one had warned her about and she hadn't studied for. Destined to gaze at the page miserably with no idea what she was meant to do…

She shot to her feet as Henri pushed away his empty plate, clearing the table quickly as he leaned back in his chair, a not altogether pleasant smile on his face as he surveyed his domestic kingdom. She turned on the tap - more water, hot this time –

Sylvie jumped as she felt Henri's breath on her neck. He stood behind her, too close, and held her arm tight, trapping her hand under the running water.

'You went out today,' he said. Not accusing, just stating a fact. The water was beginning to run uncomfortably hot.

'Yes Henri,' she said, trying to twist her arm away. 'I had a doctor's appointment.'

'Why? Are you ill?' Her hand was starting to turn red.

'No, it was about my medication.'

She managed to rip her hand away and turn on the other tap, adding cold water. Henri relinquished his grip but she could feel his eyes burning into the back of her head.

'You're not due another prescription until the 17th,' he said, running a proprietorial finger up and down her bare arm.

'I know, Henri.' She spoke carefully. 'But I don't like the way it makes me feel. The pills make me feel – disconnected. Woolly headed.'

Henri snorted. 'Little Bird, that's not the pills. You ARE woolly headed.'

Sylvie stood her ground. 'The doctor said I've been taking them too long. He said I should start weaning myself off them.'

Henri sighed. 'We've talked about this. You know what happened last time.'

'The doctor said that was because I stopped suddenly. He said I should do it gradually. He's given me a lower dose.'

'Hmm...' Henri reached up and softly twisted a strand of her smooth chestnut hair in his fingers. 'You and your friend the doctor, you've got it all worked out, haven't you?'

'Please, Henri - '

He pulled the strand of hair tight, not tight enough to hurt, just tight enough to exert his power over her. *I am bigger than you, and I could hurt you if I wanted to.* He laughed and let go, stepping away and spreading his hands in a gesture of sudden good nature. The magnanimous husband humouring his obstinate little woman.

'But of course I shall do whatever is best for my wife!'

He sat back down at the table and waited for dessert, raising his eyebrows at the plate of *tarte tatin* Sylvie placed in front of him. 'My favourite! To what do I owe this?'

Sylvie sat opposite him and said nothing. He smiled and began to eat. Waiting.

'The doctor also said it would do me good to get out of the house more.'

Henri looked up from his plate, his eyes steady on hers. 'Did he now? Well, well...'

She plunged on nervously. 'I want to work, Henri! I'm not used to sitting around.'

'You have work. You iron my shirts, you cook my dinner, you keep my house clean. You don't need to work. I look after you.'

'I know you do, Henri, and I'm very grateful…' He snorted, but she ignored it. 'I'm not asking for much – just a little part time job.'

Henri put down his spoon with the air of a long-suffering spouse. 'A job doing what, Sylvie? What exactly can you do?'

'Well – I know about art –'

'You know about art. Fat lot of good that did you last time.' Sylvie said nothing, but stared down at the kitchen table.

'Put this out of your head, Little Bird. That imbecile doctor has unsettled you. Now let me finish my food in peace.'

Henri had spoken. Sylvie went to the kitchen window and looked out as the final feeble rays of sun dissolved into the night.

CHAPTER 2

It was still dark as Philippe wheeled his bicycle out of the staff entrance and across the Coeur de Napoleon. Behind him the glass pyramid of the Louvre glowed warmly, a beacon of art and civilisation at this very uncivilised time of the morning. He was used to working 12-hour shifts but he felt quite strongly that Man wasn't meant to be on his way home to bed at 6am, just as the rest of the city began to stir.

But needs must. He'd never intended to become a night watchman at one of the most famous museums in the world, but there were worst places to work and dirtier, more stressful jobs.

He jumped on his bike and cycled up the Rue du Louvre. He was 30 years old, with an open, friendly face; unlikely to set the world (or even *les Mesdemoiselles* of Paris) on fire, but nice looking. Not a mean bone in his body. If you were unkind it might even cross your mind to call him a bit of a loser, but that would be like kicking a puppy.

He made his way through streets where refuse collectors and sweepers were already at work making the city presentable, getting (in the words of his mother) her face on. The road sloped upwards, Philippe pedalling hard towards Montmartre where the Sacre Coeur loomed above the inhabitants of Paris, keeping a watchful eye on their sins.

He finally reached the old apartment block, carrying his bike into the foyer and up the winding stairs, past peeling paintwork and the breakfast smells of his just-rising neighbours. He could hear his mother pottering around inside her bedroom as he opened the front door.

'Is that you, Philippe?' she cried, as was their early morning routine. He thought briefly (also part of the routine) about saying no, it wasn't, but he was too tired to deviate from the script.

'Yes, Maman!' he called, wandering into the kitchen. He tore off his uniform jacket and threw it on the kitchen table.

'Don't leave your jacket on the table,' called his mother. '*Tante* Isabeau is coming over later and I want the place to be tidy.'

He sighed and picked it up again. 'Ok, Maman.'

'And don't leave your shoes under the table.'

How does she do that? he wondered to himself, straightening up and shoving his feet back into his shoes. 'Good night Maman!' he called.

He took off his uniform, shirt stained with the efforts of his cycle home, threw it on the bedroom floor, then lay back on his single bed. Now he was home, the sleep that had been threatening to overwhelm him for the last hour of his shift had deserted him. He looked around the room, which had been his home for the first 22 years of his life, and had been again for the last two. It hadn't changed much, down to the same old bed and the same curtains covered in footballs that he'd had for his 8th birthday. The football posters on the walls were just updates of the ones that had been there season after season, all except for the one of Eric Cantona in his prime, the one his dad had given him on that same birthday, the day Eric scored his last-ever goal for France.

His mother had offered to redecorate the room – get him a new double bed in case he had 'company' (the accompanying wink worked like anti-Viagra and made him all the more certain he wouldn't be bringing any women home with him) – change the curtains, fresh coat of paint... But Philippe, in the distant, optimistic days when he'd just moved back in with her had said no, no need, it's temporary. He hadn't expected to still be there two years later. And redecorating it now would feel like an acceptance of his Fate, like giving up and admitting to the world that he was indeed a bit of a loser who was destined to live with his mother forever. So instead he would lie there in a melancholic and slightly self-pitying fugue, waiting for sleep to take him away from there.

He reached out to the bedside table for his phone, slipped in some ear buds and selected a song to drift away to...

CHAPTER 3

As Philippe finally slipped into an exhausted but fitful sleep, the rest of the city got to work. Businessmen put on suits and descended into the Metro, daydreaming in the claustrophobic tunnels of calling in sick and spending the day in bed with their wives or secretaries or in some cases, both. Shop workers pinned on name badges and turned 'Closed' signs to 'Open', staring out of the window at a grey sky which promised yet more rain and wishing it was closing time already. Teachers smoked cigarettes behind the school gymnasium and half-joked about bringing back the guillotine for persistent misbehavers.

Henri favoured well-cut Italian suits and expensive leather brogues for his work uniform, but neither did anything to alleviate the general impression his appearance gave; that he was an educated, arrogant bully. In his younger days he'd done better to hide it, to the extent that he had completely taken Sylvie in – although he had caught her at a time when grief had weakened her resolve and left her susceptible to the charm he was still capable of exuding when he wanted something. Not that he bothered charming her any more. He didn't need to. He had everything he wanted.

Sylvie felt the tension lift from her shoulders as she heard the front door close. It was only when Henri left the apartment that she realised how tightly wound she was, how taut with nerves, how their home wasn't floored with tiles and rugs but eggshells that would shatter under her feet if she did something that displeased him. She was vaguely aware, in the anti-depressant fog of her brain, that it wasn't her fault, despite what Henri always said; that she wasn't clumsy or stupid, that she was perfectly capable of looking after herself and had done for years before she'd met him – but then that fog would envelope her again and she'd find herself staring out of the window, or at a piece of lettuce under the cold tap, dreaming about the past. Maybe it wasn't the pills, after all. Maybe the accident had changed her permanently and she really was useless.

But for the next eight hours or so, the day was hers. Not to do exactly as she wished; Henri would question her when he got home, and he'd know somehow if she'd gone out unexpectedly. But it was still hers.

She looked at her reflection in the mirror. She looked older than her 32 years, she thought. Her clothes were well cut – Henri wouldn't have let any wife of his look poor – but her skirt was a modest length and her sensible pearl-buttoned cardigan left everything to the imagination. She looked like a 1950s housewife. She opened the wardrobe and rummaged around at the back, underneath a pile of scarves, and pulled out her best-kept secret: a pair of jeans. Henri didn't like women to wear jeans; he liked them to look like 'real women'. Sylvie had been tempted to ask what a fake woman looked like, but of course hadn't dared. Henri had obviously never been to the drag show at *Chez Michou*; none of the 'fake women' there would've been seen dead in denim. Except maybe the Dolly Parton lookalike, and only then if there were rhinestones involved.

The jeans clung to her curves. She was pleased to see she still *had* curves; she still went in and out in the right places. One day, she would wear those jeans and go out somewhere frivolous; maybe meet a girlfriend for coffee and cake on the Champs Elysees. If she had a girlfriend, that was.

She put the jeans back in the wardrobe.

In the kitchen she turned the radio on and tuned it to a station that played pop music. Henri, of course, had no time for music other than classical or opera. He would listen to it intently, betraying not even the slightest hint of enjoyment. In Henri's opinion, culture might be good for you but it wasn't meant to be entertaining. And it certainly shouldn't make you tap your fingers on the kitchen counter, or wiggle your hips from side to side. Henri would not have approved.

She danced around the kitchen, taking out mixing bowl and scales; creaming together butter and sugar in time with the music; scraping in vanilla pods as the song changed, and ladling in flour. She cracked in an egg, beat it in, then turned to pick up another egg, gasping in shock as she saw Henri standing in the doorway watching her with an amused sneer on his face.

The egg cracked on the cold tile floor. She grabbed a paper towel and bent down to mop it up.

'Henri, you made me jump!' she said. She felt absurdly guilty that he'd caught her enjoying herself. 'You're home in the middle of the day. Is there something wrong? You don't normally come home for lunch.'

'I left a file here,' Henri said, holding up a bundle of papers. He hadn't – he'd taken that file from his briefcase on entering the apartment unnoticed – but he sometimes thought it was good to keep Sylvie on her toes, not knowing when he would pop up and catch her out. Today though he had a different purpose.

He went over to her, sticking a finger into the mixing bowl and licking it clean. 'Oh and while I'm here, I've got some good news for you. I've got you a job.'

Sylvie stared at him in astonishment, immediately suspicious. 'A job?'

Henri smiled at her obvious discomfort, sticking his dirty finger back into the bowl and carelessly swiping out another dollop of cake batter. He slowly sucked his finger as she watched, stringing out the moment for as long as possible before answering.

'Yes, a job. See Little Bird, I do listen to you. I spoke to one of my clients who works at the Louvre and told him my wife 'knows about art', and he's found an opening for you.'

Sylvie was even more astonished. 'At the Louvre? Oh – Henri!'

'A job surrounded by art that will utilise your many fine skills...' He laughed, making it clear that as far as he was concerned an employer would be hard pressed to find *any* fine skills in his wife. 'You start work at seven o'clock this evening. Don't wear anything fancy.' He indicated the mixing bowl. 'Needs more sugar.'

And with that, Henri turned abruptly and strode out of the apartment, leaving her in confusion.

CHAPTER 4

Some people live their life by clocks. They carefully measure out their day in units of 60 minutes; they have schedules and To Do lists that actually get done. They have a routine, and they are always punctual or better still, ten minutes early.

Philippe however was not one of those people, and at 5.50pm when he should have been passing the *fontaine de Theatre Français*, he was only just hitting Rue la Fayette. He flew through the city streets, weaving in and out of cars and buses, narrowly avoiding a group of British tourists who were looking the wrong way as they crossed the road, and somehow made it to the staff entrance of the Louvre just as the clock towers of Paris began to strike six o'clock.

He fumbled his bike padlock shut and rushed inside, swiping his ID pass, skidding through the barrier and throwing himself onto his seat behind the security desk as the last chimes faded.

His colleague Stephanie – who *was* one of those people - watched, lips pursed, head shaking.

'Man, you push it more and more everyday,' she said, reaching out to turn down the collar of his jacket which was sticking up untidily.

'I'm not late,' protested Philippe. 'Our shift starts at six. Look, it's six. On the dot.' He held his watch out to show her but she pushed it away, exasperated but laughing.

'You might want to do something about your hair before she comes down,' she said. Philippe looked affronted.

'I don't know what you're talking about,' he said, turning away and smoothing down his unruly brown mop with the slightly sweaty palm of his hand. She rolled her eyes.

'Yeah, right...here they come.'

'They' were the daytime staff. The ticket sellers and tour guides, the café cooks and baristas and waiters, the gift shop checkout operators and the museum guards who Philippe felt rather looked down upon, or at least pitied, their night time counterparts. And with good reason, he supposed. They actually got to see some action occasionally; potential art thieves casing the joint, terrorist threats, or (more likely) tourists who had been driven mad with the long queues to get in and were itching to take it out on someone. Whereas the most excitement Philippe had had in his two years of night shifts was the time he'd accidentally caused a power cut by falling asleep in the CCTV control room, holding (dropping) the cup of coffee that was supposed to be keeping him awake. The resulting explosion, though minor, had taken some time to repair and knocked out the door alarms and cameras for 15 minutes. It had taken rather longer for him to live down.

'They' also included the office staff. The ones who wore smart suits instead of an ill-fitting uniform made of what felt like old sacking. Philippe discreetly scratched his groin and wished that the label inside his jacket said Armani instead of *'fabriqué en Chine'*.

So the ticket sellers and tour guides and café and gift shop workers began to leave, rushing to catch buses or heading for the Metro, turning their tired feet homewards. Philippe casually watched them go, now and then smiling or saying goodnight, but mostly keeping an eagle eye on the elevator doors that would release the administrators and accounts assistants and executives from the offices on the upper floors.

Stephanie watched him, and shook her head again.

'Could you make it any more obvious you're waiting for her?' she scoffed.

'I'm not waiting for anyone!' he said hotly. Stephanie was having none of it.

'The curvy blonde from HR,' she said. 'She's well out of your league anyway.'

'All I said was, I think she's pretty - '

'Let me use a footballing analogy so you'll understand,' said Stephanie. She was becoming a bit too enthused on the subject of his shortcomings, he felt. 'She's Paris St Germain and you're, I dunno, Valenciennes.'

Philippe was hurt. 'Oh come on, I'm not that bad! I must be at least St Etienne...'

Stephanie looked at him pityingly. 'You've got a nice face, but you're not *première ligue* material. Brest at best.'

Philippe straightened his itchy jacket defensively and got haughtily to his feet.

'Right, well if you're going to be like that then I'm taking my poor second division face out of here and getting a cup of horrible coffee from the vending machine. Do you want one?'

'Yes please,' said Stephanie.

'Tough,' said Philippe. And then froze.

She had long blonde hair that fell in waves over her shoulders, waves that were mirrored in the curve of her waist and hips as she stepped out of the lift and undulated towards him, encased in a snugly tailored black suit and white silk blouse. Tasteful but expensive diamond studs and a single gold strand necklace glinted against her tanned (even in January), supple skin. She was an intoxicating vision of femininity, and she knew it.

Philippe became aware that he was staring at her, mouth open – *catching flies,* his mother would've called it - and was vaguely conscious that Stephanie was too.

The blonde piece from HR drew level with the security desk without even a sideways glance at them. Stephanie recovered her senses first and called out.

'Good night, mademoiselle! Have a nice evening!'

The blonde looked around in surprise, then smiled at Stephanie. She had perfect straight white teeth. '*Merci*, and you!'

Philippe could've been invisible for all the notice she took of him. She left the building and Philippe went to get a horrible coffee before Stephanie could gloat.

CHAPTER 5

Same night (though a little later), same place (but on a different floor), Sylvie stood and looked at the mop in her hand, bemused, while her new colleague Farheena – a bright, friendly young woman with a hijab and an irreverent sense of humour - explained the job.

'So now we've dusted and vacuumed, we'd normally get the buffer out and give the floor a good polish. But the old one's clapped out and those tight *bâtards* in Management won't buy us a new one, so...' She smiled apologetically at Sylvie and held up a bucket of soapy water, patting her on the back as Sylvie took it with a resigned sigh.

'It's not that bad,' said Farheena. ' *Les directeurs* all bugger off home the minute the public leave, so at this time of night it's just us cleaners and a few night security guards. They're alright. They'll come round and check on you now and then but most of the time it's really peaceful. Mopping can be quite Zen when you get into it.'

'Are you mopping too?' asked Sylvie, conscious that there was only one mop and a whole lot of floor. Farheena rolled her eyes.

'Fuck that, I'm off for a smoke,' she said, and laughed at Sylvie's look of dismay. 'I'm kidding! I'm doing the exhibition hall down the end there. Come and find me if you need anything, ok?'

'Thanks Farheena,' said Sylvie, and watched her walk through the gallery.

Sylvie had been to the Louvre many, many times in the past, but it had always been full of people, full of life and noise. And now it was almost silent; almost, but not quite, because she could still hear the low but ever-present hum of traffic outside, and the clock of the nearby church which chimed every hour, much to the annoyance of local residents.

She began to clean, stopping every now and then to dunk and wring the mop, move the bucket, look back at how much she'd done and in front at just how much floor was still left to wash... She stopped again for a moment to rest her chin on the wooden mop handle, and looked up at the portrait on the wall next to her.

Sylvie knew the face in that painting nearly as well as her own reflection in the mirror.

'The Empress Marie Louise by François Gerard, painted in 1810. See, Papa? I was listening.'

Her father used to call their regular Sunday morning trip to the museums and art galleries of the city 'her apprenticeship'. A passionate lover of art, he wanted to instil those same feelings in his young daughter, partly so he could leave his antiques shop to her one day but mostly because he wanted her to experience and enjoy the beauty of the work for herself. Sylvie, keen to impress the father she adored, took in his every word and committed them to memory. She smiled as she remembered how she made him test her.

'Incroyable, Sylvie!' said her father. 'Well done. You know why I am teaching you all this?'

'Oui, Papa,' answered young Sylvie. 'Because one day the shop and everything in it will be all mine!'

Her father had smiled at her enthusiasm. 'That's right! And when your customers ask you about the beautiful paintings in your shop, you'll be able to tell them where they came from, who painted them - '

'And how much they cost!' young Sylvie said brightly. He laughed.

'Well, that too. But you need to tell them about the people in the paintings, and the stories behind them. That's what they're really buying, the stories.'

They moved to the next painting along, a portrait of two sisters.

'You see these two young ladies?'

Young Sylvie had thought they looked miserable; she still thought so now.

'They may look miserable,' said her papa, 'but their lives were easy compared to others'. They were rich, and they would've spent their evenings at grand balls, dancing with handsome, eligible young men.'

And then he'd grabbed his young daughter's hands and whirled her around.

'Handsome young men just like me!'

Sylvie could see it so clearly in her head; she could even hear the invisible orchestra her father had conjured up before waltzing her along the gallery, oblivious to the gaze of the other visitors. She grabbed the mop and swirled it around the floor, humming and whirling past the paintings and statues in time to the music in her head, dancing in the unblinking gaze of the portraits staring down at her from the walls.

But the paintings weren't her only audience. Philippe, in an attempt to alleviate the boredom of an uneventful night shift and stop himself falling asleep on duty (again), had decided to do a quick sweep of the Denon wing. A brisk walk up and down the stairs, shining his torch into shadowy corners and having a quick chat with any cleaners he came across could sometimes waste as much as an hour.

He entered the gallery and his heart almost stopped at the sight before him. The lighting in the gallery was dim, with shafts of moonlight through the glass roof throwing the darkness into sharp relief and casting wild shadows around the sculptures dotted throughout the corridor. But none so wild as the ethereal creature that danced alone, spinning gracefully and laughing, talking to the faces who lined the walls.

He watched spellbound for a moment before realising that this wasn't some magical spirit who had stepped out from a portrait, but a young woman with a mop. A young woman who would almost certainly be hugely embarrassed if she realised he was watching. He stepped backwards into the shadows of the doorway, intending to turn around and carry on his walk elsewhere; but he found himself unable to leave, unable to tear his eyes away from her. She looked so...free. As if the walls of the gallery would be unable to contain her if she ever decided to just fly away. He shook his head in disgust at his own whimsical thoughts but stayed in the doorway, watching.

Sylvie reached the end of the gallery. The invisible orchestra became silent. She smiled at her foolishness, but at least it had made mopping the floor more enjoyable. She curtsied to the mop in gratitude and laughed. It might have been the pills or it might have been the accident, but whatever it was, Henri was right; she was away with the fairies half the time. She sighed and trudged back along the wet floor to collect the bucket, leaving small but dirty footprints in her wake.

Philippe silently turned and fled, but the picture of Sylvie in his head stayed exactly where it was. And when he went home that morning and lay on his childhood bed, listening to music and waiting for sleep to claim him, she danced again.

CHAPTER 6

Sylvie woke the next day feeling refreshed and full of energy, after the best night's sleep she'd had in a long time. She cheerfully took her pills, promising herself that this time it would be different; the lower dosage, coupled with her new job, would soon free her of her dependency and restore some clarity to her often-muddled brain. She would get her life back. On the edge of that thought, dark clouds lurked – she was aware that the drugs weren't the only thing keeping her down – but she pushed them away; some problems were easier to deal with than others.

Henri hadn't asked her anything about her new job but he'd been in a happy enough mood that morning as he left for his office, so Sylvie was hopeful that her new three or so hours of freedom every night would continue for some time.

She spent the day going through the motions; it was a shopping day, so she went to the market and then to the *patisserie*, where she treated herself to a small box of macarons (to take home, of course), then went back to the apartment and threw herself (not literally) into the huge pile of ironing that awaited her return. She found herself counting down the hours until work; an hour of ironing (listening to illicit pop music again), two hours of housework, an hour to prep dinner before Henri came home… But she still managed to find the time to sit down, enjoy a cup of tea (along with most of the macarons, despite kidding herself that she was only going to have one) and dream about the old times that being in the museum again had brought back to life; trips with her father, memories of her mother…happier times.

Sylvie thought there had never been two people more in love than her mother and father. They were fated to be together, her father had told her. Julia Boudain – who had started life as Julia Thorpe – grew up in a small village deep in the English countryside. Stifled by such provincial beginnings she'd escaped to London, where she'd studied Economics. After what she later described as the most boring three years of her life, she'd scraped through her final exams and ground out a degree that she had no intention whatsoever of using in her future career. She'd decided instead that she was going to spend the rest of her life travelling and having adventures, to make up for all the restrictions and boredom Life had so far imposed upon her.

Her first – and last – stop was Paris. On the first night of what was only meant to be a three-night stay (Paris is far too expensive for the lowly backpacker to stay for much longer than that), she found herself in a restaurant attempting to order dinner using only her schoolgirl French and a phrasebook. The handsome young man at the next table – who was also eating alone, having been stood up by his girlfriend – came to her rescue and stopped her ordering a plate of *tetines* – cow's udders – instead of the terrine she was really after.

Once it had become apparent that his girlfriend wasn't going to show (which, he later admitted, he was relieved about because he'd planning to finish with her over dinner), the handsome young man joined her and, despite the fact that his English wasn't much better than her French, they managed to talk and laugh all night, until they were the only ones left and the waiters were putting the chairs up on the other tables, glaring at them and hoping they would take the hint.

The next day Julia extended her stay by another week. By the end of the month, it was obvious that rest of the world would just have to explore itself, because she was staying in Paris. And by the end of the year, they were married.

Julia had left her daughter with an inquisitive nature, a very British sense of humour, and a deep and abiding appreciation of the restorative qualities of a nice cup of tea. Much to her coffee-drinking husband's amusement she had always insisted that tea tasted better brewed in a pot – none of your sticking a bag in a mug and swirling it about with a spoon nonsense here, thank you very much – and so when Sylvie had come across an old blue and white china tea pot at a flea market one Sunday, she'd immediately bought it without even haggling over the price. It was her way of paying homage to her half-British roots. She liked the idea of being half passionate Parisian, half English eccentric.

Finally it was 6.30 – time to leave. Sylvie carefully washed and put away her tea pot, placed an exquisitely prepared plate of food on the table (she didn't want Henri to accuse her of letting things slip at home) and called out. 'Dinner is on the table, Henri. I need to go.'

Henri, reading in the lounge, looked up in surprise. 'Go where?'

"To work of course!' she said, that familiar feeling in the pit of her stomach slowly beginning to rise. She wanted – needed – this job. She picked up her jacket and bag as he entered the room, slowly folding his newspaper.

'You're going back to clean toilets?' he asked. There was an edge of disapproval in his voice. Now she knew why he hadn't bothered asking her about it.

'Of course I am,' she said, carefully. 'Didn't you think I'd stick it out?'

He snorted. 'Little Bird, I know you better than you know yourself. You get these crazy ideas in your sweet little head and then pouf! The next day you've moved onto something else. Of course I didn't think you'd stick it out.'

She stared at the floor. She didn't want to argue with him and make him stop her going out, but that wasn't fair. The long-imprisoned Sylvie Boudain, schoolgirl rebel, algebra failure and Edith Piaf fan, screamed inside her head in silent frustration. She had to say something.

'I'm not like that at all,' she said, in a tiny voice. He laughed.

'Sylvie, Sylvie, it's not a bad thing that you're so flighty!' he said. 'I just don't want you getting any ideas in your head about a career or that kind of nonsense. You're not cut out for it. Remember what happened last time, hmm? Remember who came to your rescue that time?'

'I know Henri, and I am grateful - '

'Good. Come here then and let me kiss you.'

She stood in front of him, all thoughts of fight or disagreement gone. He seemed pleased, pleased enough to make a magnanimous gesture. He kissed her forehead and stood back.

'Go on, then. Off you go to clean up other people's shit. Just remember that you've got work to do in this house too, taking care of me. And I don't just mean cooking - ' He picked up a lettuce leaf from his plate and dangled it in disgust. 'If you can call it that.'

'Thank you, Henri!' She kissed him on the cheek and rushed away before he could change his mind.

Philippe had also spent a restless day. His dreams had been full of strange dancing women. The blonde from HR was in there somewhere, but soon got lost in the shadows and turned into his mum, which was possibly the most disturbing thing in the whole dream. But just there, on the edge of his vision, was Sylvie. He didn't know it was her of course, he hadn't even seen her face properly, but he couldn't get her out of his head.

When he got to work he was so out of sorts that he didn't even look out for the golden Human Resources goddess. Luckily Stephanie was too busy looking out for her herself to comment.

By 6.30 all the day-time staff had gone home and the evening cleaners had just begun to trickle in. Philippe sat at the desk reading a book; he had to keep occupied to stop himself going mad with – restlessness? frustration? romantic longing? – whatever it was that was causing him to ache inside. It was a good book, but he still found himself going over and over the same page. His eyes took the words in but they seemed to get lost on route to his brain, so he had no idea what was going on.

Stephanie was busy at the computer when Sylvie entered, harassed. The brief scene with Henri had held her up, and it was already almost 7pm. She'd been hoping to arrive a little early and maybe have a chat with Farheena, even meet some of the other cleaners, but here she was, out of breath and fumbling around in her bag. She stopped at the security desk.

'I'm so sorry, I can't - ' she began. The other security guard, the one with his nose in a book, spoke without looking up – he was obviously getting to the end of a sentence and didn't want to lose his place.

'You have to swipe - ' said Philippe, and finally looked up. It was her. He knew it immediately. The dancing woman of his dreams. Gulp!

Philippe took a deep breath and put his book down, very calmly – on the outside. On the inside his stomach was doing the Macarena and his heart was thudding. The dancing woman looked at him with a gently quizzical smile on her face. He swallowed.

'You have to swipe your pass, mademoiselle,' he said. He was amazed to hear his voice sounding so normal.

Sylvie smiled at him. He seemed a bit nervous, she thought, but friendly. And he liked books. *Never trust a man who doesn't read*, her mother had told her once, only half joking. Her father had read, mostly about artists he admired and the odd bit of history, but her mother had devoured all kinds of stories and, stuck at home looking after her husband, that was how Sylvie saw the world these days; through the pages of books. Books which Henri was happy to have around (like opera and classical music, he felt they represented 'culture' and added an air of classiness to the apartment) but which he never picked up himself.

'I'm so sorry,' she said, fumbling in her bag again. She seemed to have a lot of stuff in that small bag. 'It's in here somewhere. I left home in a hurry,' she explained. 'I hate being late.'

'Me too,' said Philippe. Stephanie snorted incredulously. He ignored her and walked around to help Sylvie, taking stuff from her hands and putting it on the desk. She smiled at him gratefully.

'Thank you so much. I'm not usually this disorganised.'

'Oh God I am!' cried Philippe. 'I can never find anything at home. My mother says - ' He stopped abruptly, hoping she hadn't heard that.

She had.

'Do you live with your mother?' she asked.

'Me? Ha! As if.' To change the subject he took the object she was holding in her hands from her. A book. 'Oh! 'The Shadow of the Wind'!'

She looked pleased. 'Do you know it?'

'Yes!' he said, enthusiastically. 'It's a wonderful book. Exciting and dramatic and romantic - '

'All the things Life should be,' she said, with a wistful smile. And suddenly they both felt it.

A meeting of kindred spirits.

Their eyes met for a moment, and then – Sylvie's pass fluttered out from between the pages of the book. Philippe bent down to retrieve it, scanning her name on the card. *Mme Sylvie Cloutier.* Married. Damn.

He swiped the pass for her, giving himself time to adjust the disappointed expression on his face, and handed it back to her.

'Here you are, Madame Cloutier. Have a good evening.'

Sylvie felt her face turn ridiculously hot. 'Oh, please, call me Sylvie! Thank you so much for your help - ' she peered at the name tag on his uniform jacket ' – Philippe.'

'You're welcome, Sylvie,' he said, and all at once it didn't matter that she was married. Not in a sordid, seedy way; he just felt very strongly that she was going to be an important part of his life. Someone special.

They smiled at each other, neither wanting the moment to end; the outside world had faded away into the background and all that was left were these two slightly bruised but hopeful souls facing each other.

Philippe opened his mouth to speak, but then – the bells of Saint Germain l'Auxerrois, the church across the road, begin to chime.

'Oh!' cried Sylvie, suddenly shy and flustered again. 'I'd better get to work! I don't want to get the sack on my second day!'

She stuffed everything back into her bag and rushed away, wondering to herself what on earth had just happened there. Philippe watched her go, then turned to see Stephanie staring at him, amused.

'Oh. My. God,' she said in disbelief. 'What are you like?'

'I don't know what you mean,' he said, treating her with the contempt he felt she deserved – even though he knew exactly what she meant. He'd just lost himself in a scene that was straight out of the trashy romance novels his mother sometimes read.

It was only when he went to sit down that he realised he was still clutching Sylvie's book to his chest.

CHAPTER 7

The evening passed in a blur for Sylvie. She listened to Farheena talking, the younger woman prattling on at high speed about the cleaning manager's foibles, about the miserly wages they were paid, about her university course, her family... Sylvie usually loved hearing about other people's lives – because hers was so boring, she realised with a shock – but tonight, no matter how hard she tried to listen, she found her attention wandering. She nodded in all the right places, even asked her new friend the odd question, but her heart wasn't in it and she was relieved when Farheena left her to it.

As she dusted and polished Sylvie tried hard not to think about the security guard downstairs, the security guard with the shy smile and kind eyes, who lived with his mum and liked a good book. He wasn't exactly romantic hero material. But then again, how would she know? There had been a time when Henri had seemed like a romantic hero to her, and now...

She shook her head, angry with herself. She was a married woman. She had had some problems, and her husband had been kind enough to look after her (if her mind had been able to face-palm right then, it would've done. *'Kind'? 'Look after'? If that was kindness...*) Sylvie polished harder, taking out her confusion and frustration on the poor defenceless sign on the wall in front of her.

The Empress Marie Louise... She stopped and looked up at the regal face, dropping to the floor in a curtsey.

'Good evening, your majesty,' she said. Marie Louise looked at her imperiously but didn't speak. Sylvie laughed at herself and went to get the bucket.

Farheena came back as Sylvie was halfway through mopping the floor.

'Aren't you finished yet?' she asked. 'You do know it's nearly 10 o'clock, don't you?'

Sylvie rested the mop on the edge of the bucket.

'I'm nearly done,' she said. 'I'm not in a hurry anyway.'

Farheena's eyes widened in understanding and she nodded. 'Ah, it's like *that* is it? Is there no one waiting for you at home?'

'Just my husband.'

Farheena nodded again. 'I see... Well, don't hang around here and let the cheap bastards get unpaid overtime out of you. I can think of a hundred better places to avoid going home from.'

The church clock struck 10.

'You'd better go before you turn into a pumpkin or something,' said Sylvie. Farheena smiled.

'Ok, I can take a hint!' she laughed. 'But don't stay too long. See you tomorrow!'

Sylvie watched her leave, then turned back to her mop.

Philippe was on tenterhooks as the evening cleaners started to leave. He hopped from foot to foot impatiently, clutching Sylvie's book and looking out for her amongst the mainly women who were heading home to their husbands and families or, in a couple of cases, cats. Lots of cats.

No sign of her. He frowned, but then smiled as he recognised the young Asian woman heading his way; he'd spoken to her a few times when he'd been on his rounds and he was pretty sure she normally cleaned the gallery where he'd seen Sylvie dance.

'Hey!' he called out. Farheena stopped. 'Do you know the new lady? Sylvie? Is she on her way down?'

Farheena looked at him appraisingly. She knew him, of course, but he seemed a bit more awake than usual. Eager. Hmm. It was like that, was it? After just one night? Sylvie was a quiet one, but don't they always say it's the quiet ones you have to watch?

'She's still working,' she said.

'She's dedicated,' Philippe said. She laughed.

'Nope, she just doesn't want to go home. Denon wing, first floor.'

'Thanks!' cried Philippe, already halfway there. Farheena and Stephanie watched him go, then looked at each other, Farheena raising her eyebrows. Stephanie shook her head.

'Don't ask,' she said.

The gallery was dimly lit by the time Philippe reached it, the overhead lamps turned off. The illuminated security signs and the pale winter moon through the skylight cast a soft glow, soft but still bright enough to glisten off the wet wooden floor. There was no sign of Sylvie.

Disappointed, Philippe turned away, determined to catch her on her way out when she finally left. The soles of his shoes, worn smooth by age and by his habit of wandering the museum at night, skidded on the wet floor. He smiled and looked around, tempted; then stepped back, took a run up and slid the length of the gallery on the polished wood.

There are three ways to stop a slide along a wet floor. One, you run out of slide and just gradually, gracefully grind to a halt; two, you run out of floor and hit a wall; or three, you lose your balance, flail around in an ungainly manner for a few seconds, think you've regained your balance for a few more seconds, and then end up on your *derriére* anyway.

Philippe went for number three.

'Ow!' He sat up and rubbed his elbow, which he'd banged on a heavy marble statue on the way down, then realised he was being watched. He turned to see Sylvie, holding an empty bucket and shaking with suppressed laughter. He grinned ruefully, surprised to find that he although he felt like a bit of an idiot, he wasn't completely mortified. Although she was laughing at him, it didn't feel mocking or malicious.

She dropped the bucket and rushed over to help him up.

'Oh my goodness, are you alright?' she said. 'I'm so sorry, I should really have a wet floor sign up - '

He scrambled up, smiling at her.

'Oh no, it's my own stupid fault,' he said. 'I haven't been able to resist a wet floor since I was a kid.'

She looked at him, quizzically.

'My mother - '

'The one you definitely don't live with?' she smiled. He laughed.

'Yes, that's the one. She used to be the cleaner at my school when I was little. I had to hang around after lessons and wait for her to finish, and I used to get bored...'

A brief vision of his mother clutching a mop popped into his head. She'd just finished washing the floor of the school gymnasium. It was a particularly good one for skidding along, except for the fact that there was often equipment in the way. Philippe had seen the wooden vaulting horse from close quarters – *very* close quarters, gazing up groggily from the floor – more times than even his mother realised. He could still feel the egg-shaped bump on his head from one particularly violent crash.

'Go on, say it,' he said, resigned.

'Say what?'

'What everyone says. You live with your mum, what a loser - '

Sylvie looked horrified. 'I'd never say that!' she protested. 'I'd live with my mum again like a shot if she was still around.'

Philippe smiled and picked up her bucket. They slowly headed down the gallery to where Sylvie had left her cleaning kit.

'I haven't always lived with my mum,' said Philippe. 'I moved out years ago when I got married - '

Her heart skipped a beat. So he was married too. Might as well forget all that romantic hero nonsense –

' – but that ended in complete disaster so I moved back. Temporarily.'

Sylvie composed herself. 'Well, that makes sense. Paris is a very expensive city. Given the choice between renting a grotty room somewhere or moving back home, I know what I'd choose.' *Except I don't have either option.*

'Exactly!' Philippe felt less embarrassed about his living arrangements now. She struck him as the sort of person who didn't judge others on material things. 'And just because I live with my mum, it doesn't mean I've reverted back into being an overgrown teenager...'

'No?' said Sylvie, chiding him good-naturedly. 'So she doesn't do your washing or make you a packed lunch for work?'

He grinned. 'That would be really sad, wouldn't it? Almost as sad as having my bedroom exactly the same as it was when I was a kid, even down to the old childhood curtains with footballs on them...'

She laughed. 'Oh dear, maybe you are a loser after all.'

They reached the end of the gallery. Sylvie picked up her cleaning things. They both stood in silence for a moment, wanting to speak but unsure of what to say.

Philippe suddenly remembered the book tucked under his arm and held it out to her.

'Oh yes, I was bringing this back! You left it at Security earlier.'

She smiled and took it, gratefully. 'Thank you! I'm so forgetful sometimes. Henri - ' She stiffened.

'Is that your husband?' asked Philippe, hoping for a 'no'.

'Yes,' she said. 'He says I'm woolly headed. He says I'd be dangerous if I had a brain.'

Nice guy thought Philippe. 'You were just in a rush,' he said. 'Well, I'm holding you up. I should let you go.' *Back to your husband...*

'No hurry,' she said. 'I have to get all this put away first.'

Philippe took the mop from her and looked back along the gallery. The moon had disappeared and it was dark and shadowy. He remembered her dancing the night before.

'Some people would find it creepy working up here on their own,' he said.

'I'm not on my own though, am I?' she smiled. 'I've got loads of old friends up here.'

'You have?' Maybe she *was* woolly headed... She laughed at his puzzled face and walked over to a painting. He followed.

'This is Marie Louise. She looks terribly refined, but I think she's desperate to let her hair down. Underneath all that finery there's a wild cat lurking.' She turned to another painting. 'And there's Joan of Arc. A rabid feminist who refused to take nonsense from anyone. A kind of 15th century Germain Greer. With a sword.'

Philippe laughed loudly and looked at her in admiration. 'How come someone who knows all this stuff is working as a cleaner?'

'Long story...' she sighed. 'My papa used to bring me here every Sunday. These paintings are like childhood friends.'

'Not very chatty ones, though.'

'No, but they're very good listeners...'

CHAPTER 8

So that was how it began. Friends.

Sylvie looked forward to going to work and, after his initial surprise at her sticking at it, Henri didn't seem to mind. It had occurred to him that there were certain advantages to having the house to himself in the evenings, advantages that Sylvie didn't need to know about. It had also crossed his mind that, if his wife had ever had any thoughts about becoming independent or even leaving him, this part-time job would serve as a timely reminder of what level she'd sunk to, of exactly what kind of 'career' she could look forward to after so long away from work. He wasn't sure however if it also served as a reflection on him; that not only was his wife working, she was working in such a lowly capacity. On a rare social outing – one of the seniors in the accountancy firm he worked at was retiring, and they held a party in his honour - he forbade Sylvie from telling anyone about her new job. But it came out anyway after a few drinks.

'Madame Cloutier,' said Henri's boss Monsieur Guiton, an elderly but dapper man with kind eyes. 'I believe you used to run Boudain's Antiques?'

Sylvie smiled up at him. 'Oh yes, I did!'

'A wonderful shop,' said Monsieur Guiton. 'My wife was one of your best customers! Such a shame you decided to close. I don't suppose you have any plans to re-open?'

Sylvie looked at him, not quite sure what to say. She hadn't decided to close; it had been rather forced upon her. She opened her mouth to speak but Henri, by now full of brandy and alarmed by the turn the conversation was taking – he didn't want her getting any ideas about re-opening her shop - spoke before her.

'It was too much for Sylvie, after her – you know – *accident*,' he said. Why he said it like that – like it wasn't an accident that had caused her problems, but rather some kind of mental weakness – Sylvie didn't know. 'But she's overcome her problems and gone back to work. Why don't you tell them what you do now?'

She was confused; he'd told her often enough that he didn't like the thought of any wife of his going to work, let alone being a cleaner, so did he actually want her to say something, or was it one of his jokes? Evidently he didn't really want her to speak, because he spoke for her.

'My wife, who 'knows about art' and used to fancy herself as something of an expert, well now she's an expert at scrubbing the toilets at the city's most prestigious museum,' he explained, waving his glass around drunkenly and leering lecherously at a well-upholstered brunette in a tight-fitting dress who stood nearby. The brunette smiled uncomfortably. Sylvie stared into her drink.

'I remember your father,' Monsieur Guiton said, touching her softly on the arm. 'Such a nice man.'

Henri, who had moved closer to the brunette, brayed with laughter at something she'd said, making her glance around awkwardly. But his eyes stayed firmly, humourlessly, on Sylvie. She swallowed.

'He was a wonderful father and a great teacher,' she said, tears springing to her eyes.

'You must miss him?'

'Yes,' she whispered, willing herself not to cry. Henri would be furious with her if she embarrassed him like that.

Monsieur Guiton squeezed her arm gently and looked into her eyes. For a moment he looked like he was going to speak again, but then he just smiled sadly and walked away.

Every day Sylvie would do her chores around the house, counting the hours until it was time to leave. *Time to see Philippe.* She would take her pills, the lower dose not making a noticeable difference to her fuzzy brain yet, but it was early days and she was hopeful. She felt more cheerful but also, conversely, more anxious; her life had changed, for the better she thought, but in the process the tiny bit of newfound freedom her job had given her had brought the bars of her gilded cage sharply into focus.

Every evening at 6.15 Sylvie would call Henri to the table for his dinner. It was a little early for him, but as he'd made it quite clear that he wouldn't cook his own dinner he had to accept an earlier mealtime. Henri had taken to making her a last cup of tea before she left; he insisted on it, and often even poured it from the old blue and white tea pot for her. She wasn't quite sure if this new development was sweet or suspicious; apart from the fact that he was usually a coffee drinker himself, he'd rarely offered to do anything for her after the early days of their relationship. He claimed it was because he wanted to spend a few minutes of quality time with her; he'd been at work all day and whereas in the past they'd have spent the evening watching the television (the programmes chosen by Henri, of course), they now spent hardly any time together. The cynical, non-woolly part of Sylvie thought it more likely that he enjoyed keeping her on tenterhooks, wondering if tonight would be the night he would finally forbid her from going out. But he never did.

Philippe's routine had also changed. Gone were the hurried flights on his bicycle through the streets of Paris, getting to work by the skin of his teeth in a uniform that had seen better days. Now he actually had a timetable.

Philippe would get up around midday and eat whatever his mother had left in the fridge for him. He had told her that she didn't need to cook for him any more – Sylvie's joke about her making him a packed lunch had hit a nerve – but all that had done was stop her dishing it up and leaving it on a plate for him; now, everything was left in plastic containers ready for him to assemble himself. *I'm a big boy now,* he thought to himself, looking proudly at the plate in front of him.

Gone were the screwed up, sweaty shirts on his bedroom floor. Well – most of them, anyway; there was every possibility that there were one or two lurking in the deep dark recesses under his bed, breeding with the odd socks and discarded pants that seemed to be indigenous to that shadowy region of his room, spawning God knew what horrific fashion *faux pas*. Most of them now ended up in the laundry basket, and some even made it to the washing machine without his mother getting involved.

Philippe would do a few chores, or in fine weather he'd take a book and find somewhere nice to sit – there was a café at the foot of the Sacre Coeur which served great coffee, and the walk there afforded a wonderful view of the city below. He'd read and try not to think about Sylvie. He usually failed.

Then he'd head home, where his mother would be back from work. She'd fuss around and make sure he'd eaten, tempting him with homemade *madeleines* and cakes. Then time to shower and shave, deodorise, put on a freshly laundered shirt and attempt to tame his unruly brown mop of hair, all under the watchful eye of Eric Cantona.

'Don't look at me like that, Eric,' he said one day, fed up with the ex-footballing legend's steely-eyed and slightly disapproving expression. 'Just because I'm making an effort.'

The poster of Eric said nothing but his silence spoke volumes.

Then Philippe would kiss his mother goodbye and cycle sedately to the museum, carefully padlocking his bike to a lamppost outside the staff entrance. He made sure that he was always at his desk ready to greet Sylvie as she arrived.

This hadn't gone unnoticed, or unremarked. The first time Stephanie had arrived at the security desk to start her shift, only to find

Philippe already seated and calmly bidding the departing day time staff a good night, she stopped in shock with her mouth open in surprise.

'What are you doing here?' she said, flabbergasted. He smiled at her.

'Good evening, Stephanie.'

'Am I late?'

'No.'

'Are you sick? Am *I* sick? You've ironed your shirt. What's going on?' She seemed completely bewildered. 'I know – you're an alien replacement, aren't you? I've seen Invasion of the Body Snatchers.'

Philippe smiled at her condescendingly and got to his feet.

'I am rising above your childish insults and going to the coffee machine. Would you like one?'

'That does it,' said Stephanie, shaking her head. 'I've fallen through a wormhole or something.'

She wasn't the only one who'd noticed a difference. The Head of Security, Monsieur Fournier, complimented Philippe on his newfound sense of responsibility.

'Well I have to admit, Philippe, I only took you on as a favour to your mother,' Monsieur Fournier said to him one evening. 'But you seem to have turned over a new leaf recently. Smartened yourself up. Always here ready to start your shift on the dot. Well done.'

Philippe smiled, a little embarrassed; his recent punctuality had nothing to do with work but he was damned if he was going to admit it to his boss.

'Well, I thought it was about time I started to take things seriously,' he said. His manager smiled.

'Good man!' he said, patting him on the back. 'Say hello to your mother for me.' And at that he strode away, but not before Philippe saw the redness in his cheeks.

At 6.45pm Sylvie would arrive. She made a point of getting to work in plenty of time to change her shoes, get her cleaning kit ready...

at least, that was what she told herself, but even she didn't believe it. She was a terrible liar. She knew it was actually so she had time for a chat with Philippe.

They would talk about their day, or about what they were reading. They liked a lot of the same books; books with a sense of romance and adventure, with stories that swept you up like a Kansas farm girl in a twister and deposited you somewhere exotic, somewhere far removed from every day life, away from low-paid jobs and toxic relationships.

One evening she arrived with a present for him.

'It's the follow up to 'The Shadow of the Wind', have you read it?' she asked, holding out a book.

'No,' he said. His fingers brushed against hers as he reached out for it, making his whole hand tingle.

'It's wonderful,' she enthused. 'It made me cry. I've read and reread all of his books loads of times. They make me ache.'

He smiled gently at her wistful face and she blushed.

'You must think I'm *dérangé - '* she said, embarrassed.

'No no, not at all!' he cried. 'I know exactly what you mean. I get that ache as well, all the time.'

They stared at each other, the only two people in the world for a moment, until Farheena arrived and swept Sylvie away upstairs.

Later on Philippe would find some excuse to wander up to the Denon wing, usually around 8.30pm when Sylvie had finished her dusting and polishing and would be taking a brief rest before starting on the floor. They'd stroll along the gallery and she would tell him about the paintings on display, sharing with him the stories her father used to tell her. She was amazed to find that she remembered them all, that the information was still up there, hidden away – she just needed the encouragement of an interested audience to look for it.

Sometimes Philippe would swipe a couple of his mother's homemade cupcakes on his way out of the apartment and he'd share them with Sylvie, laughing as she bit into them with obvious enjoyment. He wiped pink frosting from the tip of Sylvie's nose and ate it, making her giggle.

Even Mathilde – the curvy blonde from HR – had noticed the change in Philippe; she noticed that the gormless security guard had stopped gazing at her, doe-eyed, when she left for the day. She was pleased, if also secretly a little affronted to have been so easily tossed aside. He wasn't her type.

CHAPTER 9

It was raining again. It had hardly stopped all winter – there had been major flooding in several parts of the country – and so far spring was showing all the signs of continuing in the same damp vein. Philippe lay on his single bed reading the book Sylvie had given him, the watery early morning light filtering through the footballs on his curtains and dimly illuminating the Eric Cantona poster. He finished the page he was reading and threw the book down, dramatically but very carefully and only after inserting a bookmark.

'Oh Eric, I can't sleep! I can't eat. I can't stop thinking about her!'

Eric rolled his eyes – not an easy thing for a poster to do. 'Which one is it this time?' he asked, dismissively. 'The sexy blonde or the ex-wife?'

'Don't say it like that!' protested Philippe. 'It's different this time. Sylvie's different.'

'Yeah, married different,' said Eric, shaking his head. 'That's *sooo* much better.'

'No need for sarcasm, Eric,' said Philippe. 'I know she's married. But she's not happy, is she? I know she isn't. I could make her happy.'

Eric didn't reply. Philippe wasn't sure if that was a sign of contempt or agreement.

Sylvie meanwhile was getting frustrated at the seemingly slow progress her withdrawal from anti-depressants was having. The doctor had made a point of telling her not to cut down too quickly; she'd tried in the past to just stop, and it hadn't ended well. Henri had already voiced his concerns about her quitting – he didn't want her slipping back into the deep depression she'd suffered after the accident, he said, making it sound like a foregone conclusion that without the pills that's exactly what would happen. But Sylvie knew that, even if it still often felt like her head was stuffed with cotton wool, even if she had trouble concentrating on things and found herself drifting away into a daze, she was getting stronger. She might only be spending her evenings cleaning, but on those evenings she was surrounded by some of the most beautiful art in the world; paintings which she remembered from happier times, fragile creations of pigment and canvas and paper which had nonetheless survived through wars and famines and terrible disasters, and which lived on for hundreds of years even after the artists who had made them and the subjects who had sat for them had died. If they could survive, couldn't she?

'Day dreaming again, Little Bird?' Henri's contempt interrupted her thoughts, bringing her back to the here and now like a shot of adrenaline in a cardiac patient. She turned away from the window, unaware she'd even been staring out of it, and picked up the just-boiling kettle to fill the teapot.

'You're not going to work in that skirt,' said Henri. As usual it wasn't a question, but a statement of fact.

'I was going to - ' began Sylvie, but Henri held his hand up to silence her.

'It's too short. Do you want everyone to see your fat arse when you bend over? Go and change it. I'll finish the tea.'

Sylvie's cheeks burned. It *was* shorter than her other skirts because she'd taken a pair of scissors to it that day, fed up with dressing like someone twenty years older than her, but it was hardly obscene. Obscene would be the red leather mini-skirt with the side lacing that left little to the imagination that she'd been fascinated (and tempted) by as a teenager, the one in the window of the fetish shop over the road from Boudain's Antiques. The shop had always attracted crowds of giggling window shoppers but very few who were brave enough to venture inside. A shame, because if they had, the elderly and rather motherly owner Madame Giroux would've offered them a small glass of Pernod and a hefty discount on anything they wanted. She opened her mouth to tell Henri this but thought better of it. He might stop her going if she contradicted him.

When she came back into the kitchen five minutes later Henri was all smiles. He held out a cup of tea.

'I haven't got time now,' she said. Henri's face darkened. She took the cup and drained it quickly.

'There, that's better,' he said. 'Can't have my wife going to work without something warm inside her.'

Sylvie waited for him to make a crude joke about giving her something else warm when she got home, and was relieved when he didn't.

She hurried through the sodden streets and over the Pont des Arts, the padlocks that decorated the bridge glinting in the rain. She wondered how many of the couples who'd left a padlock there as a symbol of their eternal love were still together. *Shackled* she thought, and laughed bitterly to herself. *Getting cynical in my old age*. But then Henri had put one there for her, the day he'd proposed. Maybe she had every right to be cynical.

The heavens opened as she reached the middle of the bridge, the rain coming down even harder. It seemed to have been raining for months. She ran for cover, the imposing façade of the Louvre waiting for her on the bank. And inside, waiting for her rather less stoically, was Philippe. The thought caused a little warm glow in her tummy.

CHAPTER 10

It was nearly ten o'clock. Sylvie finished her cleaning and gathered her things together in the gallery. She said good night to Farheena – who always popped down for a chat at the end of the night, and usually at the beginning of the night, and quite often during the night whenever she got bored – and waited, fiddling around with her mop and looking busy as her friend left, smiling knowingly to herself.

Philippe passed Farheena on the stairs, smiling casually, then raced up to the gallery to find Sylvie. He slowed down as he spotted her but it was too late; she'd already seen his eagerness. He looked sheepish.

'Busted!' she laughed.

He laughed too then. 'I'm just keen to carry on with my lessons,' he said. She shook her head.

'No, I've taught you about all the paintings on this floor now,' she said. 'Everything I remember, anyway. There's nothing left for me to tell you.'

He smiled softly. 'I don't know about that. There's so much I don't know about you.'

She stared at him, tempted for a moment to just tell him everything, but she knew that once she'd opened the floodgates she would be swept away. Who knew where she'd wash up?

Thunder rumbled in the distance.

'Oh, this weather!' she said, blatantly changing the subject. Philippe took the hint.

'My maman reckons this has been the wettest spring for 20 years,' he said. 'I just hope it clears up for the European Championships.'

She looked puzzled.

'The football,' he said. 'You don't follow it? Your – your husband, he's not into soccer?'

'Oh, no,' she said. 'Henri's not a very sporting person.'

'Each to their own,' said Philippe. 'I enjoy it, but I'm not a fanatic. My father, now – he was mad about it. But he supported an English team. Manchester United?'

'Oh yes,' said Sylvie, grateful for inane small talk. It was probably best to avoid getting too intimate. 'Even I've heard of them! David Beckham, Eric Cantona...'

'Yes. My father was a massive fan of Eric Cantona. He'd more or less retired when I was old enough to get into soccer, but my father still used to rave about him.' To the point where Young Philippe had felt like he knew Eric better than his own *papa*.

'What happened to your father?' asked Sylvie. 'You talk about your mother all the time - '

'Not *all* the time!' protested Philippe, slightly embarrassed. Sylvie laughed.

'Yes you do. It's sweet. But you never mention your father.'

'No...' Philippe shuffled his feet awkwardly. 'My father wasn't around much when I was growing up. He – went away a lot because of his work. In the end my mum had enough and they split up. She raised me more or less on her own, even when they were still together. He was pretty useless.'

'My father was the complete opposite,' Sylvie said warmly. 'He did everything for me after my mother died. He tried so hard to stop me missing her. It didn't work, of course, but it was nice of him to try.'

'What happened to him?' asked Philippe, gently. She sighed.

'He had a stroke. He wasn't even that old, but he was a typical Frenchman – he never visited a doctor. He had high blood pressure and he smoked like a chimney.' She stared up at the glass roof, watching the rain beating against it, remembering. 'He was in hospital for months. I went to see him every day. I wanted to bring him home, but he didn't want to be a burden to me. He wanted me to keep the shop going, to have a life...'

'You had a shop?'

'Yes. Antiques and art.'

'So that's how you know about the paintings and everything. What happened to it?'

Sylvie turned away from him. 'I ruined everything. It's a long story.'

There was another flash of lightning.

'I should probably get going,' she said, picking up the bucket. Philippe reached out to her.

'Wait!' He started after her and skidded. They both looked down at the wet floor. He smiled, an idea forming in his head; he didn't want her to leave when she was obviously feeling sad. 'Take your shoes off.'

She laughed. 'What?'

'Take your shoes off. You're wearing pantyhose, yes? It works better on socks, but they'll do.'

She laughed again as he slipped off his own shoes and followed suit.

'Now we take a run up and...'

She shrieked with laughter as he grabbed her hand and they skidded the length of the gallery together, wobbling and ending up in a giggling heap together at the end. Sylvie jumped and grabbed him tightly as there was a massive crash of thunder and a flash of brilliant lightning.

'Oh! What was that?' she shrieked, still giggling. He pulled her closer and looked into her eyes.

'Electricity,' he whispered. Their laughter subsided as they gazed into each other's eyes. He touched her cheek, so soft and smooth, trembling, and moved in close enough to feel her warm breath on his own skin. Sylvie closed her eyes, giving in…

There was another massive crash of thunder, making Sylvie jump again. She leapt up, away from him.

'I really need to go,' she said. 'It sounds like the storm's getting worse.'

'Sylvie - ' Philippe got to his feet too, and reached out again for her; but she danced out of his reach.

'I have to go!' she said, almost pleading.

'I'm sorry,' he said.

'No, it's fine, it's me,' she said, heading back down the gallery at speed. He reached out to steady her as she skidded again, but she stayed upright. She rammed her feet back into her shoes and grabbed the mop and bucket, flustered.

'Leave it, I'll put it away,' he said. 'Take care, Sylvie.'

She hesitated at the door, torn between wanting to stay with him and knowing that Henri would be waiting, and that if she wasn't home soon there would be trouble. Philippe smiled at her, even though his insides felt like a washing machine on high spin.

'Go on, go. Sweet dreams. I'll see you tomorrow.'

She smiled wistfully and left him to sweet dreams of his own.

CHAPTER 11

Sylvie was surprised to find Henri already in bed when she got home, despite the fact it wasn't much past ten o'clock and he was usually still up waiting for her. To her relief he grunted at her as she entered and rolled over while she changed out of her wet clothes without turning on the light, and was soon snoring. She decided to stay up a little longer.

She made herself some hot chocolate and sat at the kitchen table in her nightdress, wrapped in a blanket. With the lights on low, she stared out of the window into the dark city street watching the rain. It was getting even heavier. There had already been flooding in other parts of the country and reports of a fatality in Seine-et-Marne, east of Paris, and here in the city the river was much higher than she'd seen it in years.

She watched rivulets of water chase each other down the window pane, aware that she was trying very hard to avoid thinking about what had happened that night. She had almost let Philippe kiss her! Her heart leapt as she thought about how close he had been; how tenderly he'd stroked her skin, how his breathing (and hers) had quickened as he'd leaned in towards her...

She hugged herself a little harder, wishing it was Philippe's arms enfolding her and not the soft woollen blanket. But what would that achieve? He could kiss her a hundred times (her heart leapt again at the thought) but it wouldn't change the fact that she was married.

You don't have to stay married, the little voice in her head piped up. No, she didn't. But – where would she go? She had no money. Not any more. Her cleaning job paid very little, and she'd only got that through Henri – who would employ her, with her woolly head and daft thoughts and bad track record? No one, certainly not in any job that involved anything more complicated than cleaning floors. Henri was right; she was useless for anything other than cleaning, cooking and bed. He wasn't perfect – the little voice in her head snorted in disgust – but he provided for her. She needed him. *Yes, he's made sure of that!*

She also knew that he wouldn't let her go without a fight. He seemed to despise her, then out of the blue he would do something nice, like making her that last cup of tea and sitting down to drink it with her before she left for work. She was aware that might not sound like much, but for Henri it was a lot. And she couldn't forget that once upon a time he'd literally done everything for her. *Of course you can't forget it - he won't let you!*

And then there was the danger that Philippe wouldn't like her once he really got to know her. Henri often said that she was hard work, that he was the only one that could put up with her daydreaming. Philippe didn't know that she was too stupid to look after herself, and she wanted to keep it that way.

She yawned, tired but not wanting to go to bed, not wanting to lie on the cold half of the mattress listening to him grunting like a hippopotamus with sleep apnoea and stealing the bed linen. She watched the rain trickle down the window and wasn't even aware that it was mirrored by exhausted and hopeless tears running down her face.

CHAPTER 12

The next day was dry but cold for the end of May, the grey skies promising more rain to come. After an uneventful morning Sylvie walked along the Quai de Montebello, browsing idly amongst the posters, artwork and old books at the stalls. Below them, the slate-coloured river was as swollen as Sylvie's tear-wrung eyes; both had been in danger of flooding the night before but both had somehow held firm.

She crossed the road to Shakespeare and Company, the vintage bookshop that was one of her few legitimate pleasures. Her mother had taught her to read and speak in her native tongue, and reading the great classics of English literature by the likes of Dickens and Austen in their original language made Sylvie feel closer to her. Henri allowed her to come here occasionally, and she often tried to fit in a quick detour to lose herself among the books on her way to the supermarket.

'Sylvie?'

She turned in surprise at the sound of his voice. Philippe stood before her, smiling in delight at this unexpected meeting.

'What are you doing here?' she asked, a little breathlessly. To have him here, almost on her home turf, felt – dangerous, somehow; as if Henri, in his office just a few streets away, would be able to sense the thrill that was even now running through her at the sight of Philippe. He seemed to know everything else she did.

Philippe waved his arm towards the street behind them. 'My cousin Therese has just moved into an apartment on Rue Galande and I came to help her move a wardrobe. Of course she lives on the top floor.

Seven flights of stairs, none of them wide enough to accommodate two people and a huge wardrobe...'

'Oh dear!' she laughed.

'It's fine,' he said. 'She managed it on her own. Strong as an ox. All the women in my family are. And all the men in my family are terrified of them.'

She laughed again. Forget Henri. It was nice to see Philippe in daylight for a change. If nothing else, it proved he wasn't a vampire.

'So what are you up to? Book shopping?' he asked.

'Not really,' she said. 'Just browsing. I'm on my way to the supermarket, so I came the long way round to get some fresh air. And ok, maybe just one more book...'

He smiled. 'Just one more...that sounds familiar. My bookshelves at home are full of 'just one more' books. Fancy a coffee?'

And just like that, real life flooded back.

'I'd love to, but I haven't really got time - ' Philippe looked a little hurt. She spoke again, quickly. 'No, really, I would love to! But I've got to do the shopping, and I'm only supposed to take an hour, and - '

'What do you mean, you're only supposed to take an hour? What would happen if you took longer?' He was puzzled. He didn't *think* she was trying to make excuses not to have a drink with him, but... Sylvie's cheeks flushed and she looked down at the pavement.

'Henri – he doesn't like me to go out unless he knows where I am and who I'm with.'

'What?' Philippe still didn't get it. 'You mean you have to ask his permission? You're an adult, Sylvie, if you want to get a drink with a friend that's up to you. He can't stop you. And how would he even know, anyway?'

'I don't know, but he always does!' she cried. 'He knows exactly where I've been, and how long I've taken - '

Philippe was shocked. He opened his mouth to swear, then looked at her. She was clearly upset, and telling her that she shouldn't allow her pig of a husband to run her life probably wasn't going to help. He bit his tongue.

'Which supermarket are you going to?' he asked gently.

'The one on Rue Lagrange,' she said.

'That's lucky, I need to go there too. Shall we?'

She stared at him, still unsure for a moment, until the little voice inside her head pointed out that she was only going to the supermarket, just as Henri expected her to, and that if a friend happened to be going there at the same time so what? He could hardly bar other men from being in the shop at the same time as her.

He stood aside to let her move on. She smiled up at him, uncertain this was a wise thing to do but determined to do it anyway, and together they walked to the supermarket.

Inside, Philippe picked up a basket and turned to her. 'Do you have a list?'

She smiled and waved a piece of paper.

'I'm fully prepared,' she said.

'For anything?' He grinned at her, eyebrows raised.

She had a fleeting but intense vision of him grabbing her in a passionate embrace, sweeping her off her feet and ravishing her then and there amongst the pickles. Slowly unbuttoning the dress she wore, sliding it down over her shoulders...and then staring in astonishment and disappointment at the unbecoming and slightly greying underwear she'd slipped on that morning. She wasn't prepared for *that*. She could feel her cheeks starting to burn.

'Not quite,' she said, and he laughed.

'What's first on the list?'

'Olives.'

Together they scoured the shelves for her groceries, Philippe reaching up to the higher shelves for her. He passed her a jar and she smiled, gratefully.

'It's so nice having someone to help me!' she said.

'Doesn't your husband ever come with you?' he asked. He hated hearing about her husband, but he couldn't seem to stop asking her. It was torture, but it was also, he thought, a case of knowing your enemy...

'Henri? In a supermarket?' she laughed, even though it really wasn't funny. 'Good Lord no. That's what he's got me for. What was it he said? 'You don't get a dog and bark yourself'.'

Philippe could feel his hands tightening into fists. What a great guy this Henri sounded! If he ever met him –

'He's a romantic, then?' he said, the lightness of his voice completely at odds with the darkness of his thoughts. Sylvie smiled ruefully.

'He used to be.'

They moved on to the fruit and vegetables. Sylvie, unwilling to talk too much about Henri, steered the conversation into different waters.

'Tell me about your ex,' she said. He looked at her in surprise.

'Is this you changing the subject?' he said. 'Ok, I suppose you've told me a little bit about your past, I should tell you about mine. I warn you though, I'm not a very interesting person.'

She smiled at him. 'Let me be the judge of that.'

'Where to start?' They stopped for a moment as Sylvie inspected some apples. 'We met at school. Childhood sweethearts. We split up briefly when she went away to university and I went to college here, but when she came back we carried on where we left off. We moved in together when we were twenty-two. Looking back on it now we were far too young, but at that age - '

'At that age you know everything,' interrupted Sylvie with a wistful smile. He laughed.

'Everything and nothing. I worked hard – I was a waiter at a really good restaurant near the Opera house – Le Palais, do you know it?'

'Yes!' said Sylvie, impressed. 'I went there once with my father.'

'I enjoyed it. I'm not the cleverest person in the world, but I know how to talk to people, to make sure they get what they want and have a nice evening. The maître de was a really nice guy who took me under his wing. He was grooming me to take his job when he retired in a year or two. But apparently a lowly waiter wasn't good enough for my ex.'

'What happened?' asked Sylvie.

'I thought we were happy, but as she ended up fucking my then-best friend behind my back, she obviously wasn't.'

'Oh, bananas,' said Sylvie.

'I thought she was, yes,' said Philippe. She gestured behind him, apologetically.

'No, I mean – can you pass me a bunch?' He passed her the bananas and they smiled ruefully at each other. 'So what happened when you found out?'

'Eventually, all hell broke out. But I didn't find out for quite a while. Not until she had his baby and let me think she was mine for a year.'

Sylvie stopped in the middle of the aisle, mouth open in shock, causing an elderly male shopper to almost walk into her. He swore but she was too shocked to hear him. Philippe glared at the old man – there was no need to be rude - and took Sylvie's arm, steering her out of the way. Her mouth was still open.

'Oh my god, Philippe, that's just nuts!' she said. He absent-mindedly picked up a bag of walnuts and put them in the basket.

'It was the worst moment of my life,' he said, as she discreetly took the walnuts out and put them back on the shelf. 'I'd spent a whole year thinking that little girl was mine, feeding her, changing her nappy, loving her – and suddenly she was gone, along with my wife. My whole life fell apart in one night.'

Impulsively, Sylvie reached out to softly touch his arm. He reached up and took her hand, squeezing it gently. She let him hold it for a moment before pulling away.

'What did you do?' she asked. He sighed.

'Made things worse, of course,' he said. 'I was drinking heavily. I started turning up for work drunk. Eventually Monsieur Laurent – my mentor at the restaurant – had had enough and wouldn't cover for me any more. I lost my job, I lost my apartment, I lost everything. So I went home.'

'The drinking - ' she began, tentatively. He stopped her.

'I don't drink alcohol at all now,' he reassured her. 'I went back to my mother and she said I could stay as long as I needed to, but only if I stopped drinking and got another job. She gave me three months to get my shit together or I was out.'

'So you cleaned yourself up and started working at the museum.'

He smiled and passed her a pack of toilet paper. 'Didn't have much choice. I don't want to end up like - ' he stopped.

'Like who?' she said. 'Like your father?'

He grinned at her. 'Women's intuition or a lucky guess?'

'Lucky guess.'

They moved to another aisle, by now almost at the end of Sylvie's shopping list. Philippe watched her from the corner of his eye, not wanting to be creepy or lecherous but unable to tear his gaze away from her. He was fascinated by her. She was clearly an intelligent woman; their conversations at work, about books and art and the world in general, were proof of that. And sometimes she seemed to forget herself when they were together, laughing at his stupid jokes and relaxing in his company. But sometimes – like today – she was nervy and on edge; alert, as if she was constantly on the lookout for someone to spot her doing something she shouldn't. Sometimes when they talked he would start to feel annoyed with her, because she was always putting herself down; she seemed completely unaware of her own worth. And those were the times when he wanted to grab her, to shake her (gently) and tell her that she was the most amazing, interesting, funny, thoughtful, beautiful woman he'd ever known.

He took a deep breath. He wouldn't get a better chance than this.

'Your turn,' he said. She looked puzzled. 'Tell me. What is it with your husband?'

She immediately became flustered and turned away. They'd been having such a nice time – why did he have to bring up Henri and spoil everything?

'I – he just looks after me,' she said. Now he looked puzzled. 'I can't cope on my own. I'm too stupid, I'd probably burn the house down or something - '

'You're not stupid!' he cried, almost angry with her. 'You have to stop putting yourself down. What makes you think you couldn't cope?'

'I had an accident a few years ago. I have to take all these pills and they make me a bit fuzzy. At least, I thought it was the pills, but I've been trying to cut down and it's made no difference - ' the words tumbled out in a rush. 'I think maybe it's me, I'm fuzzy, not the tablets.'

'You don't seem fuzzy to me,' he said. 'You're clever, and warm and funny...'

She looked down at the floor, unable to meet his eyes because hers were full of sudden tears. He reached out and tenderly lifted her chin, staring into her face. 'Sylvie, I think you're wonderful.'

She looked at him for a moment, her insides all at once consumed by the fluttering of a million butterflies, a warm, tingling sensation. The man who had occupied her thoughts almost constantly since she'd started that little part time job – the one Henri had got in order to teach her a lesson and show her that she was only good enough to mop floors – this kind, considerate man who was as much of a dreamer as she was, thought she was wonderful.

And it made no difference, because she was still trapped. She struggled to contain her emotions, not wanting to make a scene in the local supermarket where they knew her and knew she was a married woman. Even now, they were probably judging her; maybe they were even ringing Henri to let him know she was here, with another man. It would explain how he always knew where she was.

'Please don't say that,' she whispered, miserably.

'Sylvie – you must know how I feel about you?' Philippe looked almost as miserable as she felt. He knew he shouldn't have said anything but it had kind of slipped out. 'And I think you feel the same way too.'

It was true. And it was too much. Sylvie looked at him longingly, burst into tears and rushed out of the shop, leaving behind her a basket of shopping and a stunned sales assistant, who was restocking the tinned tomatoes.

'What's up with her?' the assistant asked, bemused. Philippe glared at him and rushed after Sylvie, but she was all ready half way down the street.

Philippe kicked himself and slowly made his way home.

CHAPTER 13

Sylvie hastily dried her tears as she heard the front door open, splashing cold water on her swollen eyes to take the redness away. If Henri saw that she was upset he'd comment on it, and probably not in a sympathetic way.

But he barely even looked at her as he entered the kitchen. She was glad. She felt sure he'd be able to read her thoughts if he looked into her eyes.

Henri was in a foul mood. He'd had yet another disappointing day at the office; a major client who he'd introduced to the company, who he'd wined and dined and whose boring stories he'd listened to intently and whose stupid jokes he'd forced himself to laugh at, who was rolling in money and had a list of business interests as long as your arm – their account had been given to another, less senior, member of staff. Old man Guiton, who must be almost a hundred years old by now and well due for retirement, clearly no longer knew how to run the business properly and would be doing everyone (but particularly Henri) a favour if he just lay down and died. The frustration and resentment had been building all day and Henri now needed someone to take it out on.

'You look like shit, Little Bird,' he said. 'You look tired. I think maybe they're working you too hard at that museum.'

'I'm fine, thank you Henri,' she said, hastily putting the kettle on to boil. He smiled thinly.

'Yes, well you would say that, wouldn't you?' He shook off his wet overcoat and took it out into the hallway, hanging it on the hook by the front door, then sat at the kitchen table. 'You wouldn't want to miss an evening's mopping, would you?'

She ignored the sarcasm and carefully measured tea into the pot; they were beginning to run short of it. Henri noticed.

'You went to the supermarket today,' he said. 'Did you forget the tea?'

'No - ' she began.

He cut her off rudely. 'This is why I only drink tea when I make it myself. You make tea as weak as an old lady's piss.'

She swallowed hard. 'I did go to the supermarket, but I forgot my purse,' she said. He looked at her, sternly.

'You got all the way to the supermarket?' he said. 'And you did the whole shop before you realised you'd forgotten your purse?'

She stared at the floor, cheeks flaming. 'Yes.' She risked an upwards glance.

Henri stared at her, unspeaking for a few seconds, then burst into laughter. Anyone listening would've imagined that he'd just heard the world's most hilarious joke. And then he stopped abruptly.

'You're tired. You're not going to work tonight,' he said.

'But - '

'You're not going.' That was it. The final word. She poured boiling water into the teapot, imagining for a second pouring it into his lap. In her mind's eye she saw herself, Edith Piaf-like, gleefully tipping the scalding hot liquid all over his nether regions as she belted out '*non, rien de rien, non, je ne regrette rien'.* But Sylvie knew she WOULD regret it; he'd make her. He watched her, satisfied that any sign of rebellion had been crushed before it had had time to develop, and then spoke again. 'Oh, I've left my newspaper by the front door. Be a good girl and get it for me, will you?'

Be a good girl. Edith Piaf seethed but said nothing. 'Of course, Henri.'

She stepped out into the hallway and grabbed the rolled up newspaper, which was slowly transforming into soggy mush on the floor under his dripping overcoat, and silently turned back to the kitchen.

She stopped in shock. Unbeknown to Henri, she could see him in the kitchen from here; see him stand up, pour the tea into a china cup and then add a fine powder before stirring it vigorously. And all of a sudden she knew why the lower dosage of her medication hadn't been working. The high strength pills which had been left over from her previous prescription – the ones Henri had promised to return to the pharmacy – were still in his possession, and once crushed and put into her hastily drunk pre-work cup of tea, were still getting into her blood stream. And once those had run out, how hard would it be for him to buy more? Henri had connections all across the city, and it probably wouldn't be that difficult to source illicit medication or stolen prescriptions.

Frozen to the spot, she knew that she had to move, to keep playing Henri's game until she had worked out what to do. The old Sylvie would've confronted him – *the old Sylvie would've kicked his arse* said the little voice in her head – but this Sylvie, the here and now Sylvie, had nowhere else to go.

'Where's my paper, Little Bird?' Henri called. He sounded so – normal. Not like a man who'd been drugging his wife. Sylvie was suddenly furious.

'Here!' she said, flinging it on the table. He glared at her.

'Careful, my sweet,' he said flatly, the innocent words barely masking the threat. 'You nearly knocked your tea over. Here.' He held out the cup.

'I'm not thirsty,' she said, smiling sweetly. 'I had one just before you came in. You drink it.'

His thin smile flickered slightly – if she hadn't been looking so closely, she wouldn't have spotted it. Oh, he was a cool one. 'Don't be silly, you know I prefer coffee.' He poured hot water into another cup, adding a spoonful of instant coffee. 'Don't waste it. Drink up.'

He placed the tea in front of her and picked up his own cup.

'I really don't - ' said Sylvie.

'Just fucking drink it!' he shouted, almost spitting the words into her face. She flinched away and reached for the cup, but her hand trembled so hard that she knocked it over. Tea soaked the newspaper. Henri swore and lunged at her, but she dodged away, grabbing the tea towel and mopping at the paper.

'Leave it!' he shouted.

'It's not that wet - '

'Fuck the newspaper! You did that on purpose!' She couldn't remember seeing him this furious before. Somehow, it made her feel stronger.

'Of course I didn't!' she protested. 'Why would I spill it on purpose?'

For a moment he just looked at her. How much did she know? Not much, he thought; too stupid, too Prozac-addled and too worn down. He forced himself to calm down before he blew it.

Henri smiled at her, the over-worked, stressed out but penitent husband placating the little woman. 'I'm sorry, Little Bird. I have a lot on my plate at work, and then I come home and find you too tired to do your duties here. It's my fault, I shouldn't have let you take that job. Sit down. You're staying home tonight.'

CHAPTER 14

Philippe got to work early. There was nothing else for him to do, other than sit at home and despair, cursing himself for being insensitive or over-eager or just misreading the situation with Sylvie completely – he still wasn't sure which. He was sure however that he'd upset the one person he never wanted to see cry. He sat behind the security and heaved a deep sigh.

'Oh for God's sake!' Stephanie wasn't unsympathetic, but she'd seen only too clearly where this infatuation with Sylvie was heading; he'd had no chance with the blonde from HR, but at least she wasn't a married woman... And what was Sylvie up to? Leading him up the garden path when she had a husband at home.

'You don't understand,' said Philippe, miserably. He was right. She didn't. He sighed again and stared at the door, as if staring hard enough would make the time go quicker and Sylvie turn up sooner.

'Ah Philippe, I'm glad you're here already!' Monsieur Fournier appeared behind him. 'I need you up in the Denon wing. We've got the contractors up there, fitting the new security case on *La Joconde.* They've already overrun so I need someone up there keeping an eye on them and hurrying them up.'

'Ok...' Philippe dragged himself out of his chair and headed up to the gallery. Fournier looked at Stephanie, eyebrows raised.

'Really, don't ask,' she said.

La Joconde – or the Mona Lisa, as she's probably more widely known – was hung in a small room off the main gallery, where the most famous painting in the world looked down upon the roughly 8 million tourists and art lovers who visited the Louvre every year; many of whom didn't even bother with the rest of the museum once they'd done the obligatory selfie in front of her.

Philippe had been slightly disappointed with Mona the first time he'd seen her. She was one of the most recognisable images on the planet, a colossus of the art world. Songs had been written about her; films made, heists planned and foiled. But in the flesh, she was diminutive and surprisingly small after all the hype. The famous enigmatic smile looked to Philippe like a wry grin, as if she was bemused by all the fuss being made over her.

A team of contractors were carefully removing the housing of her display case, gently sliding the heavy glass from the front, as Philippe approached.

'*Bonsoir, les gars*!' he called. The lead contractor, a nervous man in his 50s, jumped in surprise and let go of the glass, making his workmates grab at it in panic.

'Don't sneak up on people like that!' he snapped. Philippe shrugged.

'I didn't think I had,' he said. 'What are you doing?'

The contractor rolled his eyes. 'What does it look like?'

'Are you replacing the glass?' asked Philippe. 'I didn't realise it was broken.'

'It isn't,' said the contractor, as the other men slowly placed the sheet of glass on the floor, sighing in relief. 'It's bullet resistant. Very difficult to break once it's installed, if it's done right.'

'Do you mean bullet proof glass?' asked Philippe.

'No, bullet resistant,' said the contractor. 'Common misconception. No glass is completely bullet proof, but once it's in place it'll stop most firearms in their tracks. It's basically layers of glass and plastic. Bullets themselves aren't dangerous, it's the speed and the force they hit you with that does the damage. If you tried to shoot through bullet resistant glass, the bullet would penetrate the first layer of glass, but then the next layers would absorb the force and slow it down. Chances are it wouldn't make it out the other side.'

'Ah, right,' said Philippe. 'So why are you replacing it?'

The contractor looked at Philippe, sizing him up, glad to talk to someone who seemed genuinely interested in his life's work. It didn't happen very often. His wife certainly wasn't interested, despite the pains he'd taken several times to educate her on such a fascinating subject. Little did he know that Philippe was just desperate to take his mind off Sylvie for five minutes. His employees carefully began to unwrap the new sheet of bulletproof glass.

'It can discolour in UV rays. Obviously the painting's not in direct sunlight, but it's been in this same case for over 20 years now so the glass was starting to yellow.' Philippe peered closely at the old glass. It had a very faint tinge of yellow to it, but he thought he wouldn't have noticed if it hadn't been pointed out to him. The contractor read his thoughts.

'It's not very noticeable yet, but obviously when it's in front of such an important artwork it needs to be perfect, so it doesn't detract from the painting.'

'Of course,' said Philippe. 'And if it keeps her safe…'

The contractor laughed. 'As safe as she can be. Between you and me, even this toughened glass wouldn't stop a really determined thief, but by the time they'd got through it they'd be surrounded by armed police. The alarms and the cameras are what's really protecting her.'

'They'd never make it out of the building,' said Philippe. 'The museum would be full of armed police before they got to the front door.'

'Exactly!' said the contractor. Both men turned to watch the other workers slowly lift the new sheet of glass into place.

'So how much longer do you think you'll be?' asked Philippe, discreetly checking his watch. He wanted to be back in Security when Sylvie arrived.

'Well, installing the glass correctly can be a tricky process - ' the contractor began, but then he was interrupted by a loud crash and cries of alarm from his workers.

They'd dropped the glass.

'*Merdé!*' muttered the contractor. Philippe crouched down next to him as he inspected the glass.

'It looks fine,' said Philippe, but the contractor shook his head.

'No, it's chipped around the edge,' he said, mournfully. 'If it's not absolutely precise it won't fit the display case properly. It needs to seal the painting in.'

'Can't you just put the old bit of glass back in while you get a new one made?' asked Philippe. But the contractor shook his head again.

'No, the old piece has got crazing on it, see? From where we took it out.'

'So what are you going to do?' asked Philippe.

The contractor stood and looked at his workmen, who all decided it was nothing to do with them and looked away, muttering about how it must be time to go out for a smoke. Finally, he turned back to Philippe. 'I'd better have a word with your boss,' he said. 'We've got ordinary glass in the van, which we can just cut to size and fit temporarily, but of course it's not bullet resistant...'

Philippe left the contractor in a heated discussion with Monsieur Fournier and hurried back to the Security desk. It was almost 7 o'clock and he hoped that he hadn't missed Sylvie; he wanted, needed, to talk to her and make sure that she'd forgiven him for upsetting her earlier.

When he got back to Security and looked questioningly at Stephanie, she shook her head; Sylvie hadn't arrived yet. 7pm came and went, and still no Sylvie. Philippe began to feel uneasy, then terribly worried.

And then, just as he felt he was going to explode with the tension, she walked in. Her face was tear stained, her clothes were soaking wet, and her feet were bare. Stephanie, who'd been busy lecturing him on something (he wasn't listening) stopped mid-sentence, mouth wide open. Philippe looked up and saw Sylvie, bedraggled, and his heart stopped.

He rushed around to the other side of the desk and stopped in front of her. She looked up at him.

'He hid my shoes,' she said in a small voice. Philippe didn't understand.

'What?'

'Henri. He hid my shoes. He didn't want me to come tonight – he forbid me to – so he hid all my shoes. And my coat.' She looked at him defiantly, but then her face crumpled into tears. He gently put an arm around her and spoke to Stephanie.

'I'm taking Sylvie up to the canteen,' he said. Still open mouthed, Stephanie nodded and watched them go. She hoped he knew what he was letting himself in for.

CHAPTER 15

The canteen was silent at that time of night; the day time staff had gone, and the night time staff hadn't been working long enough for a break yet. Philippe sat Sylvie down on a chair and went behind the counter, reappearing with a bowl of warm water and a couple of tea towels. She seemed to be in a daze, sitting limply, not speaking but watching his every move. As if her act of defiance - coming to work barefoot - had taken all the fight out of her.

Philippe knelt in front of her with the water. City streets were no place to go without shoes, especially on a night like tonight. She flinched slightly as he gently picked up her foot and rested it on his thigh, but gradually she relaxed as he started to wash it, moistening one of the tea towels and dabbing it tenderly on the aching soles of her feet. He didn't speak, trusting her to tell him what had happened when she was ready.

When she did speak, it was brief and to the point. 'I hate him.'

Philippe put down the tea towel and looked at her, guiltily. 'Was it because of earlier? I shouldn't have ambushed you like that - '

'He's been drugging me.'

Philippe sat back, the wind knocked out of him. 'What?'

'You know I told you I take anti-depressants? And I've been weaning myself off them? He's been crushing them up and putting them in my tea.'

'Holy fuck, Sylvie! How the hell did you end up with him?'

She smiled at him sadly. 'It's a long story…'

Julia Boudain liked to say that her husband Matthieu, proprietor of Boudain's Fine Art and Antiques, had the soul of a poet rather than a businessman. He had a feeling for Beauty and Truth rather than a desire for profit, and more than once she'd had to stop him practically giving away a piece for well under the guide price because he wanted it to go to someone who would really appreciate it, rather than someone who could simply afford to buy it. And because she loved him and his poetic soul, more than once she'd turned a blind eye and left him to it.

Luckily their daughter Sylvie had inherited her father's soul and her mother's brain along with the shop, and she instinctively had that gut instinct for a good bargain and an under-appreciated work of art. After her father died, Sylvie threw herself into the business. She loved it. Like her father, she loved finding the right home for the right piece (and vice versa) and, like her mother, she always got the right price for it. She also delighted in tracking down new stock, travelling across the country to house clearances and auctions, to flea markets and antique fairs. She had a good eye and a lovely way with her customers, many of whom became regulars.

Henri Cloutier was an old acquaintance of her father's. Not a friend – Matthieu would never have socialised with an accountant! – but someone who he'd done business with, although he normally dealt with Henri's boss at the accountancy firm. Henri popped into the shop one day to pay his respects to Sylvie and to look for a piece of artwork or antique furniture for his new apartment in the 6th arrondisement. Sylvie knew the area; it was very expensive, although not quite as expensive as the neighbourhood her shop and the apartment above were located in. Not that Sylvie even gave it a thought. The building near the Pompidou centre had been in her family for generations, well before the modern museum had been built and had made property prices rocket, and she intended to keep it in her family for as many future generations as possible. Financial worth was never a consideration.

Henri began to come into the shop at least once a week, to browse and to have a chat with Sylvie, but he never bought anything; and eventually it began to dawn on her that the only thing Henri really had his eye on was her. He was a nice enough man, though not really her type. But he knew how to win her. He talked about her father, about the shop, he listened to her stories about her childhood and their visits to the museums, and eventually – in the nicest way possible – he wore her down. She wasn't used to living on her own and had been feeling lonely, and Henri came along at the just right time to play that to his advantage.

He took her out to dinner a couple of times, but Sylvie soon realised that he felt more for her than she did for him. She'd resolved to end the relationship – had already dropped some gentle, subtle hints, not wanting to hurt him – when the accident changed everything.

The crash happened on the way to a house clearance in Mauregard. It was big enough to close the motorway and make the evening news. The articulated lorry that smashed through the central reservation and flattened Sylvie's ancient Peugeot van came off relatively unscathed, but the same couldn't be said of Sylvie.

She woke in a hospital bed after drifting in and out of consciousness for three days, and stayed there for two months.

'Two months?' Philippe was horrified.

'I thought they were the worst two months of my life, but I was wrong,' she said. 'I had a lot of broken bones, which was bad enough, but I also had a brain injury. A cerebral edema - ' She saw his look of confusion. 'Swelling on the brain. It can be life threatening, or cause long term damage. Which is why I still take medication now…'

'But – it gets better, right?' he asked, concerned. Sylvie smiled sadly.

'Sometimes the symptoms lessen and eventually stop altogether. Sometimes they don't.'

'Symptoms like…?'

'Depression, for starters. Problems with concentration - '

'Woolly headedness.'

She laughed softly. 'It explains a lot, doesn't it?' He shook his head.

'It doesn't explain how you ended up with that bastard.'

She sighed and sat back in her chair.

'Two months is a long time to be stuck in a hospital bed. I'm an only child, I've got no family. I did have friends, and they did come to see me but…well, they have jobs and kids and husbands, and half the time I wasn't very talkative, so eventually they stopped coming to see me. But not Henri. He came and saw me every single day. He'd sit by my bed, even when I was sleepy or grumpy or so out of it I didn't know he was there. He'd sit and read the paper, or he'd bring stuff from work. He was the only one who didn't desert me.'

Sylvie was propped up in her hospital bed, just as she had been the day before, and the day before that, and the day before that… It was getting so she could barely remember a time when she *hadn't* been stuck in that awful bed, with its hard, slippery mattress and stiff cotton sheets. She stared out of the window and felt for the millionth time that day that if she didn't get out of here soon she would go insane.

'How's my Little Bird today?' said Henri, sitting down beside her. She felt herself stiffen; she loathed that nickname. 'Wings still healing?'

'Sick of being caged up in this fucking bed!' she snapped. He looked at her disapprovingly.

'Don't swear, Sylvie,' he said calmly. 'Ladies don't swear.'

She bit back the scathing reply that lurked on her tongue. She didn't want him to think she didn't appreciate his visits, even if he was a bit of an old woman sometimes. If it weren't for Henri, she really would've gone insane by now. She forced herself to smile at him.

'I'm sorry, Henri,' she said. 'It's just – I'm so sick of this hospital bed! They say I'm getting better, but they can't let me leave because I live alone. They said how could I think about going home when I still need someone to help me take a pi – to go to the bathroom! If I have to wait until I'm fully recovered I'll be here for the rest of the year!'

He smiled sympathetically at her. 'Is that the only reason they're keeping you here?' he asked. 'Well, we can soon sort that out.'

And that was how Sylvie ended up moving in to Henri's apartment. She'd wanted to go back to her own home above the shop – there were two bedrooms, so there was plenty of room for him to stay – but Henri said (and claimed the doctors agreed with him) that living so close to her business would be too stressful; she would be constantly wanting to know what was going on downstairs. Henri arranged for someone to work in the shop part time and promised to pop in once or twice a week to check that everything was ok.

She was still unsure whether she was doing the right thing or not, but when the day came and Henri wheeled her along the squeaky clean linoleum corridor and out into the fresh air – air that smelt of sunshine and the river and the lunch time menu at a nearby café, air that smelt so good after the institutional fragrance of disinfectant, bleach and stale urine – her misgivings shrank. And when Henri halted her wheelchair at the bottom of the long and winding staircase up to his apartment, lifted her in his arms and carried her ever so gently up and up and up to his front door, they evaporated completely. He'd carried her over the threshold and into his bedroom, tenderly lying her down on his bed, then turned to go; but she was so overwhelmed with relief at finally being out of that terrible hospital room, and with surprise and gratitude at how caring he was, that she reached out her hand to stop him.

He had made love to her, so careful not to hurt her shattered body. She'd realised then that she'd completely misjudged this man; yes, he could be fussy and old fashioned, he was undoubtedly set in his ways, but he had a good heart.

Those first few weeks had been magical. He would fuss around her, bringing her tea and making her tasty snacks to nibble at while he was at work (he'd offered to take time off, but when it came to it Sylvie realised that she couldn't handle a nursemaid 24/7), finding her books to read and jigsaws to complete. The second weekend they'd gone for a stroll around the Tuilleries, on the way home stopping on the Pont Des Arts for a moment while Henri supposedly searched his pockets for his wallet (he claimed to have left it in the park café). But to her surprise he instead pulled out a padlock and got down on one knee in front of her wheelchair, and in front of a gawping crowd of tourists had proposed to her. She was too overwhelmed to do anything more than gasp a quick 'yes!', and to the applause of the modest crowd he'd written their names on the padlock and attached it to the bridge as a sign of their everlasting love.

He'd seemed like the perfect romantic hero, rescuing her from the confines of her hospital bed, but after another month of sitting with one leg still in plaster in his top floor apartment it felt like she'd swapped one prison for another. She was desperate to go back to work, but Henri had said the doctors still advised she avoid stressful situations, and going back to the shop after all this time would of course be difficult and tiring; plus they thought it might bring back traumatic memories of the crash. Sylvie argued that the crash hadn't happened in the shop, had it? And sitting here, bored and out of the loop, was more stressful than being surrounded by antiques and the occasional customer. But Henri was not to be swayed; he had sworn to protect her, from herself if necessary, and that's precisely what he would do.

She began to get headaches – lack of air and boredom, she thought, but one day Henri came home from work with a concerned look on his face and a bag of pills from the local pharmacy. The 'damn fool' (his words) doctor who had discharged her from the hospital with a month's worth of medication had forgotten to give her a repeat prescription, and the headaches had only started because her original pills had run out. Sylvie protested that she didn't want to take any more tablets, but finally – after days of arguing and pestering him for a second opinion – Henri arranged for his own GP to come and visit her, and after a cursory examination he'd agreed that she should carry on taking the medication for now.

The headaches abated and both of her legs were finally out of plaster, but she'd begun to feel shaky and disconnected from real life; the thought of going back to work now or even just leaving the apartment scared her. Her head felt as though it was floating an inch or two above her shoulders; no longer a part of her.

Woolly headed. At their hastily arranged civil ceremony (Henri was so in love with her that he couldn't wait to get a ring on her finger) she said her vows and signed her name – her old one and her new one – on the marriage certificate, without entirely being aware of her surroundings.

Henri told his new wife not to worry about a thing. He was happy to take care of her. He earned enough money to support them both comfortably, so why hold onto the shop? The stock probably wasn't very valuable but the building itself - especially with the large apartment above it – must be worth something, even if it was in a state of some disrepair (Sylvie wondered what disrepair he was talking about but didn't speak). Sylvie baulked at the idea of selling her old family home and business, but promised to think about it.

She took her pills as usual and that night fell into the catatonic sleep of the over-medicated, where she dreamed of her father for the first time in months. He was dancing through the galleries of the Louvre with her as he had done when she was a child, only now she was grown up, dressed Miss Haversham-style in an old lace wedding gown. She woke the next day with tears on her pillow and the firm intention of stopping her pills and getting back to work.

But cold turkey is never an easy process, and stopping the medication made her feel a whole lot worse. Blinding headaches, more shakiness and confusion... In the midst of this, Henri went over to the shop to look over the books – in preparation for her returning to work – and came back with a face like the chief mourner at his own funeral.

He found her sitting in the living room, looking out of the window at the city skyline. She knew it was bad news the minute she saw his expression.

'Henri? What's wrong?'

Henri shook his head and sat down heavily next to her. For a moment he didn't speak, couldn't even look her in the eye. Her heart pounded. She opened her mouth to ask him again, but then he spoke.

'Little Bird,' he said. 'There's something I need to tell you. Something I suspected for a while, but it's worse than I thought.'

She was seriously worried now. 'What is it? What's happened?'

'I need to tell you but I don't know if you're strong enough to hear it.'

Despite the anxiety, she felt a flash of annoyance. 'For fuck's sake, Henri - '

'Don't swear,' he said, far too calmly. 'You know I hate it when ladies swear.'

That made her want to swear even more, but she swallowed it down. 'I'm sorry, but you're scaring me. Just tell me!'

He sighed heavily and stared at her. 'I took a look at the books today.'

'I know,' she said. 'You've been keeping an eye on the business for me.'

'Not just those books,' he said, 'but your personal finances. All your paperwork is still in the apartment.'

She felt another, brief flash of annoyance – those were her personal, private things, and she'd only agreed to let him look over the shop's finances – but then told herself not to be stupid or ungrateful; he was her husband. Of course he could look at them.

'Why didn't you tell me about the tax demand?' he said. He sounded disappointed in her. She was confused.

'What tax demand? What are you talking about?' she asked. He shook his head.

'Come on, Sylvie! The letters from the tax office about your inheritance!' He noticed her puzzled frown. 'You really don't remember them? The accident must've made you forget about them.'

'No – no, I don't think - ' she started, but stopped. Her mind had been all over the place since the crash; maybe it had affected her memory as well? If she had forgotten something, how would she know she'd forgotten it? 'I don't know...what letters?'

He stood up and walked over to the window, watching the pigeons strut around the square below. 'When you inherited the shop and the apartment from your father, you were liable for inheritance tax. They say they contacted you but you never replied to any of their letters. The tax should've been paid within six months of your inheritance, but because you just ignored their letters - '

'I never got their letters!' Sylvie protested, hot with anger. He carried on.

'Because you ignored their letters, you missed the payment deadline and they've been charging you interest, as well as charging you for all the administration expenses of their tax investigation - '

'What tax investigation?' she cried, angry, embarrassed, horrified.

'Tax inspectors don't like to be ignored,' said Henri, simply. 'They've been doing a thorough investigation of your business tax records as well as your personal ones.'

Sylvie stared at him in shock. She felt utter disbelief. She'd never ignored anything to do with tax, or money, or the business; her father, not being very good with money himself, had relied on her to deal with their finances, and fortunately she'd got her mother's head for business. Her father had impressed upon her the necessity to keep the taxman happy, because little people (like them) never won against the Inland Revenue; so it was best to just follow the rules to the letter.

She shook her head. 'No, no, that's not right! Apart from the fact I know the shop's books are all present and correct - '

'How do you know, Sylvie?' he interrupted. 'You haven't been near the shop for months.'

'Apart from that, I wasn't liable to pay tax on the apartment because I was already living there with my father. My solicitor told me it was fine.'

Henri snorted with derision. 'That damn fool solicitor – what does he know? His firm specialise in getting their clients off speeding tickets, not high worth estates and inheritances! I'm an accountant, Sylvie, I deal with the tax implications of huge sums of money and inherited real estate every day, I know what I'm talking about! Or would you rather believe that shrivelled old imbecile over your own husband?'

He was getting angry, towering over her with his eyes blazing. She shrank back against the sofa. 'Of course I believe you Henri, I just think you've made a mistake...'

He grabbed her by the shoulders and shook her. 'Wake up, Little Bird! Who are you to tell me I've made a mistake? You sit around all day in a fucking dream world, and you tell me I've made a mistake? How dare you!'

She twisted out of his grip, scared of the way he loomed above her. He wasn't a tall man but he was well built, and he was very angry. She'd never seen him like that before.

He seemed to realise he'd gone too far. He abruptly let his arms fall by his side and knelt in front of her, staring into her face, not letting her look away.

'Forgive me, Little Bird,' he said, and he really did sound sorry. 'It was just a bit of a shock to see all your inheritance gone, wasted, just like that.'

It took a second or two for her to register what he'd just said.

CHAPTER 16

The plastic canteen chair under her bottom was hard and beginning to get uncomfortable. Sylvie shifted and Philippe, in the chair next to her, followed suit, the shiny surface squeaking under his uniformed posterior.

'Pardon me!' said Philippe, making her laugh softly. He took her hand as she mopped at her eyes with the tea towel. 'So was it really all gone?'

She nodded. 'Yes. Well, sort of. I couldn't deal with it. I felt so – so stupid. I'd let my parents down, my whole family. My great great grandpapa started that business. Even Hitler couldn't ruin our shop. My family, and a lot of other galleries and artists, resisted the Nazis by hiding art works from them, waiting to re-open when the war was over. All it took was one stupid woman - ' – she saw his puzzled expression – ' – me – all it took was me, missing a letter from the Inland Revenue and getting hit by a truck. I did what the Third Reich couldn't, all by myself…'

He reached out to touch her cheek but she pulled away.

'You see? I told you I was useless. Henri agreed to take care of it all. He dealt with the tax people and came to an arrangement so I wouldn't get into any more trouble. But the price was massive. He arranged for the shop and the apartment to be sold, and flogged off the stock, and used the proceeds to pay my tax bill and all the legal expenses.'

'And what happened to you?'

'What happened to me? This happened to me. I was weak. I went back on the anti-depressants – the pills I've been trying so hard to come off. He told me to be grateful to him for saving me from financial ruin and to start acting like a proper wife. He didn't want me to work, he just wanted me to run his home and look after him. He only lets me do this because it proves that I'm too stupid to do anything else.'

They sat in silence for a while, Philippe deep in thought, Sylvie exhausted. Finally she sighed and looked down at her bare feet.

'Well, I'm here, I should probably do some work...'

Philippe looked at her in wonder, smiling softly and shaking his head.

'*Fluctuat nec mergitur*,' he said.

'What?'

'The city's motto. 'She is tossed by the waves but does not sink'. That's you, Sylvie. You're like Paris. You've been through so much but you're still here.'

She shook her head. 'I'm just treading water,' she said. 'It gets tiring.'

'But you won't sink. I won't let you sink. You're the cleverest, bravest person I know.'

She smiled. 'Am I? So clever I couldn't find where Henri had hidden any of my shoes...'

He laughed and pulled her to her feet. 'We'll soon take care of that. You get started and I'll see what I can do. What size shoes do you take?'

Sylvie made her way up to the Denon wing, her feet still a little sore but her heart somewhat lighter. She knew that her problems were in reality only just beginning, but with Philippe on her side she was starting to think that maybe – just maybe – there was a way out.

In the stairwell she passed Monsieur Fournier, who had only just stopped arguing with the contractor and was still slightly red in the face; but he'd recovered enough to keep his manners and bid her a friendly *'bonsoir!'* She smiled, grateful that he hadn't noticed her bare feet, and kept walking. The contractor and his workmen, who between them encompassed a whole range of post-Fournier emotions ranging from sheepish to indignant and downright sullen, didn't even notice the slender figure with the mop and bucket as she walked down the gallery; they were too busy arguing about whose fault the whole thing was and whether or not they were entitled to over-time pay as a result.

Sylvie headed to the other end of the gallery, drinking in the peace and quiet like nectar for her troubled soul. She found a seat under the painting of a young beggar boy by the Spanish artist Murillo (she smiled to herself – her Prozac fog must be lifting, she thought, if she could remember that!) and sorted through her cleaning kit, lost in thought.

Philippe meanwhile was on a shoe hunt. He skipped out of the basement entrance of the museum and into the Carousel du Louvre, the underground shopping mall, where (as luck would have it) it was late night shopping.

Even so, most of the stores were shutting up for the night, ringing up the last purchases, hurrying indecisive customers into an ill-thought-out purchase and shooing the stragglers out of the shop. Philippe raced to the shoe shop, where a bored-looking assistant was standing in the doorway barring entrance.

'We're closed, monsieur,' said the bored-looking assistant, in a bored voice.

'You've got five minutes yet!' protested Philippe. 'Come on, do me a favour. I won't be more than two minutes. I desperately need some shoes.'

The shop assistant looked him up and down. 'Yeah. And a haircut. Actually I'd say shoes are the least of your problems.'

'*Copain*, you don't know the half of it…' said Philippe, ignoring the rude comment. 'Please, they're not for me, they're for my – my girlfriend – anything in a 38.'

The assistant thought about it for a second, then – 'We're closed.'

'Please! What about those?' Philippe pointed at a pair of shoes in the window. They were blue satin pumps, exquisitely embroidered with delicate beading. 'They look perfect.'

'They're very expensive,' said the assistant, discouragingly.

'I don't care!' Philippe was ready to plead if he had to. 'Please, a pair of them in a 38, I don't even need to look at them, just ring them up – '

The assistant sighed. He really didn't need this after the day he'd just had, but it seemed like the quite-cute-despite-needing-a-hair-cut-and-having-a-girlfriend security guard wasn't leaving without a struggle so it was probably easier to just give in. He stood back and gestured to Philippe to enter.

'Thank you so much!' said Philippe, stepping over the threshold. 'Er – exactly how expensive…?'

He found her still in the Spanish paintings section of the gallery. Sylvie had made a start on the dusting and polishing but hadn't got very far. Philippe tiptoed past the contractor and his men, who were busily cutting a thin sheet of glass to size for the display case, and approached Sylvie as she whirled the duster along a ledge.

He was tempted to just watch her for a moment, but soon dismissed that as being a bit creepy. And there was no need for him to watch her from the shadows, like he had that first night; because she was no longer a fantasy for him, but a real life, flesh and blood woman – beautiful (in his eyes at least), but so much more than that; intelligent, vulnerable, strong, funny and wistful. A woman – *the* woman – he wanted to spend the rest of his life with.

'Sylvie!' he called, quietly so as not to alert the workmen – but they were still bickering amongst themselves and wouldn't have heard him anyway. She turned to him, a wide smile on her face, and his heart did a little shuffle. He held up the pair of shoes. 'For you.'

She took them from him and studied them, a look of surprise on her face. 'They're lovely! Where did you get these from?'

He shrugged. 'They were in Lost Property.'

'Really?' she asked, suspiciously. He smiled.

'Does it matter? Just try them on!'

He led her over to a bench and sat her down, then took the shoes from her. She lifted her foot daintily as he slipped a shoe on.

'Whom so ever this shoe fits...' he began, then stopped. She frowned and bent down.

'There's tissue paper in the toe,' she said, removing it. 'And a price label on the sole - '

Philippe grabbed the shoe back and scraped the label off with a fingernail. She reached out and touched his shoulder gently.

'You didn't find these in Lost Property, did you?' she said. 'You bought them for me.'

He shrugged, trying to make it look like it was no big deal. 'I thought you'd like them,' he said. She slipped her feet into the shoes and stuck them out, admiring them.

'I love them!' she said, warmly. 'They're perfect.'

'I thought the colour matched your eyes,' said Philippe, suddenly shy. 'And I thought the beads, when they catch the light they sparkle like, well, your eyes – I've got a bit of a thing about your eyes...' She laughed, blushing, and he smiled up at her. 'I've got a thing about all of you, actually.'

She gazed into his face – his dear, sweet, open face – and reached out, her hand trembling slightly as her fingers caressed his cheek. Then she drew him towards her, making him shuffle forwards on his knees, and leant down to kiss him softly on the mouth. Her lips tingled. He returned the kiss, parting her mouth gently with his tongue, tasting her. She wrapped her arms around him, causing him to shift uncomfortably.

'Oof, my knees!' he said. She laughed and jumped up, pulling him to his feet.

'You poor old thing!' she said. He smiled and pulled her to him...

They lost themselves in the kiss that followed. Sometimes, a moment that's been so longed for, so dreamt of, so *needed*, is bound to be a disappointment. Too often the reality just can't match the fantasy.

This wasn't one of those times.

They parted – eventually – and stared at each other, nakedly. There was no longer any use in pretending that they could ever just be friends; the kiss had proved that. They had to be together now. He reached for her again then stopped himself, looking around; there were cameras everywhere, and no doubt there was a security guard in the control room watching their every move with interest.

'Not here,' he said. 'Come with me.'

They burst into the ladies' toilets, kissing hungrily and tearing at each other's clothes. Philippe lifted her up and carried her over to the sink. She wrapped her legs around his waist as he ran his fingers through her hair, marvelling at the softness of it, then pulled her towards him. Their lips met again and they kissed like their lives depended on it.

And then he stopped. She paused, breathless, worried.

'What's the matter?' she asked.

'I want to make love to you, Sylvie,' he said, earnestly. 'Not screw you in a toilet. I don't want our first time to be somewhere like this…'

She glanced around. As desperate as she was for him, she had to concede that there were probably rather more romantic surroundings. And definitely ones that smelt better. She looked at him; he was as breathless as she was, and he was clearly physically eager to take things further… So for him to stop at that point couldn't have been easy. It just proved to her – if she'd needed proof – that he was as soppy and romantic and lovelorn for her, as she was for him.

She released him from between her thighs and reached forward to pull him close again, though not quite as close as before.

'You're probably right,' she sighed, snuggling her head into his shoulder. 'It's just so hard - '

He pulled back slightly and looked down at his groin. 'Sorry, I didn't realise you could feel it from there.'

She laughed. 'No, I meant it's difficult!'

He laughed as well then, somewhat sheepishly. 'Of course, I knew that's what you meant...'

Giggling, she took his face in her hands and covered it in kisses.

CHAPTER 17

It was nearly 10 o'clock. Not much cleaning had been done, but Philippe promised to cover for her – in reality he was planning to sneak back up and mop the floor for her after she'd left. The workmen had finally finished and gone home, leaving Mona in her newly glazed but temporarily un-bullet resistant display case, and Philippe did a cursory check of her room as they walked along the gallery.

He helped Sylvie put away her cleaning kit, then they walked hand-in-hand through the staff corridors. Time to go home...

Both wanted to speak but neither really knew what to say, so they made small talk until they reached the door to the security exit. Then Philippe turned to her seriously and took both her hands in his.

'What are you going to do?' he asked. She didn't need to ask what he meant.

'I'm going to stop taking my medication,' she said. 'If Henri is putting anti-depressants in my tea, then I won't be going cold turkey if I just stop. I know - ' she stopped him as he opened his mouth to speak – 'I know I should tell him I know what he's doing, but then what? I can't just leave him.'

'Sylvie - ' Philippe began, but she stopped him again.

'I can't. Where would I go? You live with your mum. I've got no money, no family.'

'But you can't stay with him!' burst out Philippe. She smiled, sadly.

'I don't want to,' she said. 'And one day, I will leave. I just don't know when or how at the moment.'

He reached up and stroked her cheek tenderly, then kissed her. 'I hate the thought of you being with him.'

She looked down at the floor, not wanting him to see the tears in her eyes. He cursed himself for making her cry again.

'You're not working tomorrow, are you?' he said, changing the subject. 'Nor am I. Can we meet?'

'You know he always knows where I am,' she sighed.

'I was thinking about that,' he said. 'Have you got a mobile phone?'

'Of course I have.'

'Can I see it?' He held out his hand. She shrugged and gave it to him, unlocking it first. He studied it carefully, then – 'Ah ha! That's what I thought!'

He held the phone out to her. On the screen, a street map of Paris was displayed, with the time and date and a little red dot, flashing, in the middle of the Louvre - right where they were currently standing.

She gasped. 'He's been tracking my phone?'

'Looks like it,' said Philippe. 'He must've got hold of it when you were asleep and downloaded this app. I've got a similar one on my phone, linked to my laptop in case I lose it. See that number in the corner? That'll be his phone, linked to yours. If you tap it, it'll show you where his phone is. Look.' He tapped Henri's phone number and then frowned as the screen showed a blue dot in almost exactly the same place as the red one had been. 'Or maybe not. Anyway, there must be a way to turn it off.'

Sylvie took the phone from him. 'I know how to turn it off,' she said, dropping it into a rubbish bin. She smiled at him, bitterly. 'All that time he made me think he had spies everywhere, and it was just my phone. You must think I'm so stupid - '

He stopped her talking with a kiss. Behind them, a smiling and uncharacteristically discreet Farheena emptied the rubbish bin into a plastic bag and took it outside, ready for the refuse collectors to pick up the next morning.

'So,' said Philippe, ' no excuse not to meet me tomorrow now...'

She laughed. 'Just tell me where and when.'

They made their plans, the thrill of a secret rendezvous masking (for now) Sylvie's dread of going home. But eventually of course she would have to. They stepped through the door into the security foyer and Sylvie stopped in shock.

Henri stood outside the plate glass door, his face like thunder. Stephanie stood in front of him, arms crossed, barring the way with a look of disdain on her face.

'I told you monsieur, I can't let you into the building without a pass - '

'I just want to see my wife!' Henri banged on the glass in barely-contained fury. Philippe proudly watched as Stephanie stayed exactly where she was, not even flinching. She was one tough cookie.

Sylvie scurried across the room. 'Henri!'

Stephanie whirled around in surprise at the sound of her voice, eyebrows raised in amazement.

'Don't tell me this is your husband?' she asked. Sylvie nodded, not taking her eyes off Henri outside in the rain. Stephanie looked at Philippe, then back to Sylvie. 'I thought he was just some drunk madman. Do you want me to call the police?'

'What? No, of course not...' Sylvie instantly replied in the negative, although the suggestion was actually quite appealing. 'No, it's fine.'

'If you're sure...' said Stephanie doubtfully, looking at Philippe again for confirmation. He nodded.

'Let him in.'

Reluctantly Stephanie opened the security door and Henri stepped through, suddenly all smiles and *bonhomie*.

'*Merci, mademoiselle*. And finally here she is! My wife, the bird-brain!'

Philippe could feel his hands clenching into fists and forced himself to keep calm.

'What are you doing here, Henri?' asked Sylvie. He held up a pair of her shoes.

'I brought you your shoes. What sort of crazy woman forgets to put her shoes on before she goes out?' He shook his head and appealed to Philippe, man to man. 'She hasn't got the brains she was born with!'

Philippe took a step towards him but stopped as Sylvie gave a tiny, almost imperceptible shake of her head. Henri glared at him, then down at Sylvie's feet.

'Oh,' he said. 'But I see I'm not needed. You've got yourself some shoes from somewhere!'

'I lent them to her,' said Stephanie quickly. Sylvie smiled at her gratefully and slipped the blue pumps off.

'Thank you so much,' she said, handing them to her. 'You're very kind.'

'Any time,' said Stephanie, meaningfully.

Henri wasn't unaware of the glance between the two women, and he clearly didn't like it. 'Come on, then!' he said, thrusting the shoes so hard at Sylvie that she staggered backwards. He looked at Philippe, challenging him to say something as Sylvie put them on, then took her arm. 'Time to go home.'

Philippe joined Stephanie behind the desk as they watched the unhappy couple leave. Stephanie took a deep, shaky breath and sat down; the encounter had had a greater effect on her than he'd realised.

'Thank you,' he said. She gave a little smile.

'Don't thank me,' she said. 'I just hope you know what you're letting yourself in for.'

'So do I…' he murmured.

Henri held Sylvie's arm tightly, aware that they were being watched. He walked quickly, forcing her to break into a jog to keep up. Once out of sight of the two security guards he stopped dead.

'Take them off,' he ordered. Sylvie looked at him, not understanding. 'The shoes, halfwit! Take them off.'

'But – it's raining...'

'So? It was raining when you walked here earlier. You got here in bare feet, you can go home the same way.'

She took off the shoes and held them out to him. He snorted in contempt.

'You carry them, you stupid whore.'

He strode off. Shocked, she followed him without speaking. He stopped again, so abruptly she almost walked into him.

'Who was that skinny streak of piss you were with?' he spat.

'What?' Sylvie forced herself to stay calm. 'Oh, the security guard. I don't know, he was just coming down the stairs the same time as I was.'

'He looked at you like he wants to fuck you.'

'Don't be stupid - ' She stopped as he glared at her, daring her to keep talking. She swallowed hard. He laughed harshly and turned up the collar of his raincoat.

'Pity you forgot your coat too,' he said, and strode off through the rain.

CHAPTER 18

Philippe lay on his bed, staring at the rain running down the window. It was 7.30am and he was supposed to be sleeping so he'd be fresh for his rendezvous with Sylvie at 1 o'clock, but he was wide awake. He'd spent the rest of his shift worrying about her; meeting Henri, after all he'd heard about him, had only confirmed what he'd first thought – that Henri was a bully who cared nothing for his wife.

Restlessly, he rolled over and glanced at the blue satin pumps which sat on his chest of drawers. He wondered briefly what he'd say to his mother if she found them – at least they were far too small for her to accuse him of cross-dressing – then imagined Sylvie standing there in them. On top of his chest of drawers. Man, he really was tired.

He gave up on sleep and got up, picking up one of the shoes gently, caressing it as if he were caressing her foot, and then he gingerly held it to his nose and sniffed. Almost immediately he recoiled and looked at his reflection in the mirror in disgust.

'Mon dieu, Eric! What am I doing?' he cried, hurriedly putting the shoe back with its partner. 'I thought it might smell of Sylvie, her perfume - '

'And does it?' inquired the poster of Eric. Philippe shook his head.

'No. She might be beautiful but man, her feet smell...'

Philippe sat down heavily on the bed, looking up at his childhood hero.

'What would you do, Eric, if the woman you loved was in distress? You'd act like a man, wouldn't you? You'd ride in on a white horse like Prince Charming and rescue her. But that's a bit difficult when you live with your mum and all you've got is a bicycle...'

Eric shook his head in frustration. 'Stop feeling sorry for yourself and man up! Did I shut myself away and throw a pity party when I got banned from football?'

'Which time?' asked Philippe. Eric ignored the question.

'And do your own washing, boy! You make me ashamed. Your poor *maman*!'

Finally, it was 12.30. Philippe got himself ready to leave, smoothing down his hair (which immediately sprang back up again) and checking between his teeth for bits of food, not that he'd been able to eat anything. There seemed to be a bowling ball in his tummy that switched between lying like a lead slab in the pit of his stomach and rolling around like an excited (but very heavy) kitten. Nerves or excitement? Philippe wasn't sure there was much difference.

He checked for at least the tenth time that his bed linen was clean and there were no dirty pants on the floor, sprayed another burst of air freshener around the room and set off for the Sacre Coeur.

The church loomed above the city, a beautiful sentry keeping watch from the Paris skyline. Philippe made his way up the steep steps of a neighbouring street, approaching the building from behind. As he reached the church he was greeted by the sight of the whole city, laid out in front him. It was one of his favourite sights in the world; the best view of the best city on the planet. He'd travelled a little in his late teens, before he'd got married, and although he'd enjoyed it he was never once tempted to stay away, to not come back. Paris was his home.

He turned his collar up against the rain, wondering why on earth he hadn't thought to bring an umbrella, and headed for shelter under the arches of the portico.

It was nearly 1.30 when Sylvie arrived, and Philippe had been beginning to lose hope of her coming at all. His heart leapt as he saw her, struggling to hold her umbrella against the storm. She wore a thin raincoat and a hat, pulled down low over her head.

She looked cold and somewhat bedraggled, but her face lit up with a beautiful smile as he ran down to meet her.

'I'm sorry I'm so late,' she said. 'I thought you might have gone. The Metro was flooded.'

'I'd have waited all day for you,' he said, and they both knew he really would have done. 'So I thought we could go to a café for lunch, or…'

She smiled at him. 'Or?'

He hesitated for a moment, then took a deep breath. Just say it! 'My mother's visiting my auntie Isabeau in Les Mureax and she'll be out all day, so we could go back to my place…?'

She handed him the umbrella, then linked her arm through his. 'Let's go back to your place,' she said. Philippe restrained himself from punching the air and led the way back to his mother's apartment.

Up the narrow staircase, past the sound of the deaf elderly neighbour's TV set, and in through the door. His apartment was tiny, she thought; much smaller than Henri's. She realised with barely any surprise that she still thought of the place where she'd lived for nearly three years as Henri's; it would never be her home.

Philippe was nervous again, his relief at her turning up making him garrulous on the way home, but now they were here he wasn't sure what to do or say. He shook her umbrella over the kitchen sink and draped his wet coat on a dining chair.

'Just stick your coat over a chair,' he said, turning to her. 'Are your feet - '

He stopped in shock as she took off her coat, the sleeve of her jumper riding up to reveal a purple bruise on her wrist.

'What the – what happened?' He was at her side in seconds, gently taking her arm and holding it up to the light. She pulled away from him, tugging at her sleeve.

'It looks worse than it is,' she said. 'It doesn't hurt. I bruise very easily.'

'How did that happen?' he asked, although he already knew the answer.

'You saw him. He was furious I went to work. It was my own fault - '

'Of course it wasn't!' he burst out. 'He must've been dragging you along the street for you to bruise like that! God, the next time I see him I'll - '

'Hit him?' she interrupted. 'No you won't. Because you're not like him. You're kind and gentle and funny.'

'I don't feel kind and gentle at the moment,' he said. She reached out to touch his cheek.

'Please don't talk like that,' she said. 'I can't take any more anger at the moment.'

He immediately felt ashamed of himself. She was so calm and brave and strong, and he was acting like a thug. Acting like Henri. He calmed himself down.

'I'm sorry,' he said. 'I just want to make you feel safe and loved. Tell me what to do.'

She smiled at him. 'Make me feel loved. Please.'

He stared into her eyes for a moment, then took her by the hand and led her to his bedroom.

Of course, the minute they entered the room he spotted them. The dirty socks, balled up in a corner. He rushed over and grabbed them before they migrated under the bed and joined the hideous discarded items already festering there – or Sylvie saw them - but too late. She laughed.

'It doesn't matter,' she said. He smiled sheepishly, opened the wardrobe door and threw them inside as she looked around with interest.

'You weren't joking about the curtains, were you?' she said. 'And the posters!' She stood in front of Eric and looked at him, appraisingly. 'This is an old one,' she said. 'He doesn't look like that now.'

Eric raised an eyebrow but she didn't notice. Philippe looked at him, warningly.

'My father gave me that poster on my 8th birthday,' he said. 'Don't laugh, but he was away a lot and the apartment was always full of aunties and cousins – I have a lot of female relatives – and I used to escape in here whenever I wanted a man's perspective on things. I used to talk to Eric in lieu of my papa.'

'And did he ever talk back?' she asked, lightly. Eric gave him a minute shake of the head.

'Of course not!' said Philippe. 'What do you think I am, some sort of lunatic?'

She laughed at his guilty expression and took his hands in hers.

'You must be a lunatic, to get involved with me,' she said softly. He shook his head.

'Getting involved with you was the most sensible thing I've done in my life.' He lifted her hand to his lips and kissed it tenderly. 'I love you, Sylvie.'

She had tears in her eyes again, but this time it wasn't sadness causing them. 'I love you too.'

They quickly undressed and lay down on his narrow bed. As they kissed and stroked and touched each other, Sylvie marvelled at how alive she felt. It was as if she'd been sleepwalking for a very long time, and now, under Philippe's gentle hands, her mind and body were finally waking up. The woolly headedness, the lack of concentration, the despair, were all dissipating into thin air, leaving behind them this wonderful feeling that *everything was as it should be*; or at least it would be one day. This was who she should be, the Sylvie who existed with Philippe; not the timid, confused Little Bird, shut away in a gilded cage with a man who resented her. She shut out the thought that persisted in the back of her mind, that this was only a temporary respite, and lost herself in his scent, his warm breath and his touch.

Above them, *les Bleus* ran around their poster celebrating Philippe's goal, while Eric smiled and discreetly averted his eyes.

CHAPTER 19

Philippe and Sylvie lay in each other's arms. It was quite a squeeze for both of them in his single bed, but they really didn't mind. Sylvie savoured the warmth of his skin next to hers as she avoided thinking about what would happen later. She was happy in a melancholic kind of way; here, she felt as free as a bird, but she knew that soon she would have to go home and face whatever was waiting there for her.

Philippe breathed in her scent and hugged her tighter, not wanting to let her go. Together they stared at the raindrops coursing down his bedroom window.

'Run away with me, Sylvie,' said Philippe suddenly.

'Where to?' she asked.

'I don't know. Have you got any money?'

'Nope. You?'

'Nope.'

They lay silently for a moment.

'I've got an auntie who lives in Marseille,' said Philippe, thinking out loud. 'Since my uncle died she's always inviting my mother down to stay. Maybe we could go there...'

Marseille? A beautiful, vibrant city in the south of the country. She'd been there once with her father, many years ago, and she'd never forgotten the smell – of the sea, and of the rich bouillabaisse that every restaurant by the harbour had served, all of them claiming to have the best recipe. She and Philippe would wander the narrow streets of the old port, holding hands in the sunshine and eating seafood fresh from the clean blue waters of the Mediterranean. Then as the sun went down over the marina, they would gaze out to sea and dream of taking one of those yachts and sailing away over the horizon, just the two of them. Maybe they really *would* take a yacht…

She twisted in his arms to look at him. 'Marseille?' she said. 'Do you think we could?'

He looked at her, still thinking. 'Well…I don't know. My cousin Hortense moved back in with her after her husband ran off with their local priest, so - '

'Sounds complicated,' said Sylvie. Never mind. Other places had fish stew and boats.

'I've got another auntie in Rennes,' he said, brightening. 'She's got a massive house and none of her kids show any sign of moving back in with her…'

'I've never been to Rennes,' said Sylvie. He grunted.

'You're not missing much,' he said. 'Actually, come to think of it, my mother and her haven't spoken for about ten years. She's very religious and she was horrified when *Maman* kicked my father out. God knows what she'd say about me turning up on her doorstep with a married woman.'

Sylvie sighed. 'Maybe not Rennes, then. What about the aunt your mother's visiting today? What's she like?'

'*Tante* Isabeau? She's lovely, but completely bonkers. If she was rich they'd say she was eccentric, but she's not so she's just a bit barmy.'

They snuggled down again, Philippe kissing the top of her head.

'I mean it though,' he said. 'Run away with me.'

'Okay.'

But eventually it had to end. Sylvie got dressed and reluctantly went home, leaving Philippe full of more conflicting emotions than he'd ever been - ecstatically happy at the thought of her in his arms, eaten away with worry about her going back to Henri, and stricken with guilt that he couldn't do anything to help her get away.

When his mother returned from her visit she found her son sitting at the kitchen table, staring thoughtfully into space. He started and got to his feet to help her with her wet raincoat, and she gratefully dumped her bag of shopping onto the table.

'Auntie Isabeau sends her love,' she said. She reached out and stopped him as he started to unpack the shopping for her. 'She asked me how you are and I said you were fine.' She reached up and took his face in her hands. 'Are you fine? We haven't had much chance to talk lately.'

For a moment he just looked at her. What would she say if she knew he was in love with a married woman? He thought she'd like Sylvie – it seemed impossible to him that anyone could *not* like Sylvie – but her situation made it difficult. Difficult. He almost laughed. What he'd give for things to be 'difficult' rather than 'impossible', as they seemed now. He opened his mouth to tell her everything, just like he always had told her everything, but instead all that came out was 'I'm fine. I just get tired working nights.'

She looked at him, clearly not convinced, but she smiled and gave him a peck on the cheek. 'Just remember you can always talk to me if you're in trouble,' she said. 'If you're drinking - '

He stopped her quickly. 'I'm not drinking. I won't ever go back to that, I promise.'

She smiled then nodded briskly, satisfied. 'Ok,' she said. 'I know you keep your promises. You're a good boy, Philippe.'

She turned away and started to unpack the shopping, leaving Philippe wishing he'd told her.

The evening passed without incident for Sylvie, but it was hardly a relaxing night off. She'd got home with an hour to spare before Henri got back from work, and she'd spent it washing away all traces of her afternoon. She could still smell Philippe on her skin, could still feel his touch, his lips on hers… She shook her head; the last thing she needed now was to drift away into a romantic daydream and give the game away. She felt so different to how she had this morning, it seemed unthinkable that Henri could walk in and see her and NOT notice the change in his poor, confused wife. She no longer felt poor or confused, just desperate to find a way out. If only Philippe had his own place! Or even Farheena; Sylvie hadn't told her new friend much about her marriage, but Farheena had managed to put the pieces together for herself and had proved very sympathetic. But she still lived with her very large, loving and chaotic family in an apartment made for one half the size, and there was no spare room for Sylvie. She could rent somewhere of course, but if Henri used the influence he had used to get her hired to now get her fired, she wouldn't even be able to afford the rent on one tiny room in a shared apartment miles from the city centre. Cleaning, even at night, didn't pay much.

So, for now, she was stuck where she was. She just had to placate Henri until she could find some way out. She found her anti-depressants and washed them down the kitchen sink, smiling as the last one swirled around the plughole before disappearing. She also resolved to avoid any more drinks made (and spiked) by Henri wherever possible, although she knew that it wouldn't be easy. Although the doctor had warned her it was best not to go cold turkey, she was determined to cut down as drastically as she could.

She was waiting like a dutiful wife when Henri got home; dinner in the oven, with the smell of slow-roasting meat wafting across the apartment. She'd rushed around with the vacuum and sprayed polish in the air, hoping he wouldn't run a finger along the wooden surfaces she was supposed to have polished.

He looked at her, a small and not particularly genuine smile on his face.

'You've been busy,' he said, glancing around at the neatly plumped cushions on the sofa and the fresh flowers in a vase on the table. She smiled and filled her old blue and white teapot with hot water, setting it on the kitchen counter as far away from him as she could.

If he was going to tamper with it she certainly wasn't going to make it easy for him.

'I'm surprised you've had time to do anything in here,' he said, pulling out a kitchen chair and sitting down, 'what with your tour of the city today.'

She froze for a moment, then realised that without her phone he could have no idea where she'd been. She turned to him with a puzzled expression.

'What tour of the city?' she asked, sounding confused. 'I only went to the market. I've been in most of the day.'

He shook his head. 'Don't lie to me, Little Bird,' he said calmly. The pleasantness of his voice made it all the more menacing. 'You were seen in the 16th arrondisement this morning - '

Sylvie almost laughed. The refuse collectors – along with the bag of rubbish containing her phone - had been out early this morning, and their route had taken them from the Louvre, along the Champs Élysées to Porte Dauphine, and then over Pont Aval to finish at the municipal rubbish dump.

But she didn't laugh. Instead she shook her head with an even more innocent look of complete bewilderment. 'No Henri, they're mistaken. Look, I was at the market this morning – the shop receipt is on the table.'

Henri didn't move, but his gaze flickered over at the receipt. 'Don't lie to me, Sylvie,' he said again, but this time with a slight edge of uncertainty. She looked at him, wide eyed, while inside she was high-fiving herself. If she ever lost her cleaning job, surely a career in the theatre beckoned? She was clearly a much more accomplished actress than she'd realised.

'How could someone possibly think I was – where was it? – the 16th arrondisement? I don't know anyone there.' She held the receipt under his nose. 'Look, I bought milk and those flowers at the shop in Rue Lagrange at 10 o'clock this morning!'

'Hmm,' said Henri, refusing to admit defeat. 'You must have a doppelganger then.'

She poured out two cups of tea while Henri discreetly looked at his phone. *Checking up on me* she thought. She placed a cup in front of him, smiling to herself as he tried to shield the phone screen from her. He didn't need to. She knew what he was doing.

She turned back to the kitchen counter and picked up her own teacup. 'Oh that reminds me,' she said. 'I'm so sorry but I lost my phone last night.'

He looked up with a guilty start. He covered it well though, she thought, quickly replacing it with irritation.

'How did you do that, you stupid woman?' he asked. She looked repentant.

'I'm so sorry Henri, I don't know what happened but when we got back last night – after you - ' she looked up at him, then lowered her eyes, as if the memory upset or embarrassed her. 'After you went to bed I couldn't find it. I think maybe it fell out of my pocket when you drag – when you walked me home from work.'

He glared at her, not sure if she was blaming him or trying to make him feel guilty. To be fair to him (he thought), she had behaved badly and made him look a fool in front of her workmates. When they'd got home, had she apologised? No, she hadn't. She'd just looked at him, not speaking, and it was the not speaking that really got to him.

Henri had never really been in love. Not with another living being, anyway. He *did* love handmade Italian leather shoes and made-to-measure suits; he loved foie gras and champagne and the best of everything. He'd loved his apartment too for a while, although now it felt small. He'd picked the right career for someone so obsessed with material things, or so he'd thought at first; but it soon became clear that some people had far more money than they needed or even realised, money that was just sitting there in bank accounts or businesses or bricks and mortar. It was the perfect career for someone who loved dealing with money, but torture for someone greedy for more.

When the apartment had come up for sale he'd had to have it. It was just the sort of classy city pad a man in his position – eligible, successful, going places - should have. It was also ridiculously expensive and stretched his finances to breaking point – in fact he should never have been able to get a mortgage for it, on his salary – but he knew how to manipulate figures as well as people. So what if his finances looked better on paper (to the bank, at least) than they did in real life? He was a shoo in for a partnership at work now the most senior accountant, Monsieur Durand was retiring; it was just a matter of hanging in there for a couple more months before the promotion and the much higher salary was his.

Except it wasn't. Shockingly the old man hadn't appointed him as his successor, but had instead chosen Margaux Aubuchon, the stout-bodied, sensible-shoed spinster (probably a lesbian) who Henri had taken pains to avoid since the, er, *misunderstanding* in the mail room last year, and the rest of the board had inexplicably gone along with it. Henri was stuck with a massive mortgage and no way to finance it. He could've cut down, but he was used to a certain standard of living and he didn't see why his lifestyle should suffer just because some senile old bastard had been unable to recognise that it was time for new blood to take over.

Luckily for Henri, a new opportunity to better his income presented itself when he went over the accounts of Boudain's Antiques after the death of Sylvie's father. Boudain was another one who had more money than sense; money that was tied up doing absolutely nothing in that shop and apartment. Real estate values in the area had gone through the roof since the days when Sylvie's great great grandfather had bought the building to provide a home and business for his family; yet there was Sylvie, content to eek out a very modest living selling a couple of antiques every month while sitting on a goldmine. It wasn't fair. Henri had grown up in a tiny farmhouse miles away from civilisation while his parents lived hand to mouth working the land. All they'd left him with was a complete disdain for the poor and the unimaginative who couldn't see that there was a better life if they just took a few risks. And Henri wasn't afraid to take risks.

Had he ever actually loved Sylvie? Well, he had found her physically attractive, in a fragile, breakable sort of way, even though she had a bit of a dirty mouth on her. Henri's mother had brought him up to believe that women were supposed to be delicate in their manners and speech, and were certainly not supposed to have the kind of vocabulary that would make a *marin* blush. In fact, Henri couldn't remember his mother once raising her voice, not even when his papa rolled home drunk or the cow kicked her while she was milking it. Despite this, he'd imagined being able to share his home with Sylvie (or more specifically, her inheritance) relatively happily, without feeling the urge to wash her mouth out or scream in her face every time he looked at her. But he'd been wrong, and now they were both trapped.

He looked at her now and sighed. He had to tread a fine line with her. He couldn't have her getting too independent; he didn't want her getting any ideas about looking at the bank account, in case she spotted certain *irregularities*. But equally he didn't want her to stop working; it meant he didn't have to spend all his evenings looking at her simpering face, plus he'd been able to enjoy the charms of his mistress in the comfort of his own home a few times, rather than making some excuse to Sylvie about 'going to his club' and having to shell out on a hotel... Although since he'd noticed her glancing around the apartment with a somewhat mercenary, calculating expression in her eyes, he hadn't invited her again.

And meanwhile Sylvie was still watching him with those big stupid cow eyes.

'I'll buy you another phone tomorrow,' he said.

'I don't know if you should, Henri,' she said, her eyes downcast. 'I'm so stupid I'll only lose it again.'

He struggled to keep himself from swearing at her. But she looked so completely beaten down that he relented; it didn't hurt to be magnanimous occasionally and the odd bit of affection seemed to keep her docile. He patted his lap and smiled at her.

'Come here, Little Bird,' he said. Sylvie did as she was told and sat on his lap, awkwardly. He took her by the chin and turned her face to his, his touch firm but not rough. 'You see? This just proves it again. You're too feeble minded to cope on your own. Lucky for you, you don't have to. You look after my home and I'll look after everything else.' He leaned in and kissed her, almost tenderly, then shifted in his seat so she had to stand up, signalling that Henri had spoken the final word and the discussion was at an end. 'Now where's my dinner?'

Sylvie bit back a sudden, dangerous burst of laughter as she envisioned herself smashing his face into a plate of *boeuf bourguignon* and garnishing his balding pate with a sprig of tarragon, opting instead for a sweet, placid smile as she went into the kitchen. *One day*, she thought. *One day...*

CHAPTER 20

Bertrand shook his wings and peered out from the sheltered nook he'd hidden himself in, a grand, gothic and ridiculously curly architectural design on the clock tower of the church of Saint Germain l'Auxerrois. Not that he would ever have admitted to hiding – from who? that ratty-feathered *imbécile* Gerard? pah! – but he couldn't deny that at the moment, out of sight and out of mind was probably the better part of valour.

He preened his feathers, combing them out with his crooked beak. Both beak and feathers had seen better days, and were all the worse for the recent, undignified tussle over a dropped *croque monsieur* that was even now going viral among the pigeon community. The shame of it! In his younger days no one – particularly not that – that puffed up *crétin* – would've had the nerve, let alone the skill, to contest a morsel as tasty as that. He sighed, although to the untrained ear or one unversed in the language of the birds it would've sounded like a melancholic 'coo', and looked down at the street below.

It was raining – again – and it had been so insistent that the Seine had finally succumbed and burst its banks, submerging the paths that Parisians and tourists alike used for romantic walks by the river. The city's lovers would have to find somewhere else for their rendezvous, preferably somewhere undercover. Flooding had shut Metro stations and closed roads, and the streets were as empty as Parisian streets ever got. Which meant the chances of another dropped *croque monsieur* were likely to be few and far between. Bertrand coo-sighed again and closed his eyes.

Had they been open, he might have spotted Sylvie hurrying towards him. It may have been raining again but the bad weather couldn't dampen her spirits. It was an unexpected taste of freedom, and nothing was going to spoil it.

Henri had answered the telephone when it rang early that morning. Sylvie had been in the kitchen, clearing away the breakfast things, and she was amazed when he called her over; she couldn't remember the last time someone had actually rung for her.

She crossed the bridge and headed for the museum.

It's common knowledge of course that the Louvre has a lower-ground level, reached through the famous glass pyramid entrance in the Cour Napoleon or through the Carousel du Louvre shopping mall. Less well known though is that the museum has an even lower level, a basement used to store the artworks and artefacts not on display. This basement is on the same level as the old, crumbling sewer network – a labyrinth of tunnels that was currently struggling to contain the overflow of the river.

Sylvie made her way past the public entrance, past the small but disappointed crowd of tourists milling about outside and trying to decide what to do now. It felt weird, going in through the staff entrance without Philippe being there. She followed the other staff who were just arriving to the canteen.

Farheena waved at her from the other side of the room. 'Morning,' she said. 'Wasn't sure if you'd be allowed to come. I heard about the other night. What a bastard! You have to leave him.'

Sylvie smiled and shrugged off her coat.

'I am working on it,' she said.

'Good! Would it have anything to do with a certain young security guard?' asked Farheena, grinning.

'Might do...'

That certain young security guard was also on his way there. He'd foregone his bicycle and jumped on a bus, but with the Metro lines out of action the streets above ground were even more chaotic than usual, and eventually he gave up and jumped off, preferring to walk. By the time he reached the Louvre he was soaked to the skin and he'd discovered another hole in the sole of his shoe. He was feeling miserable, but when he entered the canteen and saw Sylvie waiting his spirits lifted immediately, the squelchy noises coming from his socks forgotten. He slid into the seat next to her.

'Hello!' he said, brightly. She smiled.

'Hello!'

Farheena grinned wryly and shook her head. 'God, you two are *so* obvious,' she said. Philippe laughed and grasped Sylvie's hand under the table.

'I didn't think you'd be here,' he whispered.

'Henri answered the phone,' she said. '*Madame Directeur* persuaded him it was important enough to release all of my shoes from detention.'

He laughed and squeezed her hand tightly, relieved that there were no more bruises, as far as he could see anyway.

The hum of conversation in the canteen faded as the director of the museum stood in front of them. She was an imposing, business-like woman with a great air of authority, an authority that Henri had found impossible to resist even over the telephone. She didn't normally ring her cleaning staff at home but desperate times called for desperate measures, and it had been all hands to the pump that morning as she and her team of assistants had assembled a somewhat rag-tag band of emergency workers.

'*Mesdames et messieurs*,' she said, 'thank you all for battling into work, especially those of you who wouldn't normally be here at this time of day. As you know we have a storage area in the basement, and this storage area started taking in water during last night's rain. It's imperative that we move all the pieces stored there onto the higher floors in case the water level rises.'

Monsieur Fournier, who had been loitering behind Madame Director, stepped forward.

'We will be organising you into teams,' he said. 'One team will clear space on the exhibition floors, another team will be responsible for moving the stored pieces upstairs, and the last team will try to limit any water damage in the basement. When I call your name please come forward and join your team…'

Sylvie and Farheena were assigned to the upper galleries, moving some of the lesser exhibits along with visitor benches and signage to create more room. Philippe spent the day making sure the stored items were secure in their crates, before very carefully loading them onto trollies and delivering them to their new temporary homes. Occasionally he'd cross paths with Sylvie and a smile from her was enough to stop the ache that was beginning in his arms, at least until he went back downstairs again. They broke for lunch, eating together in the canteen; the cellophane-wrapped sandwiches they shared tasting better than a five-course menu at any Michelin starred restaurant. Philippe guessed that was down to the company, rather than the cheap ham filling.

There were a lot of items to move and the work could not be rushed, so it was early evening by the time they'd finished. Sylvie was relieved that Henri had not yet had a chance to buy her a new mobile phone; he'd have rung and demanded her return hours ago if he'd been able to contact her.

Farheena peered into the last crate as Philippe moved it into position.

'Bloody hell, that is *formidable*!' she cried, reaching in to touch the item then thinking better of it. 'Oh I just want to pick it up…'

'What is it?' asked Sylvie, peering over her shoulder. Inside the crate, surrounded by padding, lay an unassuming white ceramic jar. It had a slender neck while the body was completely round – but for a flat bit on the bottom – and painted with delicate blue motifs; circular patterns made up of flowers and dragons, mostly. 'Oh, that's nice. I've got a teapot like that.'

'NICE?' spluttered Farheena, outraged. 'That's not 'nice'! That is a Qianlong moon jar from the early 1700s, worth – two hundred and fifty thousand dollars? Maybe more. 'Nice' doesn't really cover it.'

Philippe laughed. 'You like it, then?'

Farheena sighed. 'Love it. We're doing about the Chinese dynasties in History of Art at the moment. Man, the Asian market is the one to get into!'

'My papa always said that,' mused Sylvie. 'He said that Asia would be huge one day. I always meant to look into Chinese ceramics, stuff like that, but I never really got a chance to. I was so busy just running the shop that I ended up sticking with what I already knew about - French and English antiques.'

'You've got an antiques shop?' asked Farheena. 'What the bloody hell are you doing here, then?'

'HAD an antiques shop,' said Sylvie. 'I'll tell you about it one day.'

'Well it's a crying shame you haven't still got it. The Chinese are going fucking mental buying back all the art that left their country. I could get a buyer for that ten times over.'

'If it was yours to sell,' Sylvie pointed out. Farheena sighed again, even more dramatically.

'That's where my plan falls down, of course,' she said. They laughed.

Philippe stretched his aching arms and peeled off the thick gloves all the movers had been issued with. 'Well, I think we're done.'

'Yes,' said Sylvie. Neither she nor Philippe moved, but stared expectantly at Farheena.

'What?' she said. 'Oh, right. Well, I'm off then. You love birds have a good night...' She winked at them, straightened her hijab and left them. They said good night to the other staff as they finished up and left, then turned to each other.

'Alone at last!' grinned Philippe, pulling her towards him. She smiled up at him.

'Now you've got me on my own, what are you going to do with me?' she said, archly. He laughed and kissed her tenderly.

'Believe it or not, nothing smutty,' he said. 'Not here, anyway... Do you know what I'd really like to do? I'd like to take you on a date.'

'A date?'

'Yes. I'd like to take you out to dinner in a fancy restaurant, where I can gaze at you while you get tipsy on champagne and play footsie under the table. Then I'd like to walk along the riverbank hand in hand with you and kiss you under the tower - '

She snuggled her head into his shoulder. 'Oh that sounds lovely!'

' – and then I'd like to go home and fall asleep next to you, then wake up next to you in the morning and do it all over again, every day for the rest of my life.'

She looked up at him, misty eyed. 'Oh Philippe...'

He smiled. 'But unfortunately I am almost completely penniless, so how about I buy you a burger and we share a soft drink?'

She laughed. 'Sounds perfect. I'm starving.'

'Me too,' he said. He leaned in towards her and their lips touched...

...and suddenly they were plunged into pitch black.

'What happened?' cried Sylvie, eyes wide in the darkness. Philippe pulled out the night watchman's torch on his belt and shone it around, keeping a protective arm around her shoulder.

'The flooding must've knocked out the power,' he said. 'Don't worry, the back up generators will kick in after a few seconds.'

They stood in the dark. No lights came on. He shone his torch around again.

'Except of course the generators are in the basement,' he said. 'The water must've got to them too.'

'What should we do?' asked Sylvie. 'Should we head downstairs and try and find the others?'

Philippe thought for a moment, then shook his head. 'No, let's just get out of here. If we hang about we'll get caught up in a security check and be stuck here for hours. I'm not passing up my chance of a couple of hours alone with you for that. Let's go!'

They made their way carefully along the gallery. There was no moon shining through the skylight tonight, the clouds too thick and heavy with rain, and no street lights cast their glow either; it looked like the whole city was affected, not just the museum. Luckily they were in the Denon wing, so although the thin beam of the torch couldn't pick out much they were both very familiar with the layout and knew where to step. Philippe swung the torch beam around the walls, lighting up the CCTV cameras and security alarm boxes. All of them were dark and silent, their little red 'on' lights absent.

'It's a proper power cut,' he said, musing aloud. 'Everything's dead, not just the lights but cameras and alarms too.'

As they neared the end of the gallery he slowed, then stopped. He was clearly deep in thought.

'What's the matter?' asked Sylvie.

'Nothing...' he said, unconvincingly. 'I just need to check something over there. Here,' he handed her the torch. 'I can see now, my eyes have got used to the dark. I'll meet you out by the Pyramid.'

'What is it? What's going on?' she demanded, but he just gave a strained smile and kissed her cheek.

'Nothing. Go on, I'll be right behind you. Get a move on before the power comes back and we get caught here.' She hesitated, so he gave her behind a gentle push. 'Go on!'

Wondering what he was up to, Sylvie hurried out of the gallery, down the stairs and out through the security entrance, which was unmanned; she assumed everyone was trying to find out what was happening. She pushed at the door expecting it to be locked, but it wasn't and she soon found herself outside in the fresh air. She headed out into the Cour Napoleon and waited by the pyramid, which like the rest of the city was in darkness. It felt wrong for what was normally such a brilliantly lit landmark to be out.

She shone the torch around and jumped as Philippe rushed up behind her, his jacket draped over his arm despite the rain. And underneath it, the suggestion of something else...

'Let's go!' he said, striding away quickly. She turned to follow, jogging slightly to catch up.

'What's going on?' she said. In the beam of the torch his face looked yellow and sickly; but he also looked worried, and she knew that that had nothing to do with the torchlight.

'I've just done something really stupid,' he whispered, turning to her. 'Oh god, what have I done?'

She looked at him in concern as behind them the lights of the museum came on and all the alarms went off at once.

CHAPTER 21

The taxi ride back to Philippe's apartment had taken place in shocked silence but for the mournful commentary of the driver, who talked all the way there about the state of the roads, the weather, and his dire predictions for the French national football team in the rapidly approaching European Soccer Championships. Perhaps he hadn't noticed that the couple in the back seat both looked pale and worried, or maybe he put it down to a lovers' tiff. Either way it didn't stop him talking, despite the lack of a response.

Philippe was relieved to remember that it was his mother's regular night out playing bingo at *la Lotto*, and he bounded up the stairs still clutching his jacket and whatever was under there, not stopping until he reached his front door to check if Sylvie was behind him. She was.

And now they stood in his bedroom, gazing at the item that was propped up on his chest of drawers competing for wall space with Eric and *les Bleus*.

'Why - ' began Sylvie, for what felt like the hundredth time. Philippe interrupted her.

'I told you why!' he said, pleading with her to understand. 'When all the cameras went off, I thought about what Farheena had said about how much that jar was worth - '

'Then why didn't you steal the jar?!' cried Sylvie.

'Because it was right down the other end of the gallery, where we'd just come from, and I didn't know how much longer we'd have before the lights came back on!' he said. 'I told you that. I thought we could sell it and use the money to run away together. I want to get you away from here, Sylvie. I did it for us!'

She looked at his stricken face and her heart melted. She reached out for him.

'I know you did, darling,' she said gently. 'But we have a bit of a problem now, don't we? How are we going to sell her? Everyone will know she's not ours to sell.'

They looked at the painting, and she returned their gaze unblinking, that famously enigmatic smile seeming to suggest that they had no idea how much trouble they were letting themselves in for.

The Mona Lisa is probably the most recognisable painting in the world, as well as possibly the most valuable, and now it was sitting in the childhood bedroom of an ex-alcoholic security guard in a tiny top-floor apartment in the Montmartre district. She didn't exactly go with the décor, the football motif curtains and shabby wallpaper providing an unlikely backdrop for her. And it really didn't help, thought Philippe, that his poster of Eric Cantona kept winking at her and trotting out what were possibly the cheesiest chat up lines in the history of dating. *Is that an enigmatic smile on your face, Madame, or are you just pleased to see me?* Oh Eric, *please*!

'I'm so stupid,' groaned Philippe. 'Like father, like son.'

'What do you mean?' asked Sylvie. He flopped onto the bed.

'You remember I told you my father's job kept him away from home a lot?' he asked. She nodded. 'Well, it did, but only when he got caught.' He sighed. 'My father got caught a lot. He was the world's worst burglar. And probably the world's worst dad, too.'

Philippe Moreau Snr had been in his late twenties when he became a father. It was a responsibility, he told his friends at the local bar, that he was ready for. He was looking forward to playing football with his young son, teaching him how to shave, how to drink and how to pick up women. They'd all laughed and raised a glass to wet the baby's head, then another to toast the health of his beautiful wife and the new mother, Madame Moreau. There were a lot of toasts to this, that and the other that night, just as there were on many other nights.

Like many men, Monsieur Moreau didn't really 'get' babies; they didn't do much, did they, other than howl for their mother's tit and make a smelly mess of their nappies, and none of that was really a job for the father. No, he felt that his job was to be hunter-gatherer; to bring home the bacon, to put food on the table. But somehow he never managed to stick at a job long enough to get the promotions and the pay-rises, and there were long periods where he had no work at all. He would sit at the bar with his friends, drinking and bemoaning the fact that there was no money to pay the power bill, and that Philippe Jnr was growing so fast that he constantly needed new clothes. The kid was eating him out of house and home, and as for his wife... He conveniently forgot to mention that it was her string of part time jobs – cleaning, shop work, babysitting – that kept the roof over their heads and the whisky in his glass.

One night an old friend of his, newly returned from somewhere vague 'out of town', had whispered drunkenly in his ear about a special 'job' he was planning; the type of opportunity that an intelligent, nimble and more importantly fleet-of-foot man like Monsieur Moreau might do well to take advantage of. And so it began.

Moreau and his friend Vincent began what they no doubt would've drunkenly referred to as a 'reign of brilliant lawlessness and mendacity' – a spate of burglaries and frauds targeting banks, post offices and high-value retail sites – but what the police called in court 'a cack-handed campaign of petty theft leaving behind a mountain of evidence at every turn'. For a couple of months they prevailed. There was suddenly plenty of money in the Moreau household, and young Philippe, who by now was 7 or 8, reaped the rewards of having a father who 1) worked nights and 2) had a lot of disposable income that could hardly be put into a bank, seeing as it already come from one under dubious circumstances. There were outings to the zoo and ice cream and even tickets to a football match, although young Philippe hadn't been able to see much, had hated the loud roar of the angry crowd when the opposition scored, and had been afraid of the bad words coming from his father's mouth. Particularly when he got upset and those bad words were turned on him.

But Moreau was still his father, and he loved him. And then one evening he'd spruced himself up – Philippe could smell the aftershave from the other side of the room – and hunted around the kitchen for Madame Moreau's car keys.

'Where are the car keys, *chéri*?' he called out. Philippe's mother was in the bedroom, changing her clothes.

'You're not going out, are you?' she called. 'I'm off to work in a minute and I need you to look after Philippe.'

'Of course not!' he cried, winking at his son. He leaned in towards Philippe and spoke in a conspiratorial undertone. 'Never let a woman tell you what to do, boy!' he said. Then he spotted the keys, in the fruit bowl on the centre of the kitchen table. 'Ah, there they are!' he said, picking them up.

'But - ' said Philippe, worried. He didn't want to be left on his own while his mother was at work, or (worse still) with the neighbour downstairs, the one with the whiskery beard and the bad breath. He didn't like her at all.

But Moreau just smiled at him. 'I'm off to meet the lads, *chéri*!' he called. 'Don't wait up!' And with a last ruffle of his son's hair, he was off.

'But I did wait up,' said Philippe. 'I waited all night for him, and he never came home. He'd got drunk and decided to break into a bank.

Just like that, on the spur of the moment, because some woman had stood him up. *Imbecile*! It was their head office as well, there wasn't even a single *centime* in there.'

'He went to jail?' said Sylvie.

'Yes. That was just the first time. He got five years, served two. When he came out he promised my mother that he would stay sober and on the straight and narrow, but he couldn't last more than two months without getting drunk and getting into trouble again. Eventually Maman had had enough and kicked him out.'

Philippe went over to the painting and picked it up, weighing it in his hands.

'It was so easy,' he said. 'I knew it would be. I just smashed the glass and took her out of the display case and walked out of there. I'm no better than my father. He thought he was a criminal mastermind and all the time he was just a *connard*! And so am I.'

He sat back on the bed, still gripping the painting. Sylvie took it from him and carried it very carefully back to the chest of drawers, studying it closely.

'She is beautiful,' she murmured. 'To see her up close – to see the brush strokes, to smell the paint and feel where da Vinci touched her…'

For a moment both were lost in contemplation of the work of art sitting incongruously against the bedroom wall. But both were brought sharply back to reality at the sound of footsteps in the hallway.

'Philippe, are you in?' called Madame Moreau. Philippe leapt up and stood in front of his bedroom door.

'*Oui,* Maman! I was about to go to bed!'

When she spoke again her voice was louder; she was right outside the door.

'Is everything ok? You sound - ' The doorknob began to turn. Philippe grabbed it.

'Don't come in, Maman! I've – I've got a woman friend in here!'

Sylvie raised her eyebrows. 'Two women friends…' she said to herself.

From outside they heard a sharp intake of breath, then – 'I'm sorry, mademoiselle, my son is such a dark horse! I didn't know he had company.'

Philippe looked at her; *say something!* She opened her mouth, feeling awkward.

'Er – that's ok, Madame Moreau! Sorry if we disturbed you!'

'Oh no, it sounds like I was disturbing *you*!' On the other side of the door, Philippe's mother chuckled. She was relieved to find her son did have a life outside of work and books after all. 'Have a good night, and I might see you both in the morning…'

They stared at each other as they heard Madame Moreau's footsteps retreat and her bedroom door shut, then Philippe relaxed and flopped back on to the bed.

'That could've been embarrassing,' said Sylvie.

'You mean it wasn't?' said Philippe, incredulously. He looked over at the painting and groaned, holding his head in his hands, overcome with despair again as the shock of their close call with his mother faded.

'I'm going to prison,' he moaned. She knelt in front of him and took his hands away from his face.

'No you're not,' she said, defiantly.

'But what are we going to do?' he said. 'I mean, what am *I* going to do? I can't drag you into this.'

'I'm already in this,' she said. 'I tell you what we're not going to do. We're not going to lose each other, and we're not leaving Mona here with Eric and *les Bleus*.'

'Can you sell her?' he asked, hopefully. 'You had an antiques shop, you must have some contacts?'

She laughed humourlessly. 'Sure, I'll ring up a few of my old customers. Maybe the lady who bought that garden statue for 250 Euros will have a spare million to buy a stolen painting. Or the guy who bought his wife the reproduction Canaletto...'

'Okay, okay...' said Philippe. 'I get the point!'

'The first thing we have to do is make sure no one knows we've got her,' said Sylvie, thinking aloud. 'Have you got anywhere you can hide her?'

'I think so,' said Philippe.

'Somewhere your mother won't find her?'

'...Ah.'

Sylvie sighed. 'Okay, I'll take her.'

'My mother?'

'No, Mona! There's a storeroom on the ground floor of my apartment block. It's where the residents store packing crates and bits of furniture they don't have room for when they move in. We all know where the building manager keeps the key but nobody ever goes in there. She should be safe for a bit until we work out what to do with her.'

Philippe held her close and whispered words of love as she hugged him back fiercely, while on the wall next to the most famous painting in the world Eric watched them, shaking his head at their rash behaviour. Mona just smiled.

CHAPTER 21

Sylvie took another taxi home, the painting now wrapped in black plastic garbage bags to protect it from the rain. It was nearly 10pm by now, and she'd been expecting Henri to be waiting up for her, pacing up and down the apartment and winding himself up into a fury; but from the street below it looked like all the lights were off. She paid the driver and went inside.

The storeroom key was tucked under a houseplant – a straggly-looking fern in a brass pot. There wasn't normally anything of great value in the storeroom, and as most of it was furniture anything that *was* worth money was too big and bulky to steal. The building manager, Claude, had offered to have keys made for all the residents but they'd all agreed it was unnecessary, as no one could get into the building from the street without a door key anyway. Sylvie grabbed the key and let herself in, fumbling around in the dark for the light switch.

She blinked as the bare bulb flooded the room with light. A bicycle, some old drawers with handles missing, tea chests and bubble wrap from someone's move...and an old wooden armoire, ornately carved and beautiful but ultimately not loved enough by the owner to go through the pain and hassle of carrying it up several flights of twisty stairs to their apartment – especially when there was no guarantee a piece of that size would fit through the door. It was the perfect hiding place.

Sylvie opened the door and slid the painting, still wrapped up, inside; then closed the door and leaned the rusty bicycle against it to further discourage anyone looking inside, in the unlikely event that the storeroom had any other visitors. She switched off the light, locked the door, returned the key and then took a deep breath, steeling herself for a possible run-in with Henri.

But when she opened the door to the apartment, all the lights really were off; her vision of him pacing the floor waiting for her return was completely wrong and he was obviously in bed. She tiptoed past the bedroom door and into the kitchen, leaving the light off so as not to disturb him – she knew that it shone through the gap under the bed-room door, and besides the moon had finally come out from behind the clouds, illuminating the apartment clearly enough for her to fill the kettle at the sink.

She jumped as the light suddenly flicked on, making her spill water over herself. She turned to see Henri standing there, still dressed; he'd been sitting in the darkness of the living room, waiting for her after all.

'You remembered to come home, then,' he said. 'Why are you creeping about in the dark?'

'I thought you'd gone to bed,' she said. His even tone and calm expression made her nervous. 'I didn't want to disturb you.'

'You're out all day until ten o'clock and you think I'm not already disturbed?' he said, sarcastically. 'Why didn't you call me?' She opened her mouth to speak but he beat her to it. 'Oh of course, you 'lost' your phone, didn't you? How convenient. And I don't suppose anyone else had one you could borrow, did they?'

He took a step towards her and, hating herself for doing it, she took a step back. She so wanted to be brave but she was beginning to tremble, cringing away from him. She'd made him angry in the past – *no,* protested the little voice in her head, *he'd got angry in the past, there's a difference* – but he had never been physically violent towards her. Not really… But there was always a first time, and she had never seen him quite this furious before. Beneath the sarcasm she could tell he was seething, and the fact that he wasn't shouting at her made him all the more menacing. All the more dangerous.

She turned away from him, not wanting him to know she was scared, and put the kettle on to boil. He strode forward angrily at that and grabbed her arm, pulling her round to face him.

'Don't turn your fucking back on me!' he spat in her face. 'Where have you been?'

She forced herself to stay calm. 'You know where I've been,' she said. 'The museum. You spoke to the director.'

'It's fucking ten o'clock!' he yelled at her. She swallowed hard, fighting back the tears that were starting to well up in her eyes.

'I know, Henri. I'm sorry, I didn't realise it would be so late. It took ages, and then the director wanted to buy us all dinner to say thank you, and then there was a power cut and we all had to stay behind for a security check when it came back on - '

He pushed her against the kitchen sink. She was trapped.

'Don't lie to me, you stupid ugly bitch,' he growled, shoving his face closer to hers. She could smell the cheese he'd eaten that evening on his breath, and see the open pores on his nose. He had a large nose for such a short man, she thought, and it was beginning to turn red from too much alcohol. She imagined him drinking wine and brandy on his own in the dark, waiting for her, winding himself up into a fury, and felt a pang of disgust and contempt mingling in with her fear. It made her braver. She groped behind her, her fingers closing on a small but sharp fruit knife on the draining board. She brought it round quickly and waved it in his face.

He looked shocked for a moment, then laughed in derision.

'What are you going to do to me with that?' he mocked. 'Peel me?' But he stepped back nonetheless. She moved around the kitchen so that the table was between them.

'I'm tired, Henri. I just want a drink and a sit down.' And suddenly she really was tired, more tired than she'd ever been. Tired of everything.

'Of course you're tired,' he said. 'I know exactly what you've been up to, you whore.'

She stared at him for a moment, and all at once the whole thing felt ridiculous. *He* was ridiculous. A kitchen-sink Emperor losing control of his kingdom. She could feel sudden, dangerous laughter welling up inside her, and before she could stop it it burst from her. She was too exhausted to hold it back.

'Oh my god Henri,' she giggled, 'you have no fucking idea what I've been up to, you really don't.' She thought of Mona, hidden in her bin bag inside the armoire downstairs, and laughed harder.

He took a step towards her, hand raised, and her laughter stopped. She picked up a mug from the kitchen counter and threw it at him, but it missed and smashed to pieces against the wall.

'If you ever threaten me again…' she said, trying to be firm and hating the slightly hysterical edge to her voice. He smiled insincerely, trying to placate her.

'I wasn't going to hit you, Little Bird,' he said. She snorted.

'You must think I'm stupid,' she said. 'I'm tired, Henri. Just go to bed and we'll talk about it in the morning.'

He stared at her in furious incredulity. 'Don't you tell me what to do, bitch!'

'I *am* telling you, Henri,' she said, sitting on a kitchen chair. 'This is what is going to happen. You're going to bed and I'm making a cup of tea.'

He was almost apoplectic with rage now. 'I'll give you a cup of tea, you fucking whore - '

She laughed again before she could stop herself. 'That doesn't even make sense, you stupid little man.'

He approached her but she reached back and picked another mug up off the counter and threw it at him. Her aim was getting better. Her old netball teacher, Madame Leblanc – a hairy-chinned woman with a voice like a foghorn and the patience of a virgin bridegroom on his wedding night - would've been proud and amazed in equal measure.

'Don't you - ' he was spitting and raging and all she could think of was Rumpelstiltskin, stamping about in fury and splitting himself in two. *If only,* murmured the little voice in her head. She picked up the teapot and held it up, ready to throw.

He stopped at the kitchen door. 'Alright, Little Bird,' he said, getting himself back under control. He hated it when she made him lose control. 'You have your tea. You can sleep right there. But we will talk in the morning, I can promise you that. You'll keep.' He smiled at her, and the smile didn't even come close to reaching his hate-filled eyes. 'Sweet dreams, *chéri*,' he said, and then he turned and walked away.

Sylvie stayed where she was for thirty seconds, unable to move a muscle, then got shakily to her feet and shut the kitchen door, jamming it closed with a kitchen chair under the handle. *Je ne regrette rien*, she thought. And it was true; she didn't. Then she shut off the now-whistling kettle and sat down, folding her arms on the table and laying her head down to rest on them.

CHAPTER 23

Sylvie was woken by Philippe's voice, low but insistent.

'Sylvie, Sylvie, wake up!' A gentle shake of her arm made her lift her head groggily, and she opened her eyes to see his frightened face above her.

'Philippe...?' she murmured. 'But how did you - '

'They're coming for me, Sylvie!' he hissed, urgently. 'You didn't hide her properly and she got away and now they're coming for me!'

'Who?' She shook her head, trying to bring herself round and make sense of the situation. But before Philippe could answer her, the kitchen door – which was still jammed shut – began to tremble and shake... Then suddenly the door blew inwards with a rush of air and splintered wood, smoke filling the room. Sylvie coughed and swiped at the air, trying to clear it, and blinked in amazement as three armed *gendarmes* stepped through the debris into the kitchen.

'Hold it right there, Madame!' the leader cried. Sylvie could feel her jaw dropping.

'My door!' she cried. 'What the bloody hell have you done to my door? You better clear this up before my husband sees it!'

The other two policemen pointed their rifles at the two lovers as the leader called behind him. 'In here, *s'il vous plait Madame*, if you don't mind!'

Sylvie watched, amazed, as through the clearing smoke a figure emerged. A woman, whose face was almost as familiar to her as her own. It was Mona Lisa, large as life and released from her portrait, but her expression had changed and the enigmatic smile had been replaced by a look of pure, malicious evil... She smiled at Sylvie, a spiteful smile full of poisonous, malevolent pleasure, and turned to the police officer.

'That's them!' she shrieked, her high-pitched voice causing the glasses on the kitchen shelf to rattle and hum. She pointed to Sylvie and Philippe. 'He's the one who kidnapped me, and she helped! Thieves and murderers! Oh mercy!'

'Take him away!' ordered the police officer, and his two subordinates stepped forward to grab Philippe.

'Don't let them take me, Sylvie!' howled Philippe. She reached out to hold onto him but couldn't move; her arms were handcuffed to the kitchen chair. She struggled and cried out.

'No! Leave him alone! He only did it for me!' she cried, but to no avail. Mona turned her gaze back on her and smiled again.

'He's mine now, bitch,' she hissed, cackling as Philippe was dragged out of the kitchen. Sylvie struggled hard, feeling the metal cuffs digging into her skin.

'Bring him back!' she cried. 'I love him! Bring him back!'

But Mona just smiled, and floated backwards through the door. The splintered wood flew back into place, imploding into one piece again like a film being played backwards, the door coming together noisily, wood knocking against wood as the kitchen chair shot back into place and jammed itself under the door handle…

'Sylvie, Sylvie! Wake up!'

She shook her head groggily. Someone was knocking on the kitchen door. No, not someone – Henri. She slowly sat up, her muscles aching and cramped from falling asleep at the kitchen table.

'Sylvie! *Madame Directeur* just rang.' Henri banged on the door again. She got up and gingerly moved the chair from under the door handle, opening the door to let him in.

She was gratified to see that Henri looked like he hadn't slept very well either. *Good* she thought.

'The director? What did she want?' asked Sylvie, not entirely sure she wanted to know the answer. Mona, in her hiding place downstairs, waved at her inside her head.

Henri had the almost-decency to look slightly ashamed of himself. 'She said that everyone who got caught up in the power cut has to go in for a debriefing,' he said. 'She needs you there as soon as possible.'

Her stomach fluttered nervously but she kept her face blank. 'Okay,' she said. 'I'd better get ready then.' She squeezed past him, but he stuck out a hand to stop her.

'You might not have been lying to me about the power cut,' he said, ' but it doesn't mean you're off the hook about last night.'

She looked at him. He was more right about that than he realised, she thought. She shook him off and went to get showered.

The rain had finally stopped as Sylvie reached the museum. Outside the pyramid entrance grumbling tourists in cagoule raincoats gathered around a sign declaring that the museum would be closed until Tuesday due to flooding. She hurried past them and headed for the staff entrance, quickening her pace as she spotted Philippe waiting anxiously outside for her.

'Thank god!' he said, greeting her with a kiss on the cheek. 'Are you ok? Is – is she safe?'

'Yes,' she said. 'Everything's fine. Who else is here?'

'Everyone,' he said. 'It's not just us. We have to wait in the canteen to be called.'

They made their way inside and found Farheena and Stephanie in the canteen.

'Where were you yesterday?' Philippe asked Stephanie. She sighed dreamily. She looked tired but happy.

'I was...away for the night,' she said, smiling to herself. Philippe grinned at her, eyebrows raised, and she shook herself out of her day-dream. 'I turned my phone off. I'm on the day shift rota for today, so I turn up and all this is going on!'

'You must've heard about all the flooding?' said Farheena. 'Apparently there was a big power cut as well last night, after I left.'

'Yes,' said Sylvie. 'Everything went off, just as we were on our way out...'

Monsieur Fournier entered the canteen and looked around, anxiously. He spotted Philippe and approached him.

'Philippe, glad you're here,' he said. Philippe's mouth felt dry but he made himself speak, his voice sounding guilty in his own ears.

'What's happened?' he asked. 'Is everything ok?' Sylvie's hand squeezed his under the table.

'Yes...' Monsieur Fournier looked uncomfortable. 'It's just a security debriefing. Should've done it last night but everyone was too tired. Come with me.'

Philippe swallowed nervously and stood up. This was it – he was going to get caught. But then Sylvie leapt to her feet and spoke to the security chief in a low voice.

'I'm sorry Monsieur Fournier,' she said, 'But is it okay if we speak to you together? It's a bit – delicate...'

Fournier looked at her for a moment, then shrugged. 'Okay, it'll speed things up I suppose. Let's go.'

They left the canteen, leaving Farheena and Stephanie watching in concern.

Monsieur Fournier led them to the Museum Director's office, opening the door for them and standing back. They entered, nervously. The director sat behind her desk, looking business-like as usual but tired; it had clearly been a long night for her. Sylvie felt a guilty pang but it was soon replaced by worry; what did they know? Philippe had said that the power cut had affected the cameras as well as the lights, but was there a back-up power supply for them that he didn't know about?

Madame Directeur gestured to them to sit down, Philippe pulling out a chair for Sylvie before seating himself. As they sat down they both noticed with a shock the late middle-aged man standing in the corner of the office, arms folded across his chest and a look of sharp appraisal on his face. His hair was greying and he had a somewhat straggly beard, and he was dressed just short of scruffy – dark grey shirt and faded black jeans. Next to the always-impeccably turned out Fournier and the well-tailored director he looked conspicuously out of place.

Philippe and Sylvie looked at him and, leaning nonchalantly against a filing cabinet, he coolly returned their gaze. But he didn't speak and neither the director or Monsieur Fournier gave any indication of even being aware of him. *Madame Directeur* spoke.

'Okay, so you're Philippe Moreau and you're...?' she asked.

'Sylvie Cloutier,' provided Monsieur Fournier.

'Thank you,' she said. 'No need to look so nervous, we just want a little chat - '

'We have something to confess!' Sylvie blurted out. Horrified but already resigned to his fate, Philippe turned to look at her. He wasn't the only one. The director leant forward in her chair and the man in faded black in the corner stood up straight, clearly very interested. Sylvie looked at them, anxiously.

'We were here last night when the power went off,' she said, nervously. 'We were together in the Denon wing, on the first floor. But then you probably already know that from the security footage taken before the cameras went off.' She looked down at the floor, embarrassed, as the director, security chief and mystery man exchanged glances.

'Yes, we saw it,' said Monsieur Fournier, gently. He was a kind man with a soft spot for Philippe – or more accurately, his mum – and he didn't like what that horrible man the director had called in (completely unnecessarily, in his opinion) to help investigate had suggested earlier about Philippe, even if the evidence did look bad.

Sylvie carried on, her voice faltering; making it obvious that whatever had taken place, she really was very sorry about it. 'I know we should've stayed and reported to Security when the lights went out, but – well – we're having an affair - '

Philippe and Monsieur Fournier both let out their breath in relief. Fournier half-turned to the director; *there* was the explanation for Philippe and Sylvie's presence in and then subsequent disappearance from the gallery; a matter of the heart, not theft. An illicit love affair was something that every French man could understand.

'I'm sorry,' said Philippe. 'I know what the drill is on those occasions, but we had the rare chance to spend some time together and we didn't want to waste it here. When the lights went out we seized the chance and just went.'

The director and the mystery man looked at each other again, while Fournier gave Sylvie a reassuring pat on the shoulder. She smiled up at him gratefully, while inside she apologised for taking advantage of his good nature.

'Which way did you leave?' asked the director. They evidently weren't off the hook that easily. Philippe thought quickly.

'We went down the back stairs,' he said. The back stairs were in the opposite direction to the small antechamber that the Mona Lisa had hung in until last night. The mystery man spoke up, making Sylvie jump with genuine nerves.

'Why did you go down the back stairs?' he asked gruffly. 'The front stairs would've been nearer to you.'

But Philippe had already thought of that. 'We thought we might run into other people that way,' he said. Fournier nodded.

'Fair enough,' he said. 'Did you see or hear anyone else in the gallery?'

Philippe and Sylvie looked at each other, then slowly shook their heads.

'No, I don't think so,' said Philippe. 'Is everything okay? Has something happened?'

'You won't tell my husband, will you?' asked Sylvie.

'No no no,' said the director, smiling unconvincingly. 'It's just a routine security debriefing, that's all. No need to tell anyone outside of these four walls what we've talked about. But make sure you conduct your affair in your own time in future, not the museum's.'

Philippe and Sylvie looked suitably shamefaced and thanked *Madame Directeur* for being so understanding. Then they turned and hightailed it away from the museum, not speaking until they reached a small café in the Rue de Marengo. It was damp and chilly outside – plus Sylvie was still nervous that Henri might see them, despite knowing that his 'spies' were lying in a rubbish tip in another part of the city - so they opted for a table indoors where it was warm and private.

'Oh my god,' said Philippe, taking her wet jacket and hanging it with his over a spare chair. 'You nearly gave me a heart attack. I really thought you were going to confess for a moment!'

She smiled and reached across the table to hold his hand. 'I'm sorry,' she said, 'I didn't get a chance to warn you. It just occurred to me that they'd still have security footage from just before the power went out, and that they'd see us alone up there. I thought it was better to mention it before they did so it looks like we've got nothing to hide.'

'That never even crossed my mind,' admitted Philippe. 'You're so clever.'

'Am I?' Sylvie looked pleased; it was a long time since anyone had called her anything other than stupid and useless. 'I think it's just because I'm starting to wake up and think for myself again. The pills must finally be wearing off.'

They signalled the waitress for coffee, Sylvie marvelling at how natural it felt to be sitting here with him doing something so normal, so everyday, when not long ago just bumping into him in the street had seemed fraught with danger.

'Who was that sinister-looking man in the director's office?' she asked. Philippe shrugged.

'No idea. But at least we know they haven't got the theft on camera, otherwise I'd be banged up by now.'

'What about fingerprints?'

'There shouldn't be any. They gave us all gloves for moving the exhibits, didn't they? I put them back on. And I smashed the glass with a fire extinguisher and left it there. So there's nothing to tie me to the theft.' He smiled at her, then frowned for a second. She spotted it straight away.

'What is it?' she asked.

'The glass... It's normally toughened, bullet resistant glass,' said Philippe thoughtfully. 'I mean, I think you could still smash through it with something heavy like the extinguisher, but it might take a while. There's only a handful of us who knew that the display was being re-placed and that it was just ordinary glass in there.'

'But that doesn't mean that someone who *didn't* know wouldn't have had a go at stealing it,' said Sylvie.

'No...' Philippe looked unconvinced. 'But maybe that's why they're keeping it quiet.'

She looked surprised. 'Are they keeping it quiet?' she asked. He laughed.

'Come on, Sylvie! *La Joconde*'s been stolen and there's no crowd of reporters hanging around outside the museum? This café would be full of people gossiping and speculating about it. Hell, the *country* would be full of people speculating about it! It's not in the papers or on the TV.' He smiled at her. 'Think of who else knew about the glass. The director and Monsieur Fournier for starters. How much trouble would they get in if it was known Mona had disappeared on their watch, because she wasn't in a secure enough display? Bad enough that the generators failed, but the glass…' He shook his head.

'Half the works in the Louvre are loans or donations,' said Sylvie. 'People would start asking for their pieces back, if they thought the museum wasn't capable of protecting them.'

'Exactly,' said Philippe. 'So they need to keep it quiet. That could help us, Sylvie. But we need to get rid of her as soon as possible.'

The waitress, approaching their table with coffee, raised her eyebrows. Philippe smiled at her.

'The mother-in-law's out-stayed her welcome,' he explained.

'You've never liked my mother!' cried Sylvie. The waitress shook her head in weary empathy.

'They never do, Madame,' she said. 'They never do.'

They lingered over their coffees as long as they dared, but the spectre of Henri waiting at home loomed over them. As much as she would've preferred to spend the day with Philippe, Sylvie didn't dare upset Henri any more than was absolutely necessary until they had an escape plan. She had no idea what or how that escape would come about, but she had no doubt that one day it would.

They finished their coffees and said long, reluctant goodbyes, then kissed and made their way home. Sylvie headed towards the river and her home in the 6th arrondisement, while Philippe unlocked his bike and peddled through the city and upwards to Montmartre.

From a doorway opposite, the mysterious man in faded black watched them…

CHAPTER 24

The rest of the day crawled past with all the speed of a reluctant elderly tortoise wading through treacle. Sylvie kept herself busy cleaning and cooking, and avoiding Henri's hands. It was Sunday so he was at home, and he was bored. She realised that the more she cringed, the more she dodged away from the him, the more he did it; he didn't really want her, he just wanted to make her reject him so that he could accuse her of being frigid or of not fulfilling her wifely duties. Another stick to beat her with. Something to pass the time.

A brief but welcome respite came when he fell asleep, paper on his lap. In the early days of their relationship he'd have taken her out somewhere nice, but not any more. She was glad. She preferred to escape into the bedroom and be on her own, looking out of the window and across the city skyline to where she could just make out the main dome of the Sacre Coeur. She pressed her face against the cold glass and thought of Philippe, at home in his mother's apartment. Her cheeks grew hot as she thought of the afternoon she'd spent with him in his childhood bedroom, making love and talking about the future. She hoped they'd find a way to have one.

She flopped onto the bed with a heavy sigh, knocking the small framed photograph of her mother that had slept beside her since she was 11 years old off the bedside table as she did. As she bent down to pick it off the floor she frowned; there was something glinting in the darkness under the bed. On her knees, she reached out and plucked it off the carpet, looking at it closely. It was a gold earring. And it wasn't one of hers.

Most wives would be distraught at evidence of their husband's infidelity, but Sylvie just looked at it indifferently. So on top of everything else he'd cheated on her. Maybe he was *still* cheating on her. Now she knew exactly why he'd been happy for her to work evenings. Still, it had at least taken the pressure off her sexually; after the first few gentle, tender times when she'd still been in plaster, Henri had grown impatient during sex and had grabbed what he wanted without much concern for her enjoyment. She'd taken to making out shopping lists in her head as he thrust inexpertly in and out of her. In – *courgettes* – out – *plums*... The less she had to be intimate with him now, the better.

Philippe spent the day watching the TV news and waiting for the story of the theft to break, but it never did. He was convinced now that the museum would keep it quiet until absolutely forced to come clean, and he hoped that that would help them get rid of the painting. After all, everybody in the world knew what the Mona Lisa looked like; he bet there were remote tribes in the deepest Amazonian jungles who'd recognise her. And everybody in the world knew (or would probably guess) that the Mona Lisa didn't belong to a museum night watchman and a cleaning lady, and wasn't theirs to sell. He'd done some research on the internet and discovered that there was a thriving market in copies of famous works; not your bog standard tourist prints, available from the museum gift shop, but actual paintings done to such a high standard as to be almost indistinguishable from the real thing. Not quite fakes because they were never sold as the genuine painting, they nonetheless looked and felt like the original, often painted using the same techniques and materials where possible. Some of these paintings fetched very high prices, because of the level of skill involved and because they were the next best thing to owning a genuine Picasso or Monet or yes, Da Vinci. Of course, a replica Mona wouldn't net them the $1.5 billion some valued the real painting at, but it would probably bring them enough to flee Paris and start again somewhere new before the shit hit the fan and the new owner realised that their 'replica' was actually the real thing, stolen during a freak power cut...

Philippe did a few chores for his mother, who was out helping one of his many female relatives with her new baby daughter (the X chromosome was definitely the dominant one in his family), then went into his bedroom to hang up his newly laundered uniform. He shut the wardrobe and then glanced at the football posters on the wall. A thought occurred to him; he looked at his watch – which had the date on it – and shook his head.

'The European Championships start on Friday!' he said to himself. 'I'd completely forgotten about it.'

'Of course you'd forgotten about it!' exclaimed Eric, angrily. 'You've been too busy acting like an asshole!'

Philippe was slightly shocked. 'No I haven't!' he cried. 'I did what you told me to do. I acted like a man. I took control - '

'You took something that doesn't belong to you!' said Eric. 'You acted like a thief. Stupid boy!'

'I'm not – well, I'm not a boy,' said Philippe. He sighed and sat down. 'Shit. You're right, Eric. You're always right. I need to sort this out before I get Sylvie into trouble.'

He took out his phone and looked up a number; his cousin, Celine. She was a handsome, no-nonsense woman who didn't suffer fools gladly and had a family who were slightly scared of but absolutely adored her. The sort of person you could rely on to help and not ask too many questions.

He dialled her number.

They agreed to meet the next day for breakfast in a small café near the Pompidou Centre; Celine worked nearby and, if Philippe could get her to agree to the slightly mad idea that was forming in his head, it would require the temporary loan of certain items from her office…

CHAPTER 25

Philippe left home about 8am, after carefully watching the morning news on TV. He was relieved that there was still no mention of the Mona Lisa's theft. The museum was staying closed for another 24 hours until the danger of flooding had subsided and he was off the rota for that evening, so Philippe had the whole day ahead of him to execute his plan.

He took the Metro – if Celine agreed to his request, he wouldn't be able to manage his bike – to the *Étienne Marcel* stop, pausing for a moment when he reached the exit to get his bearings. He moved on, but hesitated for a split second; from the corner of his eye he was certain that he saw the mysterious man from the museum director's office, lurking by a street lamp, watching him.

He crossed the road and walked alongside a glass shop front, glancing at his reflection in the window. Sure enough, the mystery man followed. Philippe stopped for a moment and pretended to tie his shoelace, and the mystery man casually stopped to look at something in the shop window. When Philippe moved on, after a slight pause, so did he. He was definitely following.

If this had been a Hollywood movie Philippe would've known what to do. He would've hailed a taxi and jumped in, instructing the driver to drive somewhere – anywhere – fast, and lose his tail. But this was Paris on a soggy Monday morning, and Philippe's destination was about 5 minutes walk away, so he carried on walking. Let this mysterious man (who was definitely, thought Philippe, some kind of private investigator hired by the museum) – let him follow him to his breakfast meeting; see if he could come up with anything that would prove

Philippe's guilt! Nothing suspicious about two cousins meeting for breakfast.

Ignoring his follower, Philippe reached the café and went in. He was pretty sure the man wouldn't follow him inside; it would be far too obvious that he was keeping an eye on him if he did. Celine was already seated at a table near the window, smartly dressed and ready for a good day's work. She was as solid and dependable as his mother's heavy oak dresser, with a build that wasn't too dissimilar.

They kissed hello and ordered breakfast. Over coffee and croissants Philippe began with pleasantries, but Celine was a busy woman and he could see that she wanted him to cut to the chase, so he did. Some of it, anyway.

He was relieved when she didn't ask him why he needed her help – she clearly thought that the less she knew, the better – and even more relieved when she agreed. They finished their breakfast and went straight to her office, and an hour later Philippe was on his way home with a shopping bag stuffed with paper files...

Sylvie meanwhile was waiting impatiently for Henri to go to work. She'd gone from spending most of her days shut away in the apartment, cleaning and cooking, to pacing up and down to stop herself going stir crazy. If he didn't leave soon she would start climbing the walls, she thought. Or possibly start pulling her own fingernails out. She made herself sit down at the kitchen table and take a few deep breaths, not wanting him to notice how on edge she was. Then she leapt up again and washed the breakfast things, taking care to thoroughly wash and dry the cups, the plates and the old blue and white teapot. Anything to take her mind off her desperation to get out.

Finally Henri stood in the kitchen, putting on his raincoat and slowly sorting through his briefcase. Very, very slowly. It was all Sylvie could do to stop herself shoving everything into his bag, ramming it under his arm and pushing him out of the door. She gritted her teeth to keep a howl of frustration escaping her.

'You'll be late for work,' Sylvie said finally, unable to stop herself speaking. He sneered at her.

'I'm practically the boss,' he said. 'Old man Guiton doesn't know his arse from his elbow these days, let alone what time it is.' He moved closer to her, trapping her against the kitchen counter. 'I could stay here with you a bit longer if you like. I know how much you miss me when I'm away.'

She forced herself to smile at him. 'That would be lovely, Henri, but you mustn't get into trouble because of me.'

He grinned. Like he'd stay at home and spend the morning in bed with her! *Mon dieu*, she really was dumb. But it paid dividends to keep her sweet.

'You're right, Little Bird,' he said. 'I have to work to keep you in the manner to which you've become accustomed. You see how I provide for you?'

She bowed her head. It looked to him like deferral or modesty but really it was to stop him seeing the look of contempt on her face. 'I know Henri, and I am grateful.'

So she should be. He kissed the top of her head, feeling almost paternal towards her. 'Okay then, I'm off. You're not going out today.'

'Well actually, I might have to go to work to help them move everything back - ' she began.

'I said, you're not going out today,' he interrupted, his voice calm and measured. 'They're taking advantage of your simple nature. There's too much work here for you today.'

Simple nature! Inside she was fuming, but she merely bowed her head again. 'Yes, Henri. As you wish.'

He zipped up his briefcase and headed out. As soon as she heard the front door close, she ran to the window and watched him leave the building, then walk up the road and turn the corner. She slicked on some bright red lipstick – surreptitiously bought during a trip to the supermarket – and checked her reflection. Unused to wearing such a bold shade, she looked dangerously sexy and exotic to her own eyes. *Wanton*. She smiled, tidied her hair and left home.

Philippe turned the corner into Rue Bachelet, his heart skipping a beat as he saw her waiting outside his apartment. He quickened his pace as she turned to him with a smile that made him dizzy. She threw her arms around him and kissed him hard on the mouth, hard enough to take his breath away and imprint her wanton red lips on his. He laughed and kissed her back softly, then pulled away to stare into her face.

'What are you doing here?' he asked. 'Not that I'm not glad…'

'I couldn't bear the thought of a whole day without seeing you!' she cried. 'And we need to talk about the other woman in your life.'

'My mum?' he asked, puzzled. She laughed.

'No, silly! Mona.'

Philippe looked around cautiously, but there was no sign of the mystery man. 'Come inside,' he said.

They walked up the winding staircase to the attic apartment, Philippe standing aside to let her in. She hesitated.

'It's ok,' he said, ushering her through the door. 'My mother's out.'

'Good,' said Sylvie. She stepped into the hallway and stopped as Philippe put down his bag and helped her slip off her coat. They both stopped as his hand brushed her bare arm.

'How long will she be out?' asked Sylvie. It was an innocent enough question. He smiled at her.

'Long enough,' he said. They looked at each other for a moment, then they were in each other's arms, kissing passionately and tearing at each other's clothes. Philippe managed to steer her through the apartment until, still lip-locked, they were in his bedroom, leaving a trail of garments from the front door to his bed. They lay down, all thoughts of stolen paintings banished from their minds for a few moments...

Afterwards, Sylvie lay in his arms, enjoying his warmth. Philippe breathed in her scent and smiled to himself as she snuggled into his chest.

'Oh how I love hearing those three little words from you,' she sighed. 'My mum's out.'

He laughed. 'I can't help it, I'm just a born romantic.'

She smiled and sat up, scrabbling around on the floor for her clothes. 'But we can't stay in bed forever. We need to talk about Mona.'

'Yes,' said Philippe, a little nervously. 'I've been thinking about it. I know we were going to use the money to elope, but - '

'We have to take her back!' burst out Sylvie. He smiled in relief.

'Really? Thank god for that, that's just what I was going to say!' He reached down and grabbed his shirt, handing it to her. 'Here. Don't get dressed yet, I haven't finished with you.' She giggled and slipped it on as he spoke and pulled on his pants. He was as wanton as she was. 'Come into the kitchen, I've been making plans...'

Sylvie walked through to the kitchen while he grabbed his bag from the front door, where he'd dropped it. Then he tipped out all the paper files inside onto the kitchen table and began to lay them out. Sylvie picked one up.

'Blueprints?' she asked, surprised. He nodded.

'Yes. Maps of the sewer system,' he said. 'My cousin is the city's first female chief sanitation engineer.'

'You must be very proud,' she said, vaguely. 'But what has that got to do with Mona?'

Philippe found the rolled up blueprint he was looking for and spread it out for her to see.

'When we were moving things out of storage during the flood, I noticed a grate in the basement floor. It leads down to the lower basement - '

'There's a lower basement?' she asked. He nodded.

'There's a whole underground city beneath Paris,' he said. 'You must've heard stories - '

'The Phantom of the Opera, of course,' she said. 'And my father took me to see the Catacombs when I was little. I had nightmares for a week.'

He laughed. 'Yes, it's fascinating but a bit disturbing. So anyway, there's this whole underground network of sewers and catacombs, underground aqueducts – like the one that feeds the lake underneath the opera house – even abandoned Metro stations and tunnels. And there's access to them from the lower basement of the Louvre.'

'So...?'

'So, if we can get into the tunnels from somewhere else, with Mona, we can get her back into the Louvre via the basement!' Philippe looked up her, excitedly. 'You see? We can get in whenever we want to, with nobody seeing us! We just have to work out the route using these maps!'

'Okayyy...' said Sylvie, doubtfully. He looked dismayed at her lack of enthusiasm and she quickly spoke again. 'It's a good plan, it is, but...surely if it was that easy to sneak into the museum, wouldn't someone have already done it? Wouldn't there have been robberies using that exact method? I can't believe that they wouldn't have blocked the tunnels or something.'

Philippe had already had that thought – in fact, Celine had mentioned earlier that many of the tunnels which led to 'sensitive' locations had either been blocked with concrete or flooded – but in the absence of any better plans, he'd been trying to ignore it.

'It's still worth a look though, isn't it?' he said. 'Unless you have a better plan?'

'I don't even have a worse one,' she admitted, so together they lay out as many maps as they could on the apartment floor until they had the whole city under their feet.

It was a labyrinth. They began by finding the entrance points nearest to Sylvie's apartment and working their way through the tunnels until they reached the Louvre. But they never made it, losing themselves in the twists, turns and dead ends. So then they tried working from the museum and out somewhere – anywhere – where they could enter the tunnels unseen. All routes to and from the Louvre were blocked somewhere along the line; a dead end or – in a couple of cases – lakes. If it were just the two of them they could probably have made it; but carrying a painting, particularly one that had to be handled very carefully and could not be exposed to any risks? It was looking unlikely.

Philippe sighed and let go of the map he was holding down, allowing the edges of it to roll back up again. 'It's impossible,' he said.

Sylvie, one hand resting in the middle of her own map, leaned over to kiss him gently. 'It was a good plan,' she said, 'but - '

Philippe's eyes opened wide as he looked down at her hand. At her fingertips was a tunnel entrance that he hadn't noticed before; it was only faint, the ink beginning to fade away. He gently moved her hand away and stared at the blueprint, tracing the tunnel that led from the until-now unseen entrance, then turned to grin at her.

'There!' he said. She followed his finger as he traced the route. The tunnel weaved around the city, criss-crossing others, but there was no doubt that it ended under the Louvre. She looked up at him, a calculating look on her face.

'I know that place! That's not that far from here,' she said. The suggestion hung in the air for a moment.

'You're not thinking – now?' asked Philippe. She shrugged.

'Why not? Like I said, I don't have any other ideas. And we'd need to try it out first, before we risk taking Mona down there.'

'A dry run…' said Philippe, thoughtfully. 'I've got a couple of torches. You're not really dressed for it, though.'

'You must have a pair of trousers I could borrow?' said Sylvie. She was keen to try it and get the painting back where it belonged.

'You could wear the waterproof ones I've got for my bike,' said Philippe. 'Just in case it's a bit damp.'

They looked at each other, then Philippe folded up the map.

CHAPTER 26

Sylvie and Philippe stared up at the building in front of them as the taxi sped away. Philippe had insisted on a cab, worried that the mystery man from the museum director's office would be waiting outside his apartment and would tail them; but when they stepped out into the street and walked over to the waiting car there was no sign of him. Philippe began to think that maybe he'd been worrying over nothing and that his sighting of him earlier was just a coincidence. But he decided it was better not to take the risk of being followed.

The building in the 10th arrondisement had an imposing gothic façade, with a tall, elaborately decorated arched window which towered above the tourists queuing in the street to get in. The old ceramic workshop had been there since the 1860s, but had more recently been reborn as *Le Manoir de Paris*, a haunted house attraction complete with enough ghosts, zombies and monsters to give visitors bad dreams for a whole year. Sylvie thought it was an apt place to start, given that they were currently living in a bit of a nightmare.

'So where's the entrance to the tunnels?' she asked. Philippe looked around.

'I don't know,' he said. 'My cousin reckoned that some of the old entrances are bricked up – which would be a problem – but most of them just have metal grills across them, padlocked shut, in case the sewer engineers ever need access.'

'You mean like those?' said Sylvie, pointing to the entrance. Big black iron gates stood open, guarding the grand arched entrance which led into an impressively tiled foyer; and they were flanked on either side by smaller arched doorways blocked by black metal grills.

'Just like those…' said Philippe. 'But they just lead into the foyer.' He started forward and strained to get a closer look at the entrance through the crowd, several of whom were beginning to stare at him with hostility, thinking he was trying to jump the queue. He ignored them and looked closer, then moaned in frustration.

'Look!' he hissed. She looked. Of course. There was a small doorway under the grand staircase just inside the building, a doorway with an old metal grate padlocked across it. A 'Privé – Sens interdit' sign was bolted to it. To further discourage entry an old table, topped with a waxwork severed head with a fern growing out of it, had been placed in front of it.

'They probably use the tunnel as an extra store room, just like the Louvre,' she said. 'We'll have to pay to go inside.'

'Dammit,' muttered Philippe, digging in his pockets for money. Between them they came up with the entrance fee and joined the queue.

'How will we get through that padlock?' asked Sylvie, starting to regret her rash suggestion to explore. He smiled and held open the messenger bag he was carrying, showing her a flash of something metallic against the folded up waterproof trousers at the bottom.

'Bolt cutters,' he said. 'My father's. Don't ask why he had them…'

'I can probably guess,' she said.

As they neared the door they could hear shrieks and screams coming from inside. Sylvie grabbed his hand. The spooks were just actors in heavy make up, trying to pay the rent until they got their big break; but they were enough to make Sylvie, already starting to get nervous at the thought of going underground, jump.

Philippe looked around the foyer as they paid their money and entered. There were a lot of people milling around, waiting to be let into the building proper and get scared out of their wits. A far too convincing vampire and an extremely pale young woman in a bloodied nurse's uniform danced around the crowd, stopping to have selfies taken with groups of nervously giggling girls and boys who were already totally unnerved but trying hard not to show it.

'How are we going to get in there without anyone stopping us?' whispered Sylvie. But suddenly there was a commotion on the other side of the foyer. A heavily pregnant woman, shocked by a now repentant-looking demon, screamed and staggered into a chair, clutching at her bump. There was a wet patch at her feet. Everyone in the foyer surged forward with their phones out, some to help the poor woman, others to video her and stick it on Facebook. And one actually called for an ambulance.

Philippe grabbed Sylvie's arm and pulled her over to the doorway. He shifted the table out of the way and grabbed the padlock, twisting it as he reached for the bolt cutters. It came apart in his fingers. It was old and rusty and looked like it hadn't been particularly heavy-duty to start with. He turned to Sylvie, eyebrows raised in surprise, then dragged her through the doorway and down a dark flight of stairs before the excitement in the foyer had a chance to abate.

The voices from above followed them down into the echoing chamber beneath, falling away as the light from the foyer also gradually faded. Philippe and Sylvie stopped, both breathing heavily with the adrenaline. He reached into his bag and pulled out a couple of torches, then passed Sylvie the waterproof trousers.

'I'll be fine,' she said. He put them back.

Sylvie shone her torch around the walls of the tunnel as Philippe studied the map. He'd highlighted the route they needed to take and it looked relatively straightforward. He looked around, getting his bearings, but the tunnel began here so there was only way to go: forwards.

They went forwards. The tunnel here was much drier and warmer than Sylvie had expected, and much cleaner. They clearly weren't very deep underground yet, no deeper than the lower ground level of the museum. It was also still quite wide, and bore signs of having been used in the not-long distant past; cardboard boxes and moving chests stacked in one corner, probably by the current occupants of the building above. Sylvie relaxed and took Philippe's hand.

As the tunnel went on, though, the floor began to slope downwards. The air became cold and clammy and the walls, beginning to close in, were slicked with moisture. Philippe and Sylvie were forced to walk in single file. The ceiling got lower as Sylvie's pulse rate got higher.

She was just starting to feel claustrophobic when the tunnel abruptly widened into a large, cavernous space. Philippe stopped and took out a bottle of water, handing it to Sylvie before taking a sip himself.

'Okay?' he asked. She nodded.

'So far so good.'

He consulted the map again. They'd only been underground for about ten minutes and hadn't come across any other tunnels, so they must still be on track.

'I think we're underneath the *Folies Bergère*,' he said. 'There are dancing girls above our heads at this very moment!'

She laughed. 'You'd better not look up, then,' she said.

They carried on. They were deep underground now, and it was cold but quite dry.

'So is this part of the sewers?' asked Sylvie. 'These tunnels don't look man made. They don't look industrial, anyway.'

'No,' said Philippe. 'A lot of these tunnels were dug out by hand, back in the 12th century, or even earlier. They were mining for limestone.' He smiled at her expression. 'I know, I'm a bit of a history geek. I read a book about it once. I think - '

He stopped abruptly as they turned a corner. The pile of bones in front of them made him forget what he was about to say.

Sylvie gulped and grabbed his hand.

'Don't worry,' he said, hoping he sounded calmer than he felt. It was stupid of him to be shocked, he thought. They both knew what a lot of the old tunnels had been used for. 'They're only bones.'

'I know,' said Sylvie. 'I just wasn't expecting them here. The catacombs I visited were the other side of the river.'

'That's where most of them are,' said Philippe. 'But there was a leper colony here years ago, at Saint-Lazare - ' He laughed as she edged even further away from the bones. 'It was a very long time ago! Hundreds of years before they turned the tunnels into ossuaries. They moved the bones when the cemeteries started to overflow. It's not spooky, it's just history. Think of these as fossils.'

'Fossils.' Sylvie sounded doubtful.

'Yes.'

'Fossils of dead people.'

'Yeeess...' Now Philippe sounded doubtful too.

He squeezed her hand and led her onwards. The cavern began to narrow again, this time the walls lined not with moisture but with bones and skulls, picked clean and bleached ivory by time. Once you got used to them, they weren't scary at all. They were fascinating. Philippe was right, it was history. These had been people once, like them; but how different their lives had been! Sylvie read the plaques built into the walls of bones, telling the casual visiting mourner what district the late inhabitants had come from.

And then the bones were behind them and the walls were just stone again. Sylvie was glad of her warm sweater as the temperature dropped again. The tunnel began to twist and turn, snaking under the city and then sloping upwards again, and she smiled to herself as she imagined people going about their business above her head, completely unaware of what she and Philippe were up to.

Philippe stopped abruptly again.

'More bones?' asked Sylvie, but he shook his head and spoke quietly.

'I thought I heard something,' he said. Her heart leapt.

'Something?' she asked, nervously. 'Or someone?' She wasn't sure which would be worse.

He didn't answer, but held up his hand to quieten her. They stood and listened, ears straining to hear. Nothing. Sylvie opened her mouth to speak, and then –

Voices, in the distance. Lots of voices, all talking excitedly at once, and then a man's voice, taking charge.

'Okay, okay – *un peu de silence! Merci.* Let's get started.'

Sylvie looked at Philippe in alarm. He held a finger to his lips and began to creep forwards. She followed, moving as quietly as possible.

They came to another tunnel, at right angles to their own. Light spilled out into their own passageway. Philippe quickly glanced at the map, then turned off his torch, motioning for Sylvie to do the same. He grabbed her hand and led her past the tunnel's mouth; they needed to stay on course. The man's voice came again: '1,2 - '

And then they were stopped dead in their tracks by all those voices again, but this time they weren't talking over each other; they were singing. A choir of heavenly voices, amplified by the tunnels, harmonies rising and falling, swirling around their stunned secret audience of two. Sylvie and Philippe stood in the dark with open mouths, looking for all the world as if they were joining in with the beautiful sound. Sylvie crept back to the adjacent tunnel and peeped in. The tunnel widened out into a large room; at the other side, another narrow tunnel with steps cut into the stone, leading upwards. The group obviously used this subterranean rehearsal room often, as there were chairs and a table covered in bottles of water and flasks of hot coffee. At the front, a music stand, which the conductor – the male voice they had heard – stood before, reading sheet music and stirring his singers into action. There were fewer of them than Sylvie had expected, only nine or ten, but the acoustics turned their voices into a mighty choir. Sylvie jumped as Philippe joined her, putting a hand on her shoulder. She smiled at him, and they reluctantly turned away and continued their journey, the music soaring, echoing along the tunnel and gradually fading away.

CHAPTER 27

Sylvie took Philippe's hand and they ambled happily along the tunnel. The encounter with the choir had soothed her nerves, making the tunnel walls sparkle not with moisture but with magic. Philippe turned on his torch again and Sylvie followed suit.

'That was incredible!' she sighed, when the final notes had faded behind them.

'I've heard of people having parties down here,' said Philippe, 'but not singing. It makes sense, though; the acoustics are perfect.'

'There must be other entrances into this tunnel that aren't on the map, then,' she said. He nodded.

'A lot of the older buildings probably have their own private ways in,' he said. 'No one's really supposed to come down here, but there's no way they can police it if people are using their own entrances.'

'Why aren't people allowed down here?'

'Because it's so easy to get lost.'

Philippe's words hung in the air between them. She shivered. He put an arm around her and pulled her to him, kissing her on the forehead.

'Don't worry,' he said. 'People get lost because they come down here without a map. We've got an official blueprint of the whole system. We'll be fine.' He sounded confident, but inside he added, *I hope...*

They walked on. The tunnel began to widen again, the walls now more sharply cut, smooth concrete rather than hand-hewn stone. Old, but industrial. Other tunnels began to lead off. And there was water...

They barely noticed it at first. A dampness under foot. Sylvie was wearing sensible, sturdy shoes, but Philippe's trainers were old and had a few holes in them.

'Argh!' he cried, lifting his feet up exaggeratedly. Not that that would help keep them dry.

'It's only water,' laughed Sylvie. He grabbed her and tickled her to show her who was boss. Then they walked on.

Soon the water was over the top of her shoes. It was cold.

'Yuck,' said Sylvie. He smirked.

'It's only water...'

They stopped and Sylvie pulled his waterproof trousers on, tucking her skirt in and giving him a twirl. 'How do I look?'

He gazed at her smiling face. 'Beautiful.'

They walked on. The water got deeper, the walls of the tunnel steeper, taller. Their squelching footsteps echoed. Ahead of them, something splashed into the water. They looked at each other. Rats!

Ankle height.

'How deep do you think it's going to get?' asked Sylvie. Philippe shrugged.

'No idea. But we must be near the opera house, and underneath the opera house -'

' – is a flipping great lake,' she finished.

'Yes. But according to the map the tunnel skirts the edge of it. It'll be fine.'

But it became increasingly clear that it *wasn't* fine. The water got deeper, and soon Philippe's jeans and trainers were soaked and the water had found a way in up the legs of Sylvie's waterproofs, the elasticated cuff at the ankle obviously designed for a thicker leg. They waded through cold water that reached mid-shin height, and then stopped as they heard a sound ahead. The sound of running water. They looked at each other.

'That's not good,' said Philippe, consulting the map. 'There's not meant to be a waterfall…'

Sylvie groaned in exasperation. 'All that heavy rain! The Metro was flooded, not to mention the museum's basement. The water levels down here must've gone up too.'

Philippe face-palmed. 'Of course. The catacombs don't normally flood, but we're in the sewers now and they're designed to take the water away from the city… We should've waited and given the flood waters a chance to subside. I'm sorry, Sylvie. It was a stupid plan.'

She took his face in her hands and kissed away his glum expression.

'It was a great plan,' she said. 'And it might still work. There are normally walkways above the sewers, yes? For the engineers? They might still be above water. We're here now, so let's go and see.'

So they went to see. The water was knee deep now, but ahead of them were some stone steps leading to the middle of a platform that was still just about dry. They splashed through the sewer tunnel and onto the platform. Sylvie swung her torch around, studying their surroundings, as Philippe turned his onto the map again.

'I think if we go that way, we'll come out - ' he started, but then he realised that Sylvie wasn't standing next to him. He looked around; she was at the other end of the platform, staring out along another tunnel. 'Sylvie! I think we need to go the other - '

'Oh my god!' she said. 'Look! That's beautiful!'

He joined her quickly, and looked down the tunnel.

What from the other end of the platform had looked like just another sewer tunnel, widened out into a vaulted chamber. Shafts of light flooded in from skylights or metal gratings high above – bright, artificial light, rather than rays of sun; the opera house must be right above them. The water was calm and still, disturbed only by the faintest of ripples caused by movement somewhere further down the tunnel. The ripples sparkled in the shaft of light, casting an undulating reflection on the arched ceiling.

The water here wasn't the rather unsavoury, murky brown you would normally expect of a sewer; the lake had originally been built as a reservoir of drinking water for the city, although these days it was a brave (or foolish) Parisian who quenched their thirst directly from it. It looked blue and clear, and deep.

'Wow!' said Sylvie. 'I can just imagine the Phantom down here, singing to his lost love…'

On cue Philippe began to trill something operatic, flinging his arms out dramatically and serenading her. She laughed and hugged him, turning to look back at the water. He pulled her close, burying his nose in her hair – it smelt rather nicer than the sewers – and kissing the top of her head.

'We can't stand here all day,' he said finally. 'We need to go that way…'

Reluctantly Sylvie took his hand and they walked to the other end of the platform. But the platform ended in a flight of iron stairs, which descended into more water. It was dark, and it was impossible to tell how deep it was in the light of their torches.

'Are you sure it's this way?' asked Sylvie. Philippe studied the map closely again, and nodded. She sighed and went to step onto the stairs. He stopped her.

'Wait!' he said. 'We don't know how deep it is.'

'Only one way to find out,' she said, and stood on the first step.

'Wait!' said Philippe again. 'What if it's really deep? You'll get soaked. You can't go home in wet clothes.'

She looked at him for a moment, and then smiled. A mischievous smile. She slipped off her shoes and pulled down the water proof trousers. Her skirt followed, then her jumper…

Philippe laughed in amazement as Sylvie stripped and stood in front of him, shivering slightly.

'Well?' she said archly, raising an eyebrow. 'Are you coming in or what?'

He didn't need asking twice. He tore off his clothes and grabbed her, then laughing they raced down the stairs…

The water *was* deep – just below chest height on Sylvie's 5'2" frame – and it was freezing cold. Philippe yelped as the cold seeped into his nether regions and pulled Sylvie close, trying to steal her warmth. She shrieked with laughter and pushed him away, sending him splashing onto his back. Then, gasping at the temperature, she struck out for the other side of the chamber.

The icy water made her head swim for a moment, but it cleared and left her feeling more alive, more awake than she had done for a very long time. The anti-depressants hadn't just fogged her brain, they'd wrapped her whole body in cotton wool, in a soft fuzzy blanket that had dulled her senses and stopped her thinking or feeling or just being her. This was like taking a cold shower after a long and sleepless night. Sensations that had been muted for so long came flooding back. The freezing cold water caressed her skin, making it tingle. She was skinny-dipping in a manmade underground lake, with a man who wasn't her husband but who she loved with every single nerve and sinew and muscle of her body. It was ridiculous and wonderful and sublime and she never wanted it to end. She laughed with the sheer reckless joy of being alive again, of being *back*, and looked around. There was no way out of the chamber, other than retreating the way they had come.

She slowly swam back to Philippe, who was standing in the water hugging himself, still enjoying the sensation of the water on her skin. 'There's no way out from here, other than down that tunnel and into the opera house,' she said. 'We must've gone wrong somewhere. Either that or the entrance of the tunnel we need is below the water.'

'That's possible,' said Philippe. 'I don't think it's normally this deep. Can we get out now? I'm lost all feeling in my extremities.'

She grinned cheekily. 'I can wake them up for you,' she said. He laughed.

'I know you can, but can we do it on dry land?' She laughed as well and grabbed his hand, and together they waded back to the stairs and climbed up, shivering. He smiled as he watched her shaking herself like a dog to get rid of the water on her skin, and ran his hands over her goosebumps, warming her up and bringing those numb extremities back to life. She shivered again, this time not just from the cold, and together they created enough body heat to dry themselves off.

Finally, they re-dressed in their mostly-dry clothes and turned back.

'So what now? Do we just retrace our steps or is there another way out?' asked Sylvie.

'It's probably best if we go back the way we came,' said Philippe. 'The flooding's worse than we thought, and if we carry on we might just get cut off again.'

They headed back down the sewer tunnel, their torches picking out rats scurrying towards them. The rats turned tail and disappeared at the beams of torchlight.

Sylvie shuddered. 'I hate rats. We didn't see any on the way here.'

'No,' said Philippe thoughtfully. 'I wonder what's disturbed them?'

They didn't have to wonder for long. From up ahead came two male voices, footsteps treading heavily.

'Ever feel like you've drawn the short straw?' said one voice. The other man laughed. 'It's not like we ever find anyone down here, not at this time of day.'

'No, Saturday night's the best time,' said the other man.

Sylvie looked at Philippe questioningly. He opened his mouth to speak, but was interrupted by a burst of radio static.

'Zero two nine, what's your location?' came a female voice, over the distant radio. The tunnel amplified every noise, making it difficult to tell exactly how close the men were; but there was no sign of any torch-light, and no one would be down here in the dark without a torch.

'Where do you think?' said the first man, sourly. 'Knee deep in shit.'

The other man laughed and then spoke again, this time obviously in reply to the radio. 'Tunnel 29, heading west towards the opera house.'

'Oh shit,' whispered Philippe, his face looking grey and worried in the torchlight. 'Police!'

'What?' whisper-cried Sylvie, shocked but trying to keep her voice down. 'I thought you said it was impossible to police - '

'I thought it was!' he said. 'I thought the police patrols were just a story they put about to stop people coming down.'

'Well obviously it isn't,' hissed Sylvie, 'and they're heading this way.'

Philippe grabbed her hand and they turned back towards the opera house. 'I spotted another tunnel back there,' he said. 'I don't know where it goes, but we can't go back the way we came, we'll get arrested. Come on!'

Keeping their torches trained on the ground, they trotted along the tunnel as quickly as they could. They soon reached the mouth of another tunnel.

'In here!' said Philippe. They went in. It was a narrow tunnel with a low roof, which seemed to stretch far into the distance... 'We won't go too far,' said Philippe. 'Hopefully the police will see the flooding in the other tunnel and turn back, then we can follow them at a distance.'

They walked down the tunnel a little more sedately, listening for the sound of the policemen. Philippe stopped after five minutes to listen out.

Footsteps, coming closer. The policemen were laughing and joking with each other, clearly not expecting to find anyone down here but not turning back, nonetheless. And then at the end of the narrow tunnel, a tiny pinprick of light.

'*Zut*,' said Sylvie. 'They've turned in here!'

They both quickly turned off their torches, but it was too late.

'Is there someone there?' called one of the men. He was trying to sound friendly, not wanting to give his identity away. Sylvie groped for Philippe's hand in the darkness and felt him lean in towards her.

'Run!' he whispered, and then they were off down the tunnel.

'Stop!' shouted the policeman. But they didn't stop. Philippe flicked his torch on again; the police knew they were there, and it was too dangerous to go haring around in the dark. They turned down another tunnel, and another, the walls closing in on them, the ceiling getting lower and lower as they went. Sylvie began to panic. What if they got caught? What if they called Henri to come and bail her out? At the very least he'd find out about her and Philippe, and at worst the police would discover Mona hidden in her apartment building.

Philippe spotted another tunnel, the entrance set back and partially hidden by a pile of fallen rock, and pulled her into it. It was a dead end, a tiny chamber. He turned off the torch and together they crouched down, waiting for the police to reach them.

Torch beams bounced across the walls of the tunnel as the policemen thundered down it. As they reached the lovers' hiding place, one of the policemen slowed and shone his light around the chamber; but seeing there was no way out, he turned away and carried on after his colleague. Sylvie and Philippe clung to each other, letting out silent sighs of relief. They sat for five minutes, waiting for the police to turn back and for their hearts to slow down.

Suddenly Sylvie felt a breath on the back of her neck. She let out a tiny shriek and turned round; no one there.

'What is it?' asked Philippe, concerned.

'I felt something on the back of my neck,' she said, looking around nervously. 'Like a breath - '

Suddenly Philippe's eyes widened. 'Me too! There's a draught coming in from somewhere.' He looked at her. 'And now my eyes have got used to it, it's not completely dark is it? There's light coming in.' They looked around.

'Over there!' said Sylvie. There were thin pinpricks of light coming from the roof of the chamber above them.

Philippe stood and reached up, touching it. 'It's metal,' he said. 'It's a grate or a manhole cover...'

CHAPTER 28

He'd worked at the hotel for a long time now, starting as a bell boy – one of the skinny young lads who ran errands, delivered messages and carried guests' luggage up to their rooms. He'd been particularly spotty and unprepossessing in appearance, and it had taken all his skills of persuasion to get even that lowly position, but Gaspard had impressed the manager with his enthusiasm and had been taken on to cover the busy summer period.

That had been twenty years ago, and he had never left. Gaspard had worked his way up through the ranks and, although his official title was chief concierge, he really ran the hotel. He knew everything there was to know about it. He knew the names of every single member of staff. He knew the tastes of the hotel's rich, famous regular clientele; knew which suites they preferred, the pseudonyms they used and which flowers their mistresses should be sent (whether they were worth a 75, a 100 or 150 euro bouquet). He was the soul of discretion and was equally adept at dealing with midnight requests for foie gras, illicit narcotics or high-class escorts. He also knew every nook and cranny, every secret hidey-hole, in the building.

Or so he thought. He stood in the garden, the simple but beautiful green oasis in the central courtyard of the hotel. It was a chilly, damp late afternoon, and he had the place to himself; the guests were still out enjoying the city, or resting, or getting ready for a night out. The perfect spot to have a sneaky cigarette, away from the prying eyes of the manager; not the same manager who had taken him on all those years ago but a young, officious little whippersnapper who had done a degree in something or other and now thought he knew all there was to know about running the most expensive, luxurious hotel in the most beautiful, romantic city in the world. Little prick.

Gaspard took a deep drag on the cigarette, filling his lungs slowly with the poisonous but oh-so-wonderful smoke. And then he choked in surprise as the hidden manhole cover in the middle of a flowerbed full of lavender rose in the air, followed swiftly by a rather wet and dishevelled young man. The young man stopped for a moment when he saw the concierge, looking just as surprised as Gaspard was, but he recovered well and nodded to him.

'*Bonsoir*,' said Gaspard, polite and professional as ever.

'*Bonsoir*,' said the man, then he placed the manhole cover on the grass and reached down to help a very pretty, delicate and decidedly dirty young lady out of the hole.

'Thank god for that - ' she began, and then stopped as she saw Gaspard.

'*Bonsoir, Madame*,' said Gaspard.

'Oh – yes – hello!' she said, slightly flustered. The man with her replaced the manhole cover and together they stepped lightly out of the flowerbed.

'Um – how do we...?' asked the man. Gaspard pointed to the door.

'Through the bar, past Reception and out onto Place Vendome.'

The lady smiled gratefully at him. She really was very pretty, despite the smear of what he hoped was mud across her cheek.

'*Merci beaucoup*!'

Gaspard touched his cap and discreetly went back to his cigarette. He hadn't become chief concierge at the Ritz by asking questions.

Philippe took Sylvie's hand and led her briskly through the hotel, trying not to attract attention. They failed miserably, but they were past the surprised barman and the suspicious receptionist and out in the open air before anyone had a chance to question them.

On the pavement, Philippe turned to her and kissed her hard on the lips. 'One day I'm taking you back to the Ritz for dinner.'

'As long as we can go in through the front door and not a flowerbed,' she laughed.

They headed out of the square and found themselves approaching the museum. Sylvie sighed. 'So near and yet so far.'

Philippe smiled. 'We got close, but not close enough. And we can't take Mona down there, can we? She'd get ruined.' He watched as the hardier tourists, who weren't to be put off by rain, read the sign by the iconic Pyramid entrance and turned away in disappointment; the museum was still closed. 'Back to the drawing board.'

Sylvie looked at her watch. 'Oh no, look how late it is! Henri will be home from work in an hour, and I need to get changed before then. I have to go.'

They embraced tightly, neither want to let go but knowing they had to. Finally Philippe kissed her tenderly on the lips and pulled away.

'We're re-opening tomorrow,' he said. 'Are you on the rota?'

'Yes.'

'Good.' He pulled her close again. 'We'll talk about it then. We need a plan B...'

CHAPTER 29

The evening passed slowly for both Sylvie and Philippe, but without incident. Philippe tidied away the maps and put his soggy trainers in the oven to dry, alarming Madame Moreau who feared that the somewhat unpleasant odour filling the kitchen was her son's attempt to cook her dinner. Sylvie had a quick shower and threw her dirty clothes in the laundry basket, safe in the knowledge that Henri never even bothered to put his own dirty things in there so he was unlikely to spot anything untoward. She filled her wet shoes with scrunched up newspaper and hid them at the back of her wardrobe, where it was warm.

Both spent their evenings lost in thought but trying not to show it. Sylvie listened to Henri talking mockingly about one of his work colleagues and managed to add a 'yes' or 'no' in all the right places, so that he thought she was paying attention to his wit. Philippe sat quietly with his mother, who occasionally looked at him with a worried expression on her face; she was desperate to ask him about the woman he'd had in his room the other night, but she was finding him hard to read and didn't dare mention her in case it was all going horribly wrong. As soon as he could reasonably escape to bed Philippe headed off to his room, and stood staring out of the window at the night time city.

In the street below, the mysterious man from the museum director's office leaned against a lamppost and looked up at Philippe's apartment…

The next day dragged past until, finally, it was time to go to work. It seemed impossible to Philippe that he still had to go through the same routine he'd gone through for the last couple of years, when everything had changed; he'd stolen the most famous painting in the world, and the woman he loved was hiding it for him. How could he be expected to put on that uniform, as if nothing had happened? To cycle through the city on his rusty bike with its squeaky brakes when he was a (repentant and unwitting) criminal mastermind? When his mother looked into his face he was sure she would immediately know everything he'd been up to, just as she had when he was 8 years old; but she only smiled and kissed him goodbye. It was, Philippe decided, completely mental.

He paced up and down the security entrance, nodding impatiently at the day time staff as they left, not noticing the discreet and fleeting touch of hands between Stephanie and the blonde from HR as the latter left for the day, or the faint flush of colour in his colleague's cheeks.

He checked his watch for at the least the hundredth time, then looked up in relief as Sylvie entered. Sylvie had also spent the day in a fugue, counting the hours until she saw him again. It was all she could do to not throw herself into his arms, but it was best that they at least tried to be discreet.

She swiped her pass and smiled at Stephanie, who looked at Philippe and grinned.

'I'm just - ' began Philippe, but Stephanie stopped him.

'Go on,' she said. 'If Fournier asks I'll tell him you're in the toilet.' Philippe smiled at her gratefully, then took Sylvie's hand and fled with her to the privacy of the darkened staff canteen.

Ten minutes later – when they finally managed to pull themselves apart – they walked to the Facilities store room to collect Sylvie's cleaning equipment and found a group of cleaners and security guards deep in discussion.

'What's going on?' asked Philippe. One of the security guards turned to him.

'We asked Fournier if we could start our shifts later on Friday,' the guard said.

'Why?' Sylvie was puzzled. Everyone turned to stare at her.

'The European championships start on Friday,' Philippe reminded her. 'It's the opening ceremony, and then we're playing Romania.'

'Of course! I'd completely forgotten, what with – everything,' she said. Philippe shared a conspiratorial smile with her.

'Anyway,' said the guard, slightly sickened by the doe-eyed adoration on show. 'We have to start at the usual time, but the director said anyone who wants to can watch it in the canteen during the shift. Cleaners too.'

'So everyone will be in the canteen on Friday night,' said Sylvie. A thought had occurred to her.

'Yeah,' said the guard. 'Let's hope no one tries to break in until half time!'

Everyone laughed, but Philippe looked over at Sylvie, wide-eyed; the same thought had just occurred to him.

'It'll be fine,' said Sylvie, calmly. 'Even art thieves like football...'

Gradually everyone drifted off to work, carrying buckets and mops, chatting, reluctantly getting on with it. Apart from Philippe and Sylvie, who grabbed each other excitedly as soon as the coast was clear.

'Are you thinking what I'm thinking?' whispered Sylvie.

'I think I am... What are you thinking?'

'I'm thinking that Friday night would be a good time to bring Mona home, while everyone's distracted by the football,' said Sylvie. Philippe nodded.

'That *is* what I was thinking. That and how much I'd like to see you naked on a fur rug in front of the fire... But we still need to get her inside without being spotted.'

They were silent for a moment, pondering. Sylvie sighed.

'If only we could arrange for another power cut,' she said. He looked at her, amazed; she didn't realise it yet but she had just come up with the perfect solution.

'We can,' he said.

'What are you talking about? We can't just conjure one up!'

'Actually, we can. I already have.' The memory of being woken by a loud BANG, and being greeted by the distinctive smell of burning electrics and strong black coffee, flashed across his mind. It still made him cringe – he'd felt so stupid – but if he could replicate it on Friday... 'It's not that hard. We wouldn't need a full power cut, we'd just need to knock out the door alarms and the cameras for ten minutes. If we're lucky, with everyone in the canteen or thinking about the football, they might not even notice it happen.' He swept her into his arms and kissed her. 'Sylvie, I think we have a plan! But we'll need help.'

They found Farheena in the main reception area, buffing the already highly polished tiled floor. On the other side of the cavernous space, two more cleaners polished handrails and chrome posts and ticket desks, their footsteps echoing high into the famous glass pyramid above them. The pyramid was so brilliantly lit that the moonlight above had no chance of penetrating the room; it was like daylight in here.

'What can I do for you lovebirds?' grinned Farheena, surprised to see them. In low voices they told her.

'You did fucking WHAT?' she cried. Her shrill, shocked voice echoed around the room. The other cleaners looked over. Philippe looked at her mildly.

'Please keep your voice down. I am *trying* not to go to prison, you know.'

'I'm sorry, it's just – fucking hell! You stole the Mona Lisa!'

Sylvie looked around in alarm and hissed at her. 'Shh!!'

'Sorry! It's just a bit of a shock.' Farheena shook her head. 'It's like they always say, *n'est ce pas*? It's the quiet ones you have to watch.'

'So we need your help - ' began Philippe.

'Hang on – Monsieur Fournier told everyone it was in storage while the display case was replaced!' Farheena burst out, hopping about in excitement. 'Is he in on it too?'

'What? No, of course he isn't!' said Sylvie, rolling her eyes.

'No, no of course he wouldn't be. Carry on.'

'So - '

'Oh I get it, you're winding me up aren't you?' Farheena laughed and punched Philippe playfully in the arm. He grinned and tried to hide how much it hurt. 'You're joking, yeah? You haven't really.'

'For fuck's sake!' growled Sylvie, grabbing her by the shoulders and shaking her. 'Will you just stop bloody talking and listen?' Farheena stopped and looked at her, mouth open.

'That is the first time I've heard you swear,' she said. 'You're deadly serious, aren't you?'

Sylvie and Philippe nodded. She swallowed hard.

'Holy *merde.* Okay. I'm listening.'

CHAPTER 30

And now it was just a matter of waiting until Friday. Sylvie and Philippe went their separate ways that Tuesday night feeling a strange mixture of excitement, elation and abject terror. Three more sleeps and then Mona was going home – but whether she'd get home without them being caught, well, that was another matter. It was risky but their only other option was dumping her somewhere and waiting for her to be found; and for art lover Sylvie, the thought of leaving the painting where it could get rained on, or urinated on by dogs (or drunks), run over by a car or picked up by the refuse collectors made her feel physically sick. With the museum remaining silent about the theft it meant that anyone finding the painting would think it was just a worthless reproduction. It could even end up as firewood, which really didn't bear thinking about.

Wednesday crawled past, so slowly Sylvie could feel every single excruciating second of it scraping by her. The nerves in her fingertips screamed and itched; she needed to do something, anything, to take her mind off of the painting that sat, stuffed in an ornate wooden armoire wrapped in bin bags, three floors below her in the apartment building's storeroom. She could *hear* the bin bags rustling in her mind. She stalked around the apartment, glaring out of the window, taking it out on the soft furnishings as she plumped cushions to within an inch of their lives. She ironed Henri's shirts, getting through piles of laundry, washing things that didn't really need washing and scrubbing the kitchen table and just DOING instead of thinking. She drank Henri's tea when she couldn't avoid it, and tipped it out whenever she could. She tried meditation – she'd heard it was good for people coming off antidepressants – but whenever she tried to clear her mind, the image of *la Joconde* swan before her eyes, no matter how hard she concentrated on rainbows or waterfalls or Philippe or - *mon dieu*! She was being driven *dément* by all this waiting!

Wednesday night arrived. Philippe and Sylvie clung to each other in the canteen, like shipwrecked survivors clinging to a life raft, whispered words of love and comfort to each other and then got on with their work like nothing was happening. Which to be fair, it wasn't; not for another 48 hours, anyway. Thursday took much the same course, but at ten o'clock, as Sylvie was leaving, they went over their plan one last time. Spend the day acting as normal as possible – *impossible!* – then Philippe would borrow his mother's car and pick up Sylvie and Mona at 5pm, before Henri got home, and drive them to the Louvre. Philippe would leave the car in the *Louvre Samaritaine* car park, just across the road from the museum, where Sylvie would wait with the painting until the agreed time. It should be dark and quiet enough then for her to sneak over the road and around to the deliveries entrance at the back of the building without attracting too much attention, besides which most of the nation would be glued to their television sets by then, watching the opening ceremony of Euro 2016...

Sylvie left and Philippe, by now feeling sick with nerves, told Stephanie he was ill and needed to go home. He knew he needed to act normally, but he was worried that Stephanie would notice both his nervous distraction and his frequent trips to the bathroom. She looked at him curiously, but he obviously did look sick as she told him to get a good night's sleep and even offered to call him a taxi. He declined.

He cycled slowly home, deep in thought. But as he turned into his road his anxious reverie was abruptly halted by a black SUV with tinted windows which pulled up outside his apartment. The driver's door opened and out stepped the mysterious man from the museum director's office.

Philippe was suddenly, utterly and completely furious. Yes, he'd done wrong; he'd made a mistake and taken something that wasn't his, but he was trying to put things right. He hadn't planned any of this – the theft itself or the reason behind it; hadn't planned to fall in love with someone who couldn't safely be with him unless they ran away; hadn't planned to be in a low paid job, living with his mother at his time of life. He hadn't slept since the night of the theft and, quite frankly, he'd had enough. And now this ridiculous low-rent poor man's gumshoe was victimising him.

He threw down his bike and stormed over to the man.

'Right, you bastard - ' he began. The man just grinned at him, completely unconcerned by his anger. He barely even registered the passenger door of the car opening, until another voice spoke behind him.

'Hello, son.'

Philippe stopped and whirled around in surprise.

It had been almost 20 years since he'd last seen his father but he would've recognised the self-satisfied expression on the man's face anywhere. Philippe resisted his first urge, which was to punch that smug smile off his face, and stared at him.

'You've grown,' said Monsieur Moreau. If he wasn't careful Philippe really *would* punch him.

'Of course I've fucking grown!' hissed Philippe, angrily. 'I was 10 the last time you saw me! I've started shaving as well! *Connard*!'

Moreau carried on calmly smiling at him, as Philippe clenched and unclenched his fists. They were itching to spread his father's nose across his cheeks in a bloody mess.

'I hear from my friend Vincent here that you've got yourself into a bit of trouble,' he said. The mystery man – Vincent - smiled widely at Philippe.

'Why doesn't Vincent call *les gendarmes* if he's so sure of that?' said Philippe, more confidently than he felt; inside he was thinking *oh shit oh shit oh shit* –

Moreau and Vincent both laughed. Philippe was completely out of his depth now. Vincent spoke to Moreau. 'I'll leave you to it, shall I?'

Moreau nodded, his eyes never leaving Philippe. 'Yes. My son and I are going for a drink to talk about old times - ' Philippe snorted contemptuously and he smiled. 'Or maybe we should just talk about the future. What do you say, son?'

Philippe shrugged, not wanting anything to do with either man but knowing that he had no choice. Vincent got back into the SUV and drove off, leaving father and son contemplating each other silently in the quiet, dark street. Moreau looked around, up at the apartment he'd once called home, then back to his son.

'It never changes around here, does it?' he said. 'Although every time I come back it looks smaller than I remember.'

'You never come back!'

'But I do, Philippe. I've been back a few times to call on your mother and make sure you're both okay. Didn't she tell you?'

Philippe was surprised but fought not to show it. 'No. But only because she knows I don't give a shit about you.'

Moreau smiled again, but this time Philippe was stunned to see a tiny hint of regret underneath the smugness. Then again, he thought, he might have imagined it. His father suddenly roused himself and rubbed his hands together briskly.

'Right, then! Is that old soak Duval still open for business? His place was a hovel but it was always open.'

'He retired ten years ago. Someone else runs it now,' said Philippe. 'I don't really go to bars - '

'Papa will look after you. Let's go!'

Moreau turned and strode off up the road. Feeling helpless, Philippe followed.

CHAPTER 31

Philippe sat at a table at the back of the bar. It was warm and noisy, even at this time of night on a weekday, the clientele clearly having no qualms about going to work the next day with a hangover. He smiled to himself; listen to him, a born again teetotaller. If people wanted to drink it was up to them; let them, as long as it didn't ruin their lives. Or their kids'.

He watched his father at the bar. He hadn't changed that much. Even in his 60s there remained a hint of the handsome man he'd been in his 40s, only now the veins in his cheeks and nose were redder, the hair at his temples greyer – though no thinner – and he was definitely carrying more weight around his middle. But he still had an eye for the ladies, going by the easy way he flirted with the pretty young woman behind the bar; although judging by her slightly strained smile, he no longer had such a high success rate with them.

Monsieur Moreau returned to the table with two glasses, plonking one down in front of Philippe with a disgusted expression as he sat down and added the contents of the other to the half-full glass already on the table.

'One cola,' he said, with an amused expression on his face. 'I never thought I'd see the day I had to ask the barmaid to swap a glass of whiskey for a Coke.'

'Did she let you swap it?' asked Philippe. He didn't really care, but thought he should say something. His father laughed and shook his head.

'Of course she didn't! I had to drink it myself. Couldn't let it go to waste.'

'And ordered another while you were up there, so I see.'

Moreau laughed again. 'And there's your mother's voice right there! Judging me.'

'I'm not judging you,' said Philippe. 'Judging you would mean I actually gave a damn about what you do.'

'You hate me, okay, I get it!' Moreau held his hands out in a placatory gesture. 'That's fine. But don't storm off in a huff until you've heard me out.'

Philippe sipped at his drink and waited. His father shook his head.

'Don't think you're better than me because you don't drink any more. You are so much more like me than you realise. You've got an eye for a pretty girl too, yes?'

Philippe sipped at his drink again, still not speaking. Moreau sighed and knocked back his whiskey.

'Look at me! My life used to be all wine, women and song, and nowadays it's just whiskey. Oh well, it's my own fault. I mistreated your mother, and I'm sorry - ' He raised his hands again to stop a furious Philippe interrupting. 'Son, I am sorry. She didn't deserve to be treated that way, and nor did you. But she also doesn't deserve to be treated the way you're treating her.'

'I'm not treating her - '

'You are so like me. You have an eye for a pretty girl. You saw one you liked and you just took her, despite the fact she belonged to someone else.'

'She doesn't belong to anyone! She - '

'Well that depends on which pretty girl we're talking about, doesn't it?' Moreau leaned towards his son, lowering his voice. 'I'm not talking about the nervy brunette piece you've been having it away with. Very pretty but high maintenance, if you ask me.'

'I didn't fucking ask you!'

'My friend Vincent – you remember Vincent? Old, old friend. Your mother hated him. Vincent tells me that you have this other pretty young lady hidden away somewhere, he doesn't know where and it's driving him insane – and that you have absolutely no hope of getting rid of her without ending up in jail. Just like me.'

Philippe sat back in his chair, smiling humourlessly.

'How is Vincent so well informed?' he asked. 'And where do you come into all this?'

Moreau toyed with his whiskey glass. 'Have you heard the expression, 'poacher turned gatekeeper'? Of course you have. Vincent and I both work for an insurance company, specialising in finding and returning certain stolen goods. Utilising our skills for 'the other side', as it were.'

'What skills?' snorted Philippe. 'You were always getting caught.'

Moreau smiled. 'Not always. I normally only get given the smaller cases, but Vincent has proved to have a nose for this sort of work, so he gets all the juicy ones. Stolen paintings, mostly. A lot of the museums have him on a retainer. There are more thefts in the art world than you'd probably imagine; the galleries and museums like to keep it quiet. It can be embarrassing for them.'

'So what?' said Philippe. 'Are you asking me to turn over the painting and hand myself in?'

To his surprise his father burst out laughing. 'Oh my god, you know I'm beginning to doubt that you are my son after all! Of course not! Turn in my own son!' He wiped away tears of mirth. Philippe ignored them.

'You don't have to worry about me, or the – the pretty girl,' he said quietly. 'I'm taking her back.' Moreau stopped laughing abruptly.

'You're what?'

'So I won't be turning myself in or getting caught by anyone,' said Philippe firmly. Moreau glared at him in disgust.

'Now I KNOW you're not my son,' he spat. 'Do you really think I'll let you get rid of what's probably the most valuable painting in the whole world without getting at least some kind of payday out of it? *Mon dieu*!'

'But – your job - '

'It pays well, true,' said Moreau. 'Not as well as a percentage of that painting, though.'

'She's not for sale!' Philippe stood up. Moreau grabbed his arm with surprising strength.

'Don't be a fool!' he said. 'If there's one thing I do know about your mother, it's that she hasn't raised a fool. You stole that painting for a reason. You need money, yes? So you can fly away with your little lady friend. You give that painting back and what's changed? Nothing. You'll still have no money. You'll still be stuck in that ridiculous uniform, earning a pittance while her husband earns more in a month than you do in a year.' He looked at Philippe's white face. 'Yeah, I've done my homework son. Now sit down and drink your cola...'

CHAPTER 32

Madame Moreau wasn't surprised when she got up the next morning to find her son sitting at the kitchen table in his pyjamas. He normally got home and went to bed just as she was rising. She was surprised though when she realised that he'd been home since 11pm and was just getting up himself.

She automatically went to place a hand on his forehead to feel his temperature but stopped herself just in time; he wasn't her little boy any more, no matter that he sometimes acted like he was. That was her fault, she knew, for looking after him so well when he moved back in; but he'd been in pain, drinking too much and desperately unhappy. She'd helped him back from the brink and she was fiercely proud of the man he'd become again, but now she was worried; there were definitely things on his mind.

'Good morning, Maman,' he said. She smiled and kissed him on the cheek.

'Morning, sweetheart,' she said. 'Did you sleep well? You look terrible.'

He laughed softly. 'Thanks!'

She sat at the table and watched as he put the kettle on to make her tea. He really was a good boy. Throwing his no-good father out had been the hardest thing she'd ever done, but it had been worth the difficult times to see him grow up a better man than Moreau would ever be. She just hoped he was a happy man, too.

'You do know you can talk to me about anything, don't you?' she said suddenly. She felt the words on the tip of her tongue – *what's happening with your lady friend?* – but she swallowed them back. Let him tell her when he was ready to. 'I will never judge you, or give you advice unless you ask for it. But I will always be here to listen.'

Philippe had turned away to pour water into the teapot. He stopped, his back to her. She watched silently, then as his shoulders began to shake she jumped up and put her arms around him. She stroked his hair and made soothing noises as her son cried, not hard but just exhausted, tired of trying to cope with everything on his own.

'Tell me everything,' she whispered. So he did.

Almost everything.

Sylvie was exhausted too. Like Philippe, she'd hardly slept since the theft, and she was getting through the long days on sheer nervous adrenaline. She'd been up since 6.30 and had already done one load of laundry, made Henri his breakfast, smiled insincerely as he'd left, then vacuumed the entire apartment. At 9am, unable to contain herself any longer, she'd gone out for a walk. She'd tried browsing the shelves at *Bibliothèque Mazarine*; but whereas she could usually lose herself amongst the books for hours and reluctantly have to drag herself away, today she skittishly went from shelf to shelf without even noticing what was on them. She nodded to the library assistant and left, walking along the quayside for half an hour, but she started to get nervous about leaving Mona alone in the building. She went to the supermarket to pick up a few groceries and then made her way home, trying to ignore the hard knot of anxiety tying up her insides. Only a few more hours and it would all be over.

That thought made her even more nervous.

She walked slowly, wanting to get home but knowing that she would just spend the hours until 5pm pacing up and down the apartment. She finally turned into her road and looked up curiously as two removal men came out of her building, heading for the white van parked outside. The sign on the side panel read 'Charon and Sons: House Clearance and Removals'. They shook hands with Claude, the building manager, then shut the tailgate of the van, jumped in and drove off.

Claude greeted her with a smile as she reached the front door.

'*Bonjour Madame*!' he said cheerfully.

'*Bonjour*, Claude,' she said. 'Who's moved out?'

'Nobody.' He held the door open for her and as she stepped over the threshold she noticed with horror that the door to the store-room was open. 'I just got them to clear out the storeroom.'

'What?' cried Sylvie. Claude looked at her curiously.

'Is everything okay?' he asked. 'I did tell your husband – I told everyone – but he said there was nothing of yours in there.'

'No, no, that's fine - ' she said, dropping her shopping bag and rushing out into the street, just in time to see the van disappearing around the corner. *Merde*!

In the apartment, she rifled through her bag until she found a scrap of paper with Philippe's number on it (although there was no name on it, in case Henri found it). She dialled the number, praying that he would answer and not his mother.

She was in luck.

'Hello?' Philippe was surprised to hear her voice, and horrified to hear what she had to say. 'Stay right there, *chéri*, I'm on my way!'

He dumped the bag of rubbish he was carrying – after his conversation with his mother earlier, he'd taken what felt like the first step towards being an adult again and had start clearing remnants of his childhood from his bedroom – and grabbed his jacket.

'Can I borrow your car, Maman?' he called. Madame Moreau looked around the door.

'I need to go out - ' she began, but then she saw the look on his face. 'Is it to do with what we were talking about earlier?' she asked. He nodded.

'Sort of. Yes.'

She looked at him for a moment, then handed him her car keys without another word. He smiled at her gratefully and left the room at a run.

He found Sylvie waiting anxiously outside her apartment building, twisting a handkerchief in her hands, her face tearstained. She looked up as the car pulled up beside her and, seeing Philippe in the driver's seat, her mouth dropped open in surprise.

'Are you ok?' he said, jumping out. She nodded, still looking dumbfounded.

'Is that really your mother's car?' she asked.

It was a 1975 Alpine A110 Berlinette in the original Alpine blue. Idling at the kerb, the engine purred like a kitten, but on the open road – or the Champs Elysee, if the traffic was light enough – it growled throatily like a cougar who had smoked too many cigars. It was cool and iconic; the Steve McQueen of the French motoring industry. It also had a lot of miles on the clock and a tendency to overheat in traffic, but Madame Moreau had been given it by her father when she passed her driving test and had loved it so much she never got another car. Grand-père Racine had been obsessed with cars and had impressed upon his daughter the importance of maintenance, teaching her the basics; and even now she could often be found on a Sunday under the bonnet of 'Eloise' (the car's name), smoking a Gauloise while she changed the oil filter.

'Yes,' said Philippe. She shrugged.

'I just expected her to drive something more – sedate,' she said, wiping her eyes and hopping into the passenger seat.

'So what do we do now?' asked Philippe. She shook her head.

'I don't know! We can't let them keep her!'

'Why not? It gets her off our hands...'

'Think about it!' said Sylvie. 'All the while she's missing we'll be under suspicion, even if they can't prove anything.'

Philippe nodded, thinking of his father and Vincent the night before. They knew he'd taken the painting and all the time it was out there, his father would try to track it down. And he probably wouldn't believe that they didn't have it any more. His father would never leave them alone.

'And if the people who've taken it realise that she's the real thing, they'll go to the police and tell them where she came from,' Sylvie went on. 'And who in that building has a link to the Louvre? Oh yes – me.' Philippe took her hand as she continued. 'If we can get her back to the museum in one piece, before it's been too long and they're forced to announce she was stolen, then they might just let it lie.'

Philippe thought she was being a little optimistic there, but it was clearly best for everyone if they got the painting back to its rightful owner. But where was it?

'The removal van had a name on the side – Charon and Sons,' said Sylvie. 'I didn't want to ask Claude where they came from because he'd wonder why I needed to know, and he might mention it to Henri.'

Philippe handed her his phone and revved the engine. 'Look them up on the internet and we'll drive over and get it,' he said. 'Don't worry, *chéri*, we'll get her back.'

The car pulled away and they drove slowly through the city, as the phone's rather slow internet connection searched for the removals company. Sylvie groaned in frustration as the signal cut out again, Philippe patting her hand as they stopped in a queue of traffic.

'Don't panic,' he said. 'If the worst comes to the worst we can -
'

But Sylvie gave a little shriek and pointed through the windscreen. Four cars ahead the van waited at the same set of traffic lights.

'That's them!' she squealed. 'They must've had another pick up nearby!'

Philippe breathed a sigh of relief. 'Thank god for that. We'll follow them until they stop again and then tell them they've picked something up by mistake.'

The lights changed and the queue of traffic moved on. Philippe and Sylvie followed, their full attention on the van ahead. Neither of them noticed the black SUV pull out behind them.

They followed the van over the Pont de Sully towards the Place de la Bastille, then north onto the N1. Philippe looked in his rear-view mirror as they took a roundabout and saw the SUV a few cars behind them. He couldn't be sure that it was his father and Vincent, but he had a bad feeling that it was.

'*Merde*,' he muttered under his breath.

'What's the matter?' asked Sylvie.

'Do you see that black car behind us?'

Sylvie twisted in her seat, craning her neck to look out of the back window. 'The pimped-up spy mobile with the tinted windows?'

Philippe laughed. 'That's the one. I think they're following us.'

'Oh no…' Sylvie turned back and watched the van ahead of them. 'Who is it? The man from the museum?'

'Yes,' said Philippe, overtaking a Citroen 2CV that was pootling along between them and the van. 'His name's Vincent. And my dad'll be with him.'

She looked at him in shock. 'What..?'

'Long story. But we need to lose them before we get Mona back.'

The traffic on the N1 was heavier than usual as they approached the Stade de France. In the streets nearby people were already making their way towards the stadium, excited about the evening's football. They followed the van as it turned off just before the motorway onto the Rue Francis de Pressensé, along the road to a roundabout, over the roundabout – all the while aware of the black SUV still behind them.

Sylvie wondered how on earth they would lose the SUV without also losing the van.

But just over the roundabout was a slip road, closed off by workmen. The van pulled in and the driver spoke to one of the men, gesticulating wildly through the open the window. The workman nodded and moved the barrier to let the van through, then moved it back as Philippe turned the car towards it.

'Sorry monsieur,' the workman said. 'You can't come down here. The Avenue du Général de Gaulle is closed to the north, and all the other roads around the stadium.'

Sylvie watched in dismay as the van turned off the slip road and out of sight. Behind them, another car came over the roundabout and carried on up the road; and behind that, the SUV. At the wheel, Vincent faltered as Moreau shouted at him to stop but carried on; he didn't want Philippe and Sylvie to know they were following them. Sylvie and Philippe exchanged glances as they saw the SUV head past them and over the bridge. Philippe turned back to the workman.

'You let that van through!' he protested.

'Residents only,' said the workman. 'He's got a shop over there.'

'Did he say where?' asked Philippe. The workman looked at him suspiciously. Sylvie leaned across to smile at him.

'Please, I left some things out for them to pick up and they took the wrong thing by mistake,' she said. 'A painting my father left my mother. It means so much to her, she'll be devastated if she realises it's gone so I want to get it back before she notices.'

'And I'll be in trouble with the mother-in-law. Again,' said Philippe ruefully, playing along. The workman laughed.

'Oh man, I feel your pain!' He looked around surreptitiously, then leaned in to the driver's window. 'The shop's on the Place du Cornillon. Good luck with the mother-in-law!' And with that he moved the barrier to one side so they could drive past.

'Thank you so much!' cried Sylvie gratefully. The workman grinned, mock-saluted and put the barrier straight back as they drove through.

'Phew!' said Philippe. 'Two birds with one stone. We know where they're going, and we got rid of my papa.'

They turned left onto de Gaulle and drove alongside the river to a crossroads; the Place du Cornillon. The van was parked outside a shop on the corner, and Philippe pulled the car up behind it.

'What's the plan?' he asked, as they got out of the car.

She smiled. 'Same story I told the workman. We left the wrong thing out and please can we have it back. With any luck they won't even have found her yet.'

They stood in front of the shop window. Sylvie looked at the display and sniffed, unimpressed.

'Hmm! Don't think much of their 'antiques',' she said, dismissively. Philippe tugged at her sleeve.

'Maybe not. But it looks like we need a Plan B,' he said. 'Or is it plan C or D by now?'

Sylvie groaned as the owner of the shop – Monsieur Charon himself – moved the window display around to show off his very latest acquisition to its best advantage. In amongst the bad reproductions and unconvincing antiques sat the genuine Mona Lisa.

CHAPTER 33

Charon allowed himself a sly smile as the bell over the door of his shop tinkled. He'd spotted the young couple looking in his window as he adjusted the display, and he thanked the Lord that he hadn't closed up early like his son had suggested; they hadn't expected any customers this afternoon, what with the roads all around being closed off in preparation for the football. And yet here was a well-dressed young woman, who clearly had an eye for the finer things, with a beau who gazed at her adoringly and looked like he could refuse her nothing. He rubbed his hands together in anticipation as they stepped inside and began to browse. Lambs to the slaughter.

He turned around and gave them his most trustworthy, honest smile. He was very good at sincerity; he practiced it in front of the mirror.

'*Bonjour, mes amies*!' he called to them. 'Beautiful day, isn't it?' It was in reality a rather grey, overcast day, but to Charon it was definitely showing signs of improvement.

Sylvie and Philippe exchanged glances. This wasn't going to be straightforward, they could tell.

'*Bonjour,* monsieur,' said Sylvie politely. 'What a lovely shop you have! Some very nice pieces.'

'Thank you, Madame,' Charon replied, charm oozing from every pore. Or so he imagined. 'Anything in particular caught your eye?'

'The painting in the window - ' Philippe blurted. Charon smiled and reached over to lift it out.

'*La Joconde*? She's a beauty, isn't she? The best reproduction I've ever seen, very authentic. You like it, Madame?'

'Yes, I do,' said Sylvie. 'Because it belongs to my mother. It was accidentally left in a piece of furniture left out for your men to collect - '

Charon frowned. 'I believe you mean it 'belonged' to your mother. Because it belongs to me now.'

'Please monsieur, hear us out,' Philippe said. 'It was inside an armoire, yes? My mother-in-law is, shall we say, a little *dément* – I'm sorry, *chéri* but it's true – and she hides things all over the place. The painting isn't particularly valuable but it means a lot to her, and once she realises it's gone - '

'800 Euros,' said Charon. Sylvie and Philippe exclaimed loudly.

'What?' 'Bollocks!'

'You say it isn't valuable but it is to me,' said Charon. 'Look at the workmanship on it! It looks almost as good as the real thing. I've never seen another done as well. Most reproductions are just prints but whoever painted this was a talented artist. I could easily get 1000 Euros for this if I held onto it. I'm letting you have a discount.'

'800 Euros is a discount?' said Philippe hotly.

'Okay then, 900,' said Charon, smiling.

'That's not really the way haggling works,' Philippe pointed out.

'Keep talking, monsieur. I'm in no hurry to sell it. 1000.'

Sylvie face-palmed and turned to Philippe. 'Please stop trying to negotiate, sweetheart. Monsieur, let me level with you. That painting is a genuine work of art.'

Philippe looked at her in shock. 'Sylvie!' he hissed. She smiled.

'It's okay, Monsieur Charon is a man of the world, I'm sure. This painting is a genuine work of art, created by a very talented artist, as you yourself noted. It was painted by my father.'

Philippe relaxed and let out the breath he was holding. Charon shrugged.

'So?'

'So, my father always said that my mother reminded him of *La Joconde* the day they met. She had that same enigmatic smile that fascinated all the men who saw her. She was a great beauty in her day.'

'As are you, Madame, if I may be so bold,' said Charon, chivalrously. She smiled and gave a small curtsey.

'You flatter me, but *merci*. Anyway, my mother came from a wealthy family and had her pick of suitors, but the only one she was interested in was my father. But her parents didn't approve of him, because he was an artist, and not a very good one according to them. So to prove them wrong he painted that picture and pretended to them that he'd stolen the real one.'

Philippe watched her in surprise as her story unfolded. She seemed to be enjoying herself immensely, swept up in this complete fairy tale, but he did wonder where she was going with it. Charon looked at his watch.

'That's all very interesting - ' he said.

'I haven't finished,' said Sylvie, firmly. Charon looked away from his watch and back at her. 'Because the painting was so good, and because my grandparents were inclined to believe the worst of my father, they reported him to the police for stealing Da Vinci's masterpiece. Well - they raided his studio. He'd taught himself to paint by copying the most famous artworks in the world, and his apartment was full of fake Picassos, Van Goghs, Monets – you name it. He got into a lot of trouble, but the police couldn't prosecute him in the end because he'd never tried to sell them, he just liked to test his skill against the masters. They forced him to destroy all of his paintings.'

'So what about this one?' asked Charon, sceptical but interested in spite of himself. Sylvie took a deep breath and summoned up the spirit of Piaf. This was a tale of such deep but forbidden love, loss and tragedy, it would've impressed Edith herself.

'My mother loved this painting, and she knew what her parents were up to, so she hid it where no one would find it – in an old stable on a friend's farm. My father was distraught that all his work was gone, so she waited until they were married and presented him with it. And it hung in our apartment all the time I was growing up.'

Sylvie wiped a small tear from her eye and continued. 'My father died ten years ago. My mother has never been the same since. Five years ago she was diagnosed with dementia. She's become convinced that her parents – long dead – will call the police if they know that painting still exists, and so, she hides it. She hides it and then moves it and forgets where she's left it. When I realised that she must've hidden it in that old armoire – and that you'd taken it - '

Philippe looked at her in amazement as she burst into tears, and for a moment felt watery-eyed himself until he remembered that it was all complete nonsense. He risked a glance at Charon and was amazed to see the antiques dealer wipe a tear from his own eye. Philippe pulled Sylvie into a hug and stroked her hair.

'There, there, *chéri*,' he murmured, and looked at Charon hopefully. Charon took a handkerchief from his pocket and blew his nose fiercely, then shook his head.

'Sentiment is one thing, but business is another,' he said. 'I am sorry about your mother, Madame, but I am in this business to make money. I can't let you have it for nothing. 400 Euros and that's my final offer. I have overheads to cover.'

Sylvie took Philippe to one side as Charon composed himself. 'I've done my best, I think we're going to have to pay him. How much money have you got?'

Philippe rummaged in his pockets. 'Um – 27 Euros and 50 cents.'

Sylvie sighed and turned to Charon, taking off her watch.

'Would you take an exchange, monsieur?' she asked, sadly. 'It's a 1971 vintage Rolex Princess. It must be worth at least 400 Euros. My parents gave me it for my 21st birthday.'

'No, Sylvie, you can't!' cried Philippe, horrified. 'Not your watch!'

Charon took the watch. '1971, you say?' he said. He studied it closely but to Sylvie's ex-antique dealer's eyes he didn't seem to know what he was looking for.

'Are you sure about this?' said Philippe. 'It was from your parents - '

She shrugged. 'Some things are more important.'

Charon looked up at her, eyes gleaming avariciously. 'It's a deal, Madame.'

They shook hands. Charon wrapped the painting up in brown paper and they left him looking up Rolex watches on a laptop behind the counter.

'Let's get out of here,' said Sylvie, as they got out into the street. Philippe opened the car and put Mona on the back seat, then stood back to hold the door open for Sylvie.

'There's no hurry,' he said. 'We've got a few hours yet. We'll go straight to the car park and wait there for it to get dark.'

'It's not that,' said Sylvie, as he got into the driver's seat and turned the key in the engine. 'I don't want to be here when he realises that watch is a fake.'

Philippe turned to her in amazement. 'It's a fake?'

'Of course it is!' she said. 'A real one would be worth thousands. I told you I didn't think much of his antiques. Let's go!'

Philippe laughed and they drove away from the shop. 'Have I told you how incredible you are?' he asked. She smiled.

'Yes, but I don't mind hearing it again.'

CHAPTER 34

They found their way out of the maze of streets around the stadium, following a somewhat circuitous route because of the road closures. Unused to driving and not familiar with the area, Philippe took a wrong turning and they ended up on the A1 going the wrong way, towards the airport at Le Bourget.

'We're heading in the wrong direction,' said Sylvie.

'No we're not…' Philippe didn't sound too certain. She laughed.

'How come this car doesn't have a satnav? I'm telling you, I did a house clearance out this way years ago. Rundown old place near the airspace museum. Bought a fantastic Persian rug…' Her voice tailed off and Philippe glanced over at her.

'Are you okay?' he asked, concerned.

'Yes. I just – I haven't thought about stuff like that for ages, not since the accident.' She stared out of the window, as if reliving her previous trip – reminding herself of landmarks she'd forgotten. 'It's weird but it feels like I'm coming back to life. It feels like I'm finally starting to be me again.'

'That's brilliant!' cried Philippe, the car swerving slightly under the brunt of his enthusiasm. 'The more of you you are the better, as far as I'm concerned.'

She smiled at him, reaching out to put her hand on his leg. 'We're still going the wrong way though.'

He laughed and took the next slip road off, coming back out on the A1 but this time heading towards the city.

'So where did that story you spun in Charon's come from?' he asked. 'It was amazing. I nearly cried myself, until I remembered it was total lies.'

She laughed. 'I surprised myself there. It was good, wasn't it? My papa and I used to make up stories about the paintings in our shop. He used to say that his customers weren't just buying the painting, they were buying the story behind it. Sometimes he knew the story, sometimes he didn't, so we used to make them up. The more tragic or outrageous the better.'

Philippe laughed. 'I think I'd have liked your dad.'

She looked out of the window, a melancholic smile on her face. 'He'd have liked you.'

They drove on quietly for a moment.

'Talking of fathers…' she began. He stopped her.

'I don't have any endearing stories about mine, I'm afraid.' He sighed. 'All those years I wanted him to come back, and all I had to do to make him notice me was steal something valuable.'

'He knows we've got Mona?'

'Yes. Suspects we do, anyway. Him and Vincent work for an insurance company, tracking down stolen art works and returning them. He turned up outside my house last night.'

'So what does he want? To turn you in?'

'Not exactly, no…' Philippe swore as a light came on on the car's dashboard. 'Damn it, we need petrol.'

'There's a gas station if you come off at the next turning,' said Sylvie.

'Something else you remember from your travels?'

'No, we passed a sign two minutes ago…'

They took the next turn off and stopped for petrol. Philippe turned to Sylvie.

'This won't take long,' he said. 'I can only put in 27 Euros and 50 cents' worth…'

She laughed as he got out of the car leaving the keys in the ignition and began to fill the tank. She stared out of the car window, trying to ignore the painting wedged onto the cramped back seat. Even under the brown paper wrapping, she could feel Mona's eyes burning into her accusingly. She wriggled in her seat, watching Philippe through the window. Her back began to itch under that steady, unblinking gaze...

Philippe looked at her in surprise as she leapt out of the car.

'Just needed some fresh air,' she said. He smiled, finished filling up and walked across the garage forecourt to pay for the petrol, stepping aside to let a couple of young guys through the door as they left the shop.

Sylvie glanced around, anxiously. She'd been so worried about getting the painting back, and so relieved when it was finally in their possession again, but now that they actually had her sitting on the back seat of the car in broad daylight Sylvie couldn't shake the feeling that something bad was going to happen. They had to get her back to the museum as soon as possible.

The two young men walked towards her, letting out a low whistle.

'Nice car, Madame,' said one appreciatively. Sylvie smiled, not wanting to get into a conversation with them but equally not wanting to appear rude. The two men walked around the car, inspecting it, then began to walk away; but one of them had dropped his phone. Sylvie bent down and picked it up, then started after them.

'Excuse me!' she said. 'Your phone - '

As quick as a flash both men turned back, one man grabbing the phone and knocking her out of the way, the other running around to the driver's side. Philippe rushed from the shop, crying out as he saw what was happening, but it was too late. The men jumped into the car and drove off, leaving Philippe standing on the empty forecourt. He looked down and saw Sylvie sprawled on the concrete, and rushed over.

'Oh my god, are you okay *chéri*?' he asked, helping her to her feet. She nodded, shaken and sore from hitting the floor with such a hard bump.

'I'm fine,' she said, 'but Mona...?'

Grim-faced, Philippe shook his head. The car was gone, disappearing into the unfamiliar (to him) streets of Le Bourget, and *La Joconde* was gone with it. Sylvie looked at him, astonished that after all the effort they'd gone to to get her back, she was gone again – just like that – and burst into tears.

As Philippe pulled her close and hugged her, a car drew in next to them; the black SUV. Monsieur Moreau jumped out.

'Madame! Are you okay?' he asked, his voice full of concern. Philippe scowled at him.

'She's fine,' he said. Sylvie looked at Moreau in surprise, then at Philippe.

'But – you're - '

Moreau smiled jovially. 'Your future father-in-law? Yes, Madame, I am. At your service.' He gave a little nod and clicked his heels together. 'But we don't have time for formal introductions. We need to get that car back. Get in.'

He held the door of the SUV open. Sylvie looked at Philippe, who looked at the street where he'd last seen the tailgate of his mother's car disappearing and shrugged. It didn't look like they had a lot of choice.

Vincent sat behind the wheel of the SUV, smoking a cigarette. He flicked ash out of the window at the sign that said NE PAS FUMER! and nodded to Sylvie as she climbed onto the back seat, looking at Philippe as he followed with a rather more contemptuous expression. Moreau jumped into the front seat and they pulled away.

'How are we going to find them?' asked Sylvie. 'We don't know where they're going.'

Moreau ignored her. 'What do you think?' he said to Vincent. 'They looked like they'd pulled that trick before. Labossiere's crew?'

Vincent nodded, his eyes on the road. 'It's the sort of car his lot go for. Classic. They've probably already got a customer, just waiting for one to come up.'

'Do you mind telling me what the fuck you're talking about?' said Philippe, angrily. His father turned and stared at him, eyebrows raised, until Philippe shrank back in his seat.

'I can't believe your mother still drives that car,' said Moreau, amused. 'Or should I say, drove... Those two idiots were a bit too smooth for opportunistic amateurs. You probably didn't notice the car they turned up in? No? A blue Renault, probably spotted you in St Denis and has been following you ever since, waiting for a chance. They pulled up and the two passengers got out while you were filling up. Went in the shop, probably rang their boss – a thug called Labossiere – and got the go ahead, and then WHAM! Madame here gets knocked on her *derriere* and they drive off in your mother's pride and joy with the painting on the back seat.'

'How did you know we had the painting with us?' asked Sylvie. Moreau smiled at her. It was a wide smile showing all his teeth, but it didn't reach his eyes.

'Madame – may I call you Sylvie? – Sylvie. You may have lost us earlier but when you turned off near the stadium it was fairly obvious where you were going. We went over the bridge and watched you from the other side of the river.'

'So you think you know who stole the car – do you know where they're taking it?' asked Philippe, as Vincent turned the car onto Autoroute 86. Moreau nodded.

'Labossiere has a warehouse near the docks at Saint Ouen,' he said. 'They take the cars there and hide them until they can forge new registration documents for them. Then they ship them off.'

'How do you know all this?' Philippe was stunned. 'Don't tell me you used to steal cars as well as everything else!'

Moreau laughed. 'In our job it pays to know people from all sides of the industry.'

'The thieving industry.'

'If you want to call it that, yes. Like any business, it's all down to networking.'

Philippe snorted contemptuously and shook his head. Sylvie watched, confused.

'The thieving industry? But I thought you were in insurance now - '

'Yes, Sylvie, technically we are. Technically, Vincent and I are hired to find stolen property and return it to the rightful owners, for a very reasonable fee of course. But alas, sometimes we are unable to find the property in question. And sometimes it's more financially viable for us to not to return it.'

'More financially viable *not* to return it? But - '

Philippe interrupted her. 'What he means is that he doesn't want us to take Mona back. He wants to broker a deal to sell her to a dodgy art collector.'

'But – but you - ' Sylvie spoke to Vincent. 'You work for the museum! You stood in the director's office and helped her interrogate all the staff - '

Vincent finished his cigarette and threw the butt out of the window. 'Madame, a finder's fee is all well and good, but 75% of the sale proceeds would be rather more.'

'75%?' cried Philippe. 'You said 50% last night - '

'That was before you forced us to drive around Paris,' said Vincent harshly. 'Bearing in mind it was you and your lady friend who lost the fucking thing, I think you're lucky to get 25%. If you were my imbecile son you'd be getting nothing.'

'But - ' protested Philippe. Moreau grunted.

'Alright, 20%. Keep talking son, if you want to get it down to 15.'

'Am I the only one who understands how haggling is supposed to bloody work?' muttered Philippe. Sylvie squeezed his hand and gave him a small, frightened smile. He pulled her close to him and whispered in her ear. 'Don't worry, we'll get out of this somehow.'

'How?'

Philippe wished he knew. 'We'll think of something. Just stay alert…'

'*Merde*!' Vincent swore and slapped the steering wheel as the SUV slowed down. The traffic here was much heavier than usual, probably because of the football road closures, and to add to it there'd been an accident on the road up ahead. Moreau and Vincent shrank down in their seats and tried to look inconspicuous as blue flashing lights approached the car from behind, then overtook, heading for the accident. Moreau laughed and sat back up again, slapping Vincent on the back.

'Look at us! Force of habit.'

Vincent growled, unamused. 'Look at this bloody mess! Half of Paris on their way to the football, the other half avoiding it and this *imbecile* crashes his car! We're not going to be going anywhere if we stay on this road.'

'Then pull off up there,' said Moreau, mildly.

Vincent turned off the motorway and back onto residential streets but these, too, were rammed with traffic. The SUV turned into a gridlocked street and before Vincent could turn out again they were trapped by other cars following them.

'*Merde*!' cried Vincent again.

The cars in front inched forwards slowly. The SUV followed suit. Traffic was bumper to bumper, not helped by side roads being closed for the football or for roadworks. It was a perfect storm of terrible travel conditions. But at least it would give Philippe and Sylvie time to think up a plan before they reached Labossiere's warehouse.

Onwards…centimetre by centimetre…crawling to the end of the road…and onto another one, equally snarled up with cars. By now Vincent had turned red in the face and was in danger of exploding in apoplexy, and even Moreau, who was normally laidback to the point of not really giving a damn about anything, was starting to get impatient. The two men began to bicker.

'I told you we should have moved in on the painting as soon as we knew your imbecile son had it,' muttered Vincent.

'But you didn't know, did you?' said Moreau. 'You spent all that time following him around and you still didn't know where he'd hidden it. For a finder you're not very good at finding things.'

'Oh yeah? Who found the Rembrandt and let you in on the deal even though you'd done fuck all to help? I'm surprised when you get up in the night for a piss you can find your own *zizi* in the dark - '

Philippe grinned at Sylvie. The men in front might be getting wound up, but it was relieving the tension for their two passengers. Suddenly Sylvie stiffened, her eyes wide. She mouthed at Philippe: *Look!* He followed her gaze.

Way up ahead, opposite a blocked off side road, sat Madame Moreau's car. Like every other car around here it was stuck in the gridlock. Philippe squinted and whispered to Sylvie.

'Can you see what the name of that road is?'

'No…the one before is Rue Frederico Fellini, if that helps?'

It did. Philippe discreetly took out his phone and looked up the road on his map app, working out a route. He had a plan. He touched Sylvie's hand and looked into her eyes, and whispered again, very, very quietly.

'When I say run…' She nodded. 'Run!'

They leapt out of the SUV and ran towards the car. It took Vincent and Moreau, deep in argument, a few seconds to realise what had happened. Moreau turned on his colleague furiously.

'Why haven't you got child locks on those doors?' he cried. Vincent glared at him, defensively.

'Because I haven't got any fucking children!' he spat. They looked at each other for a couple more seconds, then leaped out too.

Sylvie could hear the two men chasing after them and ran even harder. Philippe had just reached the car and was yanking the driver's door open. The driver looked up at him, stunned, and just had time to open his mouth in protest before Philippe had hauled him out onto the road and kicked him.

'Sylvie! Come on!' he shouted, getting in. The young man in the passenger looked across at him in astonishment. Philippe punched him smartly on the nose, the element of surprise working for him rather than the actual force of the punch. The passenger thought about retaliating but realising his accomplice was rolling around on the floor outside thought better of it. He jumped out just as Sylvie reached the car, pushing past her and running slap bang into Vincent. Both men staggered backwards, clutching their heads. Sylvie gave the car thief a shove and sent him careering back into Vincent, and then she too jumped into the car. Philippe reversed as far as he could – which wasn't very far – and then forwards, and then back, and then forwards again until he had just enough room to turn down the side road, putting his foot down and driving through the ROAD CLOSED signs.

Behind him, an out-of-breath Moreau had only just reached the car, his years of smoking and drinking having taken their toll. He kicked the still-prone car thief and followed Philippe and Sylvie on foot, but Philippe weaved the car along the street, past the parked cars and over a still-wet patch of tarmac and was soon out of his father's sight.

Moreau gave up and watched his dreams of a large payout disappear into the early evening light. Vincent, still clutching his head, lumbered up behind him.

'Your fucking imbecile son - ' he started, but Moreau stopped him.

' – is obviously not such an imbecile, is he?' He didn't exactly feel a warm parental glow, but he was sure that one day he'd look back on this and be proud of the man his son had become, man enough to outsmart even him.

One day. But not today.

Philippe whooped as he steered the car around a corner, leaving his father way behind him. Sylvie laughed and looked onto the back seat, relieved to see the wrapped up painting still there. She grabbed Philippe's knee and smiled at him.

'You did it!' she said. 'You got her back!'

He smiled. 'No, we got her back. Now let's get to the museum before anything else goes wrong.'

Sylvie crossed her fingers tightly as they got onto the N1 and headed back into the city.

CHAPTER 35

They reached the car park as planned just after 5 o'clock. Philippe slipped out and bought coffee and sandwiches – it had been a long day – but although both he and Sylvie were hungry, neither of them could manage more than a bite. They sat quietly, not speaking, just holding hands. Sylvie tried not to think about Henri, getting home to find the apartment empty; tried not to think of how furious he would be when she finally got home that night. The end of the night felt like a long way away…

Finally the clock of the nearby church began to strike six. Philippe turned to Sylvie and embraced her, holding her tightly, breathing her in. She buried her head in his shoulder, wanting to stay like that forever, to never let go.

Eventually Philippe pulled away and took off his watch. He checked the time against his mobile phone, then handed it to her.

'Here. Synchronise watches! Be at the delivery entrance at 6.45 and look out for the red light on the security camera – when it goes off I'll open the door and take the painting from you. You go round to the staff entrance and go in while I put Mona back in her place while the cameras are off.'

'Are you sure there'll be enough time?' she asked. He nodded.

'Once the cameras go off there'll be about ten minutes before they get the system back on line,' he said. 'That should be long enough for me to get her back to the Denon wing.' He looked at her steadily. 'If I get caught - '

'Don't!' she cried, putting her finger to his lips. He moved it away gently.

'If I get caught, I'm keeping you out of it,' he said. She shook her head. 'I am,' he insisted. 'There's no need for both of us to go down. But if the worst happens, I want you to know – these last couple of months, with you, have been the best days of my life. I love you so much, Sylvie - '

'I love you too!' she said, tears springing to her eyes. They embraced again, then there was time for one last lingering kiss before Philippe opened the car door and got out.

Stephanie was waiting at the security entrance, talking to the sexy blonde from HR as Philippe rushed in. She looked up and rolled her eyes.

'I see your timekeeping's back to normal,' she said. Philippe forced himself to smile and relax.

'Sorry,' he said. 'Busy day. I haven't even had a chance to go home and change. I've got a spare uniform in my locker, I'll just go and - '

'Go on!' she sighed. 'Mathilde'll keep me company...'

The blonde – Mathilde – laughed and perched on the edge of the security desk, close – very close – to Stephanie. Philippe looked at them and, in the midst of his nerves, suddenly realised why Stephanie had been so keen to warn him off her. She'd wanted Mathilde for herself! Well, it looked like she'd got her. Philippe smiled warmly at his colleague and gave her a discreet thumbs up. Stephanie blushed, but looked like the cat who'd got the cream.

Philippe rushed off to the locker room, where Farheena was waiting. She turned her back as he slipped his uniform on.

'Everything ok?' she said. He sighed.

'You would not believe the day we've had,' he said. 'But it's all sorted now. Did anyone say anything about you getting in early?'

'No,' said Farheena. 'I just told them I was starting early so I'd be finished in time for the football. Are you ready?'

Philippe did up his last shirt button and nodded. 'I am now. Let's do it.'

Farheena held out her hand for him to fist-bump then laughed.

'I can't believe we're doing this…'

Farheena picked up her mop and bucket and headed along to the offices. She looked at her watch; 6.40pm. She took a deep breath and stepped inside the CCTV control room, where two security guards were talking about – what else? – the football. They looked up briefly as she entered the room; but nobody takes much notice of a woman with a mop.

'Come to do your floors,' she said briskly, starting to mop in a corner of the room. They went back to their conversation.

Philippe meanwhile was heading down a corridor to the Deliveries entrance. He looked at his phone; not long to go. He hoped Farheena was in position.

Outside, Sylvie had left the car and carried the painting along the street. Luckily it was getting dark and the city was almost deserted, apart from the massive crowd that had gathered by the Eiffel Tower to watch the night's proceedings on the big screens, put up for the thousands of fans who had flooded into Paris from all over Europe. Sylvie could already hear them singing from here and wondered just how loud they would get if *les Bleus* scored during tonight's game.

And now she stood in the shadows near the Deliveries entrance, waiting for the little red light on the camera above the door to go off. She thought of Philippe, waiting just the other side of the door…

Except he wasn't. Monsieur Fournier stood in front of him.

'There you are, Philippe! I've been looking for you,' he said. Philippe's heart leapt.

'Why? What's wrong?' asked Philippe.

'Your mother's on the phone for you,' said Fournier, disapprovingly. 'In the office. Says it's important.'

Philippe groaned. He'd seen that he'd missed several calls from her, but he hadn't been able to face talking to her.

'I'm sorry, Monsieur Fournier,' he said. 'My phone must be on silent. I'll call her back - '

'Oh no you won't!' his manager said hotly. 'I know your mother. She wouldn't call if it wasn't important. That woman is a saint and I won't be the one fobbing her off. You go and talk to her.'

'But - '

'Off you go, Philippe. There's a good chap.' Fournier stood back to let Philippe past him. Philippe, at a complete loss, gave up and rushed past him.

It was 6.42.

Farheena was still mopping.

'I need to do under your desks!' she said. The guards looked up at her.

'Leave it, it's fine,' said one. She shook her head.

'I can't leave it,' she said. 'Have you met my supervisor? I swear that woman has OCD, she's such a stickler. You'll get me sacked.' She apologised in her head to the supervisor, who was actually one of the loveliest women you could hope to meet. She dipped her mop in the bucket again and began to clean around the guards' feet, splashing them with water. They shuffled out of her way in irritation, scooting backwards in their chairs.

She checked her watch again; it was time. She dunked her already-sodden mop in the bucket and took a deep breath, then flicked it at the row of power sockets under the desk.

Nothing. She did it again. Still nothing.

'Shit,' she muttered. Then she nudged the bucket closer to power points and accidentally kicked the whole thing over.

There was a loud BANG and all the screens went out in the control room. The guards however didn't even notice, their attention taken by the prostrate young Muslim woman twitching on the floor.

'Bollocks,' muttered Farheena through teeth gritted in shock.

Outside, Sylvie looked at Philippe's watch then up at the camera again. She gave a mini fist-pump as the red light winked out and rushed at the door, pulling it hard. But it didn't budge.

'What?' she cried, pulling it again. It still didn't move. 'No no no!' she howled in quiet desperation, tugging at it then punching it in frustration. She looked at the watch again; where was he? One last tug; she couldn't hang around out here too long in case the cameras came back on. With a cry of frustration she left the painting leaning against the door, consoling herself that someone was bound to find it there. Then she pulled up the collar of her coat and slunk away into the darkness, just as the red light came back on again.

Philippe picked up the phone, with a feeling of despair in the pit of his stomach. He'd missed his chance.

'Hello, Maman,' he said. 'You shouldn't call me at work -'

'What's going on, Philippe?' said Madame Moreau. 'Where's my car? Your father called, he said it had been stolen and you were in trouble - '

'Everything's fine,' he said, although he wasn't at all convinced it was. 'Your car's in the car park over the road. There's no trouble, apart from Papa that is. I can't talk now, Maman, but don't worry.'

'You're sure you're ok?' Madame Moreau sounded worried. 'And this Sylvie, is she…?'

'Honestly, everything is fine,' he said, as reassuringly as possible. 'But I have to go now.' And then he said the words that made her even more certain that he was in trouble of some kind. 'I love you, Maman.'

Philippe made his way up to the Denon wing, where Sylvie had just started work. She looked up and gave a little cry of relief when she saw him, flinging down her duster and throwing herself on him. He laughed and kissed her hard on the lips.

'Where were you?' she whispered fiercely. He kissed her again.

'I'm so sorry, Fournier caught me before I got to you and I had to take a phone call. What did you do with Mona?'

'Left her outside,' said Sylvie. 'I didn't know what else to do. She'll be alright there, won't she?'

'Yes,' said Philippe. 'Someone will probably go outside for a cigarette at half time and find her. You know what this means, *chéri*?'

'What?'

'It means we did it. We got her home.'

They stared at each other for a moment, then Sylvie shrieked with laughter as he picked her up and whirled her around.

Not much work got done that night. The cleaners dusted and polished and mopped in double quick time, while the security guards – who'd by now sorted out the electrical problems in the CCTV control room – drew lots and flipped coins to see who'd get to watch the football. The museum director, herself a football fan, had arranged for a big screen TV to be wheeled into the canteen and had let it be known that she was happy for staff to watch the game as long as work still got done and art works still got guarded. By 8pm, with the opening ceremony in full swing, the galleries were deserted.

Philippe helped Sylvie put away her cleaning things and escorted her down to the canteen. It was full of people. Stephanie and Mathilde sat huddled together in a corner, while the others helped themselves to coffee and got out sandwiches and snacks. As they entered, Farheena – hair still somewhat on end after her electric shock – waved to them from her seat near the TV.

'Everything okay?' she asked. She groaned as Philippe and Sylvie exchanged glances. 'What? Did it go wrong? Did I get electrocuted for nothing?'

'No, no - ' began Sylvie, then did a double-take. 'Hang on, you got electrocuted? Are you alright?' She reached out to touch Farheena's arm and then jerked her hand back at the resulting zing of static.

'I'm fine,' said Farheena. 'I always wanted curly hair.'

Philippe and Sylvie slid into the seat next to her and settled down to watch the football.

'Are you staying for the whole match?' asked Philippe. 'It ends quite late, and Henri - '

'I'm staying,' said Sylvie, smiling much more bravely than she actually felt. But after the ups and downs of that day she couldn't bear the thought of leaving Philippe, certainly not before the painting had been discovered. Philippe squeezed her hand and she rested her head on his shoulder, exhausted.

The game began. The French team were giving it their all, desperate to win on home turf on such a special night; but Romania weren't going to make it easy for them. The workers assembled in the canteen, the massive crowd of football fans out by the Eiffel Tower and the supporters at the Stade de France cheered the players on when they made a run towards goal, and all groaned in frustrated unison at the near misses. Half time came and the armchair pundits discussed the first 45 minutes with great enthusiasm, if not with much insight.

The second half started. Philippe and Sylvie exchanged worried looks; several supporters had gone outside for a cigarette, but there'd been no mention of a package being found.

All was forgotten in the 57th minute as Olivier Giroud scored for the home team. The staff in the canteen went crazy, leaping up and down and cheering. Philippe grabbed Sylvie and kissed her hard, as Stephanie grabbed Mathilde and followed suit. The men in the canteen suddenly went very quiet and a few forgot to breathe for a moment. Mathilde broke away, laughing, and a collective sigh (of – disappointment? Maybe) went around the room. Philippe grinned at Stephanie, who looked very pleased with herself.

'I *knew* they liked each other,' said Sylvie. Philippe looked stunned.

'Really?'

'Of course! It was obvious, wasn't it?'

'Um – yes. Yes of course it was...'

The game started again and everyone settled down, several of the men trying very hard not to watch Stephanie and Mathilde and failing miserably. Sylvie and Farheena rolled their eyes.

And then in the 65th minute - Romania were on the ball – they were in the box – and then –

'Penalty!' cried the referee. A collective '*Merde*!' rang out in the canteen. And all across France fans leapt up and shouted and swore. Bogdan Stancu sent the goalkeeper the wrong way to make it 1 – 1.

Cries of despair and howls of outrage filled the room. Farheena grinned.

'Lighten up, guys, it's only a game,' she said. She laughed at the torrent of good-natured abuse that followed.

The game was getting exciting, but Sylvie couldn't enjoy it knowing that Mona was still outside. How come no one had found her? The smokers always went out to the Deliveries entrance for a cigarette and there was no way they could've missed her. Unless –

Her thoughts were interrupted by Monsieur Fournier, entering the canteen. Everyone immediately quietened down and tried to look like they hadn't just spent the best part of the evening in there, but had only just this minute popped in for a quick break.

'Settle down, everyone,' said Monsieur Fournier. 'I know you've all been in here watching the football, it's fine. But you're going to have to evacuate the building.'

'What?' cried Sylvie, grabbing Philippe's hand.

'A package has been found outside the Deliveries entrance and the police have been called in to perform a controlled explosion,' said Fournier. 'So if you'll all just - '

Sylvie face-palmed. ' Oh for – for *fuck's* sake, what else can go fucking wrong?'

Fournier looked at her, surprised, as Farheena hissed at her.

'Sylvie! Shut up!'

Philippe spoke up. 'Monsieur Fournier, isn't blowing it up a bit of an over-reaction? Hasn't anyone looked at the package to see what's inside?'

Fournier shook his head. 'Philippe, we're in the middle of a heightened security situation. It's the first night of the football and we're the most famous museum in the world. We're a genuine target, aren't we?'

'But - ' said Sylvie. She looked at Philippe, who gave a sigh of resignation and nodded. 'You can't blow it up.'

'Why not? The police say - '

'The police don't know what's in it. You can't blow it up, because… It's the Mona Lisa.' Sylvie sat down abruptly, her legs shaking. Philippe stood behind her, his hand comfortingly on her shoulder.

'What?' cried Fournier.

'But the Mona Lisa's in storage while the display's repaired, isn't she?' said Stephanie, puzzled.

'No,' said Philippe. 'I stole it during the power cut.'

'No!' said Sylvie. '*We* stole it.'

'You weren't even in the building - '

'Yes, but you stole it for me!'

'Has it been stolen then?' asked Mathilde, bewildered.

'YES!' cried Farheena and Stephanie.

'I knew you were looking more shifty than usual,' said Stephanie.

'Thanks,' muttered Philippe.

'So – you actually DID steal it?' said Fournier, marshalling his thoughts.

'Yes,' said Philippe.

'The night of the power cut?' said Fournier.

'Yes,' said Philippe.

'But he did it for me - ' cried Sylvie.

'He did it so they could run away together,' said Farheena. 'Her old man's a right bastard.'

'He is, he hid all her shoes and gave her a black eye - ' chimed in Stephanie.

'So it's not in storage?' asked Mathilde.

'NO!" cried Farheena and Stephanie. Monsieur Fournier held up a hand, wearily.

'Can you all just stop talking now?' he said. He looked around the room, making up his mind. 'Right, you lot stay here and watch the rest of the game while I go and contact the bomb squad. And you and you -' he pointed to Philippe and Sylvie ' – director's office, now!'

So the hammer blow, when it fell, fell quickly and without anything like as much destruction as Sylvie and Philippe had feared. *Madame Directeur* had been called in as soon as the mysterious package had been found, and when Monsieur Fournier carried the painting into her office the relief on her face was palpable. A quick check to make sure *La Joconde* was undamaged was enough to lift the worry that had aged her at least ten years over the last five days.

Fournier was a warm-hearted man with a soft spot for Philippe, or more accurately Philippe's mother, whom he had known and adored from afar since their high school days; so he was never going to be inclined to call the police. More to the point, how to arrest someone for a crime that hadn't been reported and was now solved? The fact that Mona was back before they'd even admitted publically that she was missing would now make it very difficult for the director to report Philippe and Sylvie, as it would lead to her having to answer some very tricky questions herself; not only from the police but from the museum's trustees and donors, who would no doubt begin to wonder just how safe their precious art works were at the Louvre.

The director sat back in her chair.

'So I think it is best for all concerned that we forget this ever happened,' she said. Fournier, standing behind her, nodded in agreement and smiled at the two hapless art thieves before he could stop himself. He quickly forced himself to look stern.

'I agree,' he said. 'It would break your poor mother's heart if she were to hear about this.'

The museum director rolled her eyes – she really couldn't care less about the state of Madame Moreau's heart – but said nothing.

Sylvie clutched Philippe's hand and beamed at the director.

'Thank you so much!' she gushed. 'We are so grateful, and so sorry, we'll never let you down again - '

The director smiled thinly. 'Of course you won't, Sylvie. You're fired.'

CHAPTER 36

Philippe tugged at Sylvie's hand and they skipped out into the Cour Napolean, laughing. Philippe felt like a great burden had finally been lifted from his shoulders; and without that weight he felt as light as a feather. As free as a little bird.

Sylvie gasped as he grabbed her and span her around.

'We did it, *chéri*!' he cried. 'We got her back safe and sound.'

'We got fired,' she pointed out. He span her around again.

'I'd rather be unemployed than in prison,' he said, stopping and kissing her on the lips. She leant against him, dizzy, and snuggled her head into his shoulder. She understood why he was so happy, but at the same time it meant they were back at square one; she was still married, still stuck with that bully, and they still had no money and nowhere to run away to.

He took her face in her hands and looked at her, smiling softly.

'I know what you're thinking,' he said. 'You're thinking we're back where we started before all this excitement.'

She laughed again at that. 'Excitement? I don't know that I'd call it that. But yes. Henri - '

'Sylvie! Look at what we just did!' There was a hint of gentle exasperation in his tone. 'We stole the most famous painting in the world, lost it, tracked it down, bought it back – then had it stolen from us, got kidnapped by my long lost papa, got free, recovered the painting - '

'Nearly got it blown up - '

'Nearly, but we saved it in time. We went through all that and got her back home, all without getting arrested! We make an amazing team, Sylvie! I think we can handle Henri.'

'But we've got nowhere to go!'

'Yes we have. Think about it. Do you really want to run away? To leave Paris? All your memories of your parents are here. My mum's here, and all my many, many aunties and cousins - I don't want to leave them because of your bastard husband.'

'But where will we go?'

He sighed and led her over to the one of the fountains by the big glass pyramid, and sat down on the low wall surrounding it. He turned to her as she sat too.

'We've been going about this all wrong. You remember that poster of Eric Cantona in my bedroom?'

She laughed, slightly puzzled. 'Of course I do!'

'I always wanted to be Eric.' He stopped her as she opened her mouth to speak. 'I don't mean I wanted to be a footballer – well, I did but I was always rubbish at football – I wanted to be a hero, someone people looked up to. When I was a kid and my papa used to go on about Eric, he made it sound like he was the only person in the team, like the rest of the players didn't even need to turn up. But of course that's ridiculous. Even Eric himself knew that he couldn't do it on his own. He knew he needed Ryan Giggs and David Beckham and the Neville brothers - ' He laughed as he saw the completely bewildered look on Sylvie's face. 'I'm sorry, it's been a long day and I'm not making any sense. I just mean – we've been trying to solve this problem all on our own, and we don't need to. We never needed to.'

Sylvie spoke slowly, thinking.

'When Henri came to meet me, the night he hid my shoes, Stephanie covered for us when he spotted the new ones you bought me...'

'Exactly! Farheena got herself electrocuted helping us get Mona back. And tonight, when the director sacked us, Monsieur Fournier persuaded her to pay us two months' salary to keep quiet about the theft. We have so many people who care about us! So many people who want to help us.'

'I think Monsieur Fournier fancies your mum,' grinned Sylvie. Philippe laughed.

'I think you might be right. And that was the biggest mistake I made,' he said. 'Not telling my mum. I was ashamed when I moved back in with her, like I was a complete failure. I didn't want to rely on her help again, after everything she did for me. But she's not just a mother, she's a woman. She went through so much shit with my papa and hearing what you've been going through with Henri - '

'You told her?'

He nodded. 'Last night. It all got to me and I told her everything. Well, not about Mona, obviously, but all about you and how much I love you. When she heard how he treats you she gave me a right telling off for not letting her know sooner. It's all sorted. You're moving in with me and my mum until we can afford a place of our own. She even mentioned selling her car to help with a deposit.'

Sylvie stared at him, tears in her eyes. 'She'd do that for us?'

'Of course she would. If it were the other way round, I'd do it for her. You'd have done it for your parents, wouldn't you? Family is everything.'

Sylvie stared at him for a second longer before falling into his arms and losing herself in his embrace as, across town at the Stade de France, Dimitri Payet chose that very moment – the last minute of the game - to snatch a winning goal for France. The city around them erupted into cheers and the sky was suddenly full of fireworks, and it felt like it was all just for them.

Romance, however, will only get you so far. Sometimes you have to be brave as well. Luckily having Philippe by her side had made Sylvie find reserves of courage she'd never realised she had. Hand in hand, they went back to Madame Moreau's car and drove to Henri's apartment.

The lights were still on; he was up, waiting for her. Sylvie looked up at the brightly lit window as she stepped out of the car and gulped, nervously. But the feel of Philippe's hand on her arm strengthened her resolve. She smiled at him and they went inside.

To say that Henri wasn't happy would be something of an understatement. Henri was a pressure-cooker of rage, and he was in danger of exploding in Sylvie's face. At the sound of her key in the lock he flew towards the front door, ready to pounce on her the moment she walked in; but she was gently moved aside by Philippe, who went in first.

Henri stopped, his hand raised to – slap her? grab her by the throat? Sylvie wasn't sure – and glared at Philippe in hostile surprise. Philippe knocked his hand out of the way, standing his ground as Henri swore and went to raise it again.

'I wouldn't if I were you,' said Philippe, calmly but with an air of authority that Sylvie had never seen in him before.

'Oh wouldn't you?' spat Henri. 'And who the fuck would you be?'

'He's my friend, Henri,' said Sylvie, trembling. He looked at her with utter contempt but didn't move, and Sylvie suddenly realised that it didn't matter what he thought or what he wanted; he no longer had any power over her.

Henri looked Philippe up and down.

'I remember you,' he said, slowly. 'You're the skinny streak of piss from the museum, aren't you? I knew you were fucking my whore of a wife.'

Philippe stepped forward furiously until the two men's faces were almost touching. His fists clenched. Sylvie tugged at his sleeve.

'Leave him, *chéri*, he's not worth it.'

Philippe shook her off. 'Don't call her that!'

'She's my wife,' sneered Henri. 'I'll call her what I fucking want, boy.'

'Henri,' said Sylvie.

'This is my house, and my wife, and you don't get to come in here - '

'Henri!'

'Oh what, you're actually going to bully someone who's not scared to hit you back this time, are you?' snarled Philippe. Sylvie had had enough of the testosterone flying around the apartment by now, besides which a suspicion had popped into her head; one which she had absolutely no evidence for but which she knew, all the same, was true.

'HENRI!' she shouted. Both men stopped their posturing and looked at her, Philippe slightly shamefaced. She took a deep breath.

'Was I really bankrupt?' she asked calmly. A look of confusion crossed Henri's face, followed almost immediately by guilt.

'What?' he said.

'I wasn't really bankrupt, was I? I didn't owe any tax. You took advantage of my accident and then kept me on those pills so I was too *abruti* to work it out.'

'You're confused - ' spluttered Henri. Philippe took a step towards him but Sylvie threw her arm across his chest, keeping him back.

'The only thing I'm confused about is how I didn't spot it earlier,' she said. 'You could never afford this place on your salary, could you? You sold my shop to pay for it. You squandered my inheritance because you felt you deserved all this – the expensive clothes, the apartment – you thought you'd be a partner at work by now. But you're not and you never will be. Harassing your female staff and being a bully isn't the way to get promotion these days, Henri.'

'You ungrateful bitch! I've kept you in - '

'In what? In a cage?' she shouted. She took a deep breath, anxious not to let anger and emotion overwhelm her, and forced herself to stay calm. 'I never cared about any of this.'

'Good, because you'll be living in the fucking gutter with him!' blustered Henri. 'If you think you're getting your hands on my money - '

Sylvie laughed. 'Well I've already been in the sewers with him and I'd take that over living in a palace with you, Henri. I'm sure all my money is either spent or squirreled away somewhere no one else can get at it, and I don't have the energy to try and recover it. But I'm leaving and you're not going to stop me.'

Henri sneered at her. 'Why would I want to stop you?'

She ignored him, walking through to the bedroom and grabbing a suitcase. He went to follow her but Philippe stopped him, blocking the doorway. Sylvie began to carelessly throw clothes into the suitcase, stopping only to wrap the photograph of her mother on the bedside table in a jumper and pack it.

'I'll take some things now but I'll be back in a couple of days to collect the rest. And I'm warning you, Henri. If one single thing of mine 'accidentally' gets lost, or smashed, or thrown out of the window, I will go straight to the police and tell them everything you've done.'

Henri laughed nastily, but it didn't quite mask the worry on his face.

'What exactly do you think you can prove?' he asked.

'Oh, nothing,' said Sylvie. 'But then I don't need to, do I? Mud sticks. I don't suppose your clients will be too keen on using an accountant who drugged, spied on and defrauded his own wife, do you?'

Henri glared at her, impotent in his rage. Philippe looked at his beetroot red face and laughed.

'Come on baby,' he said, taking the suitcase from Sylvie. 'Let's go.'

They pushed past Henri and headed for the door, Sylvie stopping on the way to pick up her old blue and white teapot and a couple more framed photographs from the kitchen.

'Good riddance, you little tramp,' growled Henri. Sylvie handed Philippe the teapot and turned back. She smiled at Henri then punched him hard in the face, hard enough to make him stagger back in surprise. Philippe looked at her in love-struck awe and amazement. Then she calmly plucked the teapot out of Philippe's hand and walked away, leaving her gilded cage behind her forever.

CHAPTER 37

It was a week later. Sylvie had settled quickly into the apartment with Philippe and his mother, who had greeted her that night with a characteristically warm but no-nonsense hug. She was grateful that Madame Moreau hadn't asked any questions, just sat her down and handed her a box of tissues to mop away the tears of exhaustion and relief that had finally burst from her. She'd made them both some hot chocolate then gone off to bed, and by the next day it felt almost as if Sylvie had always lived there.

Philippe had taken Sylvie back to Henri's apartment the next afternoon, but he had already changed the locks. He had however packed the rest of her things and left them with the building manager, Claude, along with a note telling her that as all of her things had now been safely removed from the apartment there was no need for her to ever come back, nor any reason to involve the police. Philippe had been all for calling them straight away – Henri's behaviour made it clear to him that he had indeed conned Sylvie out of her home and business – but she stopped him; without clear evidence of wrong doing the authorities would be unlikely to investigate, and even if they did it could drag on for years. Sylvie just wanted to put her ill-fated marriage behind her and concentrate on their future together. And Philippe couldn't argue with that.

Madame Moreau had gone to visit her sister Isabeau that day. After taking full advantage of having the apartment to themselves (having his mother in the next room every night was a little inhibiting), Philippe had popped out to buy some milk while Sylvie tidied the apartment; she was keen to contribute, and if she couldn't do it financially at the moment then she was determined to be as useful as possible.

She smiled as she heard the key in the door and undid her blouse, reclining seductively over the sofa. She really was a wanton hussy, and she was enjoying it.

'It's me, *chéri*!' called Philippe. She laughed; who else would it be? 'Are you decent? We've got company. Look who I found loitering on the doorstep...'

She leapt up and did up her top again as Philippe entered with Farheena. The younger woman shrieked and ran to hug her fiercely.

'Oh my god!' cried Farheena. 'I was so worried about you, and then Monsieur Fournier told me what had happened and that you'd moved in here - '

'How did he know that?' asked Sylvie. Farheena shrugged.

'I dunno, he said he'd seen Philippe's mum. But look at you! You look great! How is everything? Are you happy?'

Laughing, Sylvie disentangled herself and led her friend into the kitchen.

'Let me put the kettle on and I'll tell you everything - '

Farheena hopped around, fidgeting with excitement.

'No no no, me first. I've got some important stuff to tell. Oh my fucking *god* you are going to explode when I tell you - '

Philippe and Sylvie exchanged looks and sat down at the kitchen table. Farheena followed suit, then leapt up again.

'Where do I start? Shit, you are not going to believe this - '

'Just tell us already!' cried Philippe, laughing. She sat down again.

'Yes, you're right. Ok. Well, when you told me about that bastard selling your shop I was shocked.'

'I know,' said Sylvie. 'You wanted to down mops and storm round to give him a good kicking, as I recall.'

Farheena laughed. 'Yes. I so wish you'd let me. Anyway, after you got sacked I wondered if any of my family might have a job for you – you know I've got a massive family, right? Right, anyway, I was talking to my uncle who's a lawyer and I thought, while I'm here, might as well ask him if there's anything you can do to get your shop back.'

She stopped for breath and smiled at them, expectantly. They exchanged glances again.

'And? Is there?' asked Sylvie, hopefully.

'Well, no.' Sylvie and Philippe visibly deflated. 'My uncle said Henri couldn't have sold the property without getting a lawyer involved, and without getting you to sign the sales documents or some kind of power of attorney, handing everything over to him.'

'Hmm…' Sylvie considered it for a moment, sadly. 'I was so out of it at the time. He did give me various things to sign but I couldn't tell you what they were.'

'Either way, a lawyer would've had to witness it,' said Farheena. 'And my uncle said that if you were sick but expected to make a full recovery, no honest lawyer would've drawn up anything other than a temporary and very limited power of attorney document.'

'So what does that mean?' asked Philippe. 'That he used a dishonest lawyer? That the documents were forged?'

'I'm getting to that bit!' Farheena jumped up again and paced around the kitchen like a detective explaining whodunit at the end of a murder mystery; Hercule Poirot without the moustache, or maybe Columbo minus the rain mac. 'I wasn't sure myself what that could mean, so I thought I'd go and do a little detective work. I went to your old shop.'

Sylvie stared at her, open-mouthed. 'I haven't been back there since it was sold. I couldn't bring myself to.'

'You'll be pleased you didn't. It's a café now, serves the worst fucking coffee in the whole of the city. Anyway, I went in there and drank one of their disgusting drinks and chatted to the owner. I think he fancied me. It's the hijab, it gives me an air of mystery some men find really hot - '

'That's nice. Now tell us what bloody happened!' cried Philippe.

'Sorry. Yes, I told the owner I was looking for a property in the area, and asked him how he'd found this one because the market is really slow at the moment, and he told me that he was just renting it. And then he gave me this.'

She pulled out a business card and handed it to Sylvie. It was crumpled and the wording faded, but Sylvie knew what it said even before she stood up and walked to the window to see it better in daylight. Her hand trembled as she turned to Farheena.

'This is Henri's business card.'

'Yes and no. This is the café owner's landlord. *Henri* is the landlord.'

Sylvie wobbled and Farheena quickly pulled out a chair for her to sit down. Philippe reached across the table and took the card from her fingers.

'But if Henri's the landlord, then that means - ' Philippe looked at Sylvie, hope dawning in his face.

'That means he didn't sell it,' said Farheena. 'He *couldn't* sell it. He probably tried to and when he realised he couldn't do it legally, he lied to you and rented it out. And kept the rent money for himself.'

'All that time we thought we didn't have anywhere to live - ' said Philippe, amazed.

'It's still mine!' cried Sylvie, and then she burst into tears. 'It could be our home!'

Philippe got up and rushed to her side, crouching down to hold her close as she wept. Farheena stood, smiling awkwardly; glad to have delivered the good news but now feeling a bit like a spare part. Philippe looked up and saw her.

'Maybe some tea would be a good idea?' he said. She laughed.

'It's times like these I wish I drank alcohol,' she said. 'But tea will definitely help.'

She filled the kettle and put it on the stove. Sylvie calmed down a little and gazed at Philippe.

'We could live in my old apartment!' she said. 'There's plenty of room, and it has so many good memories. I grew up there.'

'Maybe our family can grow up there,' said Philippe gently. That prompted a fresh batch of tears, but these were calmer, happier ones. She got herself under control again.

'I'd love to re-open the shop as well, but it would take too much money to re-stock it,' she said. 'For the moment we could just keep renting it out, I suppose.'

He nodded. On the stove, the kettle began to sing. Farheena looked at Philippe, eyebrows raised.

'Tea pot and tea bags in the cupboard above,' he said. She took out a canister of tea bags and then reached for the pot.

And then stopped in shock.

'Holy *merde…*' she said. Sylvie looked up.

'Oh god, what now?' Sylvie asked. 'I don't know how much more I can take in one day!'

Farheena laughed, high pitched and on the edge of hysteria. 'Are you sure you don't have any alcohol in the house?' She very carefully, almost lovingly, took Sylvie's old blue and white tea pot out of the cupboard and caressed it, turning it over and studying it carefully for marks. She gulped and with shaking hands placed it very very carefully on the kitchen table in front of Sylvie. Sylvie reached for it but Farheena stopped her.

'Don't!' she said. 'Don't touch it. Where did you get that tea pot?'

Sylvie looked at her, confused. 'I picked it up at the flea market at Puces de Vanves, years ago. It reminded me of the one my mother used when I was growing up. Why…?'

Farheena swallowed hard. 'You might want to get my art history professor to double check, but I think your tea pot is 300 years old from the Qianlong dynasty, and it's worth somewhere in the region of - '

Outside Philippe's apartment passersby looked up in surprise and a couple of pigeons flew out of a nearby tree in a leafy explosion, as Sylvie screamed from the kitchen.

CHAPTER 38

Sylvie put the finishing touches to the window display and stood back to admire her handiwork. It wasn't quite what it had been in her father's day, but she liked it; an eclectic and, dare she say it, probably more saleable collection of art, antiques and vintage items. And in the middle of it all, a not-so-old-and-valuable blue and white tea pot in the Chinese style, and a reproduction of Andy Warhol's version of the Mona Lisa. She smiled and knocked on the window.

Outside, Philippe was finishing off some artwork of his own. He looked up at the sound of Sylvie's knock and laughed. The shop window was certainly eye-catching, and if any customers came in wanting to know the story behind it he knew that Sylvie would have a great tale to tell them. He just hoped it would be a made up one, rather than the truth...

A lot had happened in the past 18 months. They'd given the café owner notice on the apartment, moving in as soon as they could; as lovely as Madame Moreau was, her home really wasn't big enough for three adults. Philippe had worried about leaving her on her own, but when the time came she saw them out of the building with almost indecent haste. Philippe had been slightly affronted but Sylvie had pointed out that his mother had already gone above and beyond the duties of even the most devoted *maman*, and that perhaps it was time now for her to have a life of her own. Sentiments shared by his old manager, Monsieur Fournier...

The tea pot had gone to auction and sold way above the estimate, giving Sylvie the money she needed to start up her shop again. Only now, of course, Henri tried to crawl back into her life, claiming that as they were still married he was legally entitled to half of it. Farheena, who had already proved more than her worth as Sylvie's friend, got her lawyer uncle to write a polite but sternly worded letter warning Henri of the consequences of him following this course of action and, after a nervous wait of two weeks, Henri had begun divorce proceedings against her without any further mention of money; stating he just wanted shot of her after discovering her adultery with Philippe. Philippe of course saw red at this slur against her, but she gently pointed out that it was true; notwithstanding the fact that Henri had lied, cheated her out of money, drugged her and slept with various other women himself. She didn't care what was said about her in court; the people who mattered to her knew the truth, and she was happy.

Philippe waved to Sylvie, beckoning her out of the shop. He had a surprise for her. She joined him and together they looked up at his handiwork.

The sign above the shop front had been bright, plastic, garish, with the name of the terrible café written in a font which made your eyes hurt. Philippe had prised it off and was delighted to find the original sign still underneath, dirty, flaking but more-or-less still there. He'd spent the last week repairing, repainting and adding gilding to bring it back to life, covering it with a tarpaulin to protect it from the weather until it was sealed against the rain and to stop Sylvie seeing it until it was finished. And then this morning he'd added an extra little something, just for opening day.

Sylvie beamed at him, turning back to look at the sign. 'Boudain's Antiques established 1875' in burnished gold lettering against a blood red background. And underneath, a banner: 'Under old management'.

'It's perfect,' she whispered, happy but hoarse with emotion. He pulled her close and hugged her tightly.

'Come on then, Mademoiselle Boudain!' he said. 'I think it's about time you opened up for your adoring customers.'

She laughed, looking around at the street. It was empty, but it was still early; the customers would come in time. Then hand in hand they went into the shop and turned the sign on the door to 'Open'.

Bertrand the pigeon looked down on the happy couple and ruffled his feathers. From his perch on the fourth floor balcony of the building opposite, he could see a fair way down the long but very narrow medieval street. It was quiet – the Rue Quincampoix was off the main thoroughfare, which was still heaving with rush hour traffic – but Bertrand was a wise pigeon, and he knew that in a few hours' time it would be filled with tourists and art lovers making their way to the nearby Pompidou Centre, browsing the tiny boutiques and galleries (many would loiter outside the rather saucy *fétiche* shop too, but few would be brave enough to go inside) which lined the street. And then some would stop off at one of the cafés for coffee and cake, leaving a few crumbs for him to finish off. Tourist season always meant rich pickings for a pigeon who knew where to look.

He ruffled his feathers again, debating with himself about whether or not to go and visit Gerard who at this time of the morning would be amusing himself dive-bombing the Pompidou staff as they arrived for work. He was so immature. Bertrand decided to maintain his dignity and leave the daft *cochon* to it.

He took off into the air, his attention drawn to the lone figure who walked down the road. The man was well built, tall – about 6'1", 6'2", Bertrand estimated – with a closely cropped head and a shaggy beard. He had aged from his days playing competitive football at the highest level, but he still walked with that same air of confidence (some would call it arrogance), still radiated that same *je ne sais quoi* that drew your eyes to him. He stopped outside Boudain's Antiques and looked in, his interest well and truly piqued by the window display.

Bertrand completed his calculations (whoever had coined the phrase 'bird brained' as an insult to someone's intelligence obviously had no idea of the complex mathematical equations involved in a pigeon's day-to-day activities), swooped low over the lone figure and pooped on Eric Cantona's head, then flew off and out of the story for ever.

EPILOGUE

So Sylvie and Philippe got the happy ending that they deserved. When Sylvie's divorce finally came through they were married in a quiet ceremony at the nearby town hall on Place Baudoyer. If you look closely at the wedding photographs - taken across town near the Sacre Coeur, after a celebratory meal at the small neighbourhood restaurant where all of the Moreau family's important events are celebrated - you might notice that the bride's gown is stretched a little tightly across the stomach. Six months later they were back at that same neighbourhood restaurant, this time celebrating the christening of their first child Julia, who is destined to grow up with an encyclopaedic knowledge of the footballing genius of Eric Cantona and the songs of Edith Piaf. Which sounds like a great combination to me.

Farheena was delighted when Sylvie asked her to be Julia's godmother. She had graduated from her Art History course the previous year with a first class degree, and with the connections she had made when she uncovered the true pedigree of Sylvie's old tea pot she soon found a position working as assistant to a very successful art dealer. However, with her sometimes foul-mouthed enthusiasm and passion for Asian art she quickly out-grew him and became the country's foremost expert in Chinese antiquities.

Madame Moreau, finally free of her grown-up son, started life anew. She adored Sylvie and knew that her son's heart (and his liver) were safe in her hands. When her old high school friend, Monsieur Fournier, came to see her and ask after Philippe – he was apparently 'just passing', although where he was going and where he was coming from shouldn't by rights have led him anywhere near her apartment – she looked at him as if for the first time and realised what a kind, caring man he was. The last time I saw her she was driving off to the south of France in Eloise the car, with a suitcase on the back seat and her new lover next to her.

Stephanie and Mathilde moved in together and currently live happily with their two cats in Montparnasse. They continue to work at the Louvre and enjoy disturbing the male members of staff with their public displays of affection.

Monsieur Moreau crawled back under the rock he'd been drinking and whoring under for most of Philippe's life and never came back. He heard on the grapevine that he was a grandfather and felt a pang of regret that he would never get the chance to meet his granddaughter; but whiskey soon dulled the pain.

And what of Henri? Oh, I've saved the best for last. Henri married again, in a lavish and very expensive ceremony. His new bride was younger and hotter and richer than Sylvie, and he congratulated himself very much on his luck in getting rid of that irritating Little Bird. Yes he'd lost the rent money from her shop, but his new wife had a portfolio of property all across the city and just under a million in the bank, so what did he care? What Henri had failed to realise was that the new Madame Cloutier made her fortune marrying (and then burying) a succession of rich, older men. She is going to be bitterly disappointed when she realises that his wealth is just for show. Henri's days are numbered.

Thanks and Acknowledgments

This story is a love letter to Paris, and to the indomitable spirit of a city that is tossed by the waves but does not sink; but more specifically to Notre Dame cathedral, home of Bertrand the pigeon. I was lucky enough to visit Notre Dame one Easter, before fire devastated this beautiful building, and hear Mass being sung. I am a total heathen, but even I felt something spiritual and uplifting as I listened to the words (which were all in Latin and completely unintelligible to me). It made me think that maybe there is a God, and if there is, She (or He) is to be found in the beauty of the world and the people around us, rather than in some heavenly domain that may or may not be waiting for us after death.

If (as Belinda Carlisle rather than the priests at Notre Dame once sang) heaven really is a place on earth, then I've been lucky enough to befriend a few angels: six wonder women who have been my biggest supporters. I'm lucky enough to call these amazing fellow writers my friends: **Carmen Radtke, Jade Bokhari, Sandy Barker**, **Andie Newton** and **Nina Kaye,** who are beacons of sanity and support on the darkest of days. And my agent, lovely **Lina Langlee**, has cheered me up and on, and given me the odd good, stern talking to when I've needed it.

My final thanks go to my lovely family, husband **Dominic** and son **Lucas**, whose love, hugs and endless cups of tea are the answer to this writer's prayers.

Enjoy this book?
Then check out these other
great titles by Fiona Leitch!

The Bella Tyson Mysteries

Cozy mysteries with a sweary female protagonist, a little bit of love action and the odd drop of blood... Join crime writer Bella as she navigates writer's block, love in her 40s, and transatlantic murder mysteries.

Only available on Amazon.

Book 1 - 'Dead in Venice' mybook.to/DeadInVenice

Book 2 - 'Murder Ahoy!' mybook.to/Ahoy

The Nosey Parker Cozy Mysteries

Cozy mysteries set in beautiful Cornwall. Ex-copper turned caterer Jodie 'Nosey' Parker returns to the seaside town she grew up in, with her teenage daughter. She's hoping for a quiet life away from London, but will she get it? (Clue: no she won't!)

Published by One More Chapter and available everywhere books are sold.

Book 1 - 'Murder on the Menu' mybook.to/MurderMenu

Book 2 - 'A Brush With Death' mybook.to/Brush

Book 3 - 'A Sprinkle of Sabotage' mybook.to/Sprinkle

Printed in Great Britain
by Amazon